ON THE SURFACE

ON THE SURFACE

A THRILLER

RACHEL McGUIRE

CROOKED LANE

NEW YORK

This is a work of fiction. All of the names, characters, organizations, places and events portrayed in this novel are either products of the author's imagination or are used fictitiously. Any resemblance to real or actual events, locales, or persons, living or dead, is entirely coincidental.

Published in the United States by Crooked Lane Books, an imprint of The Quick Brown Fox & Company LLC.

Crooked Lane Books and its logo are trademarks of The Quick Brown Fox & Company LLC.

Library of Congress Catalog-in-Publication data available upon request.

ISBN (hardcover): 978-1-63910-815-2
ISBN (ebook): 978-1-63910-816-9

Cover design by Heather VenHuizen

Printed in the United States.

www.crookedlanebooks.com

Crooked Lane Books
34 West 27th St., 10th Floor
New York, NY 10001

First Edition: July 2024

10 9 8 7 6 5 4 3 2 1

For my mother, who taught me to read and instilled in me a voracious appetite for both fiction and Yorkshire pudding.—Rachel

For my ride-or-die husband Shane, for his unwavering support of all my injudicious schemes.—Lee-Ann

PROLOGUE

Punta Cana, Dominican Republic

TWO YEARS AGO

Emily

THE DIVE SEEMED like a good idea last night.

This morning a storm looms and the topaz blue of yesterday's sunlight-infused sea has devolved into chaotic gray chop. The troughs and crests bounce our little wooden boat with a nauseating regularity, levitation followed by spine-jarring jolts.

The wreck we're headed to is visible from the Punta Cana resorts, the primary colors of their umbrella squadrons staking their turf on wind-whipped sand beaches.

Diving a midcentury shipwreck might be worth braving poor conditions, but this Russian grain freighter that wrecked during a storm just twenty years ago certainly isn't. The guidebooks say she hit a mine and, judging by the mangled steel of the lower hull, ran aground during a storm or was deliberately scuttled.

Captain Marcos gives us the most likely explanation. "Steering trouble," he says with a broad smile.

"'Steering trouble' is code for sleeping during watch," my husband, Trip, tells me as we hit the water bow-first in a jaw-snapping landing.

"The ship ran aground because the captain was sleeping when he should've been steering?" I ask, gripping the side of the boat.

"Or sleeping it off," Marcos says with that same warm smile.

"Did they all die?" asks Ella, our dive companion introduced to us by the captain, without looking up from her phone.

"Our tug saved the whole crew, twenty-three souls," Captain Marcos says.

Good. I don't like the idea of pleasure diving in someone's watery grave. On cue, the improv troupe in my anxious brain conjures up an image of a decaying corpse trapped in the wreck, all its soft tissues unevenly eaten away by sea scavengers. An eel slithering through the skull's orbits like an underwater extra from an *Indiana Jones* movie.

"Will there be much in the way of fish and turtles?" I shout over the engine and wind, desperate to get those thoughts out of my head before we dive.

"The ship is like a reef now, there will be lots of sea life," Trip shouts back, but I catch the captain's dubious expression. "Don't you want to be able to tell people you dove a wreck?" he asks.

I can't back out; he's more excited about this than he's been about anything in a long time. We were enchanted with each other, once. Was it only a year ago? He was my one and only major rebellion against my parents. Once they realized cajoling, rage, and bargaining wouldn't change my mind, my parents acquiesced to the match and pulled off something pretty close to a Greenwich society wedding.

A year in, even civility is lost.

And here I am, clinging to the side of this beat-up, splintered old skiff, nauseated, heading to scuba dive, desperate to show my husband I still know how to have fun, take risks, and have adventures. I'm not a complete novice. I was harangued into a resort course years ago on a family vacation. The boat launches again and I brace myself with my numb, wet feet and clench my teeth.

The engine roar dulls to a putter, and I release the breath I've been holding. We've arrived.

We made love last night for the first time in ages. I have hope he may actually forgive me for my sixty-hour work weeks and the myriad other offenses he's discovered while living with me. Our six-month love affair was brief but intense. His constant romantic overtures—flowers, candy, surprise trips, and frequent texts—were overwhelming, but in a good way. He admired my drive and ambition, but also my pragmatic but anxious nature. He was nothing like the indifferent, self-absorbed professional men Bumble had matched me with, and I fell hard.

But the honeymoon is long over. And a Standish does not divorce after a year, not even if her husband has become an icy, expensive stranger.

He booked this anniversary trip as a surprise, but it's the worst possible timing. I have a brief due and have spent most of our time here working.

I reach for his hand as the boat drifts to a stop. He uses it to pull me close, kissing me with all the passion of our first kiss eighteen months ago.

As we zip each other's wetsuits for the dive, my brain is as scrambled by the kiss and his renewed affection as my stomach is from the ride.

Ella has put down her phone and comes over to check my equipment. She should be pretty, but her smile never quite reaches her arctic-blue eyes.

The captain tosses out the "divers down" buoy. "Remember folks, don't stray too far from your buddy. Don't hold your breath. Check each other's gear. Stay calm and relaxed down there and have fun."

I remember enough. It's not as complicated as you'd think: whatever happens, don't panic.

Gear on, I tumble backward off the side of the boat into the ocean, my wetsuit slowly absorbing the chilly water. I submerge and my mask fills. I use my fins to kick up to the surface, which requires effort thanks to the weighted belt and the fact that, due to my caseload, my body hasn't seen the inside of a gym for six months. I dump out my mask and try to reseal it. I put my face in the water. The mask fills again. I toss it back in the boat and ask Marcos for another.

My husband surfaces next to me. "What's up?"

"Bad mask."

The captain hunts through his bag and finds another and brings it over.

This one is marginally better.

We head down to the wreck.

I can barely see anything, it's so murky—so I'm kicking lazily when finally the structure comes into view.

Ominous and gray, covered with algae and slimy gunk.

There are no brilliantly colored fish, no turtles.

No life at all.

I use my hands to scull backward and seek out my companions. Someone is kicking up sand from the bottom and a white cloud envelops me. My nausea hasn't abated and now I'm dizzy and disoriented too.

I'm breathing too fast.

I move forward gingerly; I can't see more than a foot in front of me. I'm afraid to run into the wreck.

Have I lost my dive buddy already?

Something moves in my peripheral vision.

I turn 180 degrees but there's nothing visible in the gloom.

I'm breathing much, much too hard.

Don't panic.

There are sharks here but they're generally harmless. Of the four attacks recorded since the '60s, only two have been fatal. Still . . . one of those was a diver, and he was attacked unprovoked, at least according to the shark attack data site.

Why do I even know this? Why do I catastrophize? My therapist has told me dozens of times that researching the chances of airplane crashes, shark attacks, and whatnot doesn't make me calmer. But anxiety isn't rational. It doesn't matter how slim the risks or how slight the provocation; my brain goes screaming into full alert. It's what makes me a great attorney—and a paranoid spouse.

I attempt a few calming breaths and visualization techniques.

But somewhere nearby is that awful shipwreck. Just the thought of that lifeless, gray hunk of metal sitting on the bottom of the sea is enough to spin up my claustrophobic tendencies.

I can't get my breath under control.

I need my buddies.

Swimming forward into the glinting cloud of sand, I will myself to relax, but it's not working.

My pulse throbs in my ears.

A figure looms ahead of me. I kick harder to get to them.

I inhale.

Nothing.

I'm out of air.

That's not possible.

There is no way I've been down here long enough to run out of air.

I draw in on the regulator.

Nothing.

Don't panic.

It's my mantra as I kick for what I hope is the surface.

Don't hold your breath, you'll damage your lungs.

I blow out my remaining air, my leaden legs pumping for the surface, but I can't tell which way I'm going, and my kicking turns to thrashing. My vision goes white around the edges. A figure approaches from the murky water in front of me as my vision clouds.

I stretch out my arm toward them.

Help me.

PART I

CHAPTER

1

Serendipity, near Lee Stocking Island

Dani Fox

THE CRUISER PARTY tonight won't be at some fancy restaurant—there are none here in George Town. Nor will there be a bonfire on a deserted cay, a favorite location for these shindigs. The forecast is bad so our cruiser party will be on a few sailboats tethered together in the calm of this little Exuma anchorage. Boats have been arriving for the past week to celebrate the birthday of Sonja, the matriarch of our rag-tag, vagabond group.

"Cruisers" is such an elegant term for what is—essentially—RV living on the water. We anchor our boats here, temporarily or long term, an aquatic trailer park.

Sawyer gets annoyed when I use the trailer park analogy, but he's never known the other side of this life—motoring on white boats, as those in the biz call the big yachts. Transiting between the aqua lagoons of Bali and the white sand atolls of the Maldives. Though I suppose it's better here in the Bahamas than Miami or the Keys or Bermuda. Better and cheaper. Sure, there's noise from dawn till dusk, but the Wi-Fi is reliable, the waters calm, the cruisers entertaining, and the visuals are five-star. And when you're a content creator like me? That's all that matters. My fledgling YouTube channel, *Sailing with the Foxes,* has finally hit its monetization marks.

Sawyer comes up and wraps his arms around me. He raises his beer to the foursome passing by in a dinghy at a slow rate of speed.

We don't know them, but the vibe out here is casual and friendly. Nothing like my past life as a yachtie. Out here you don't have a crew to make repairs. Out here we rely on each other to MacGyver our way out of the constant upkeep of our monohulls and catamarans, which eat into our savings like the growing barnacles below are eating into our hull.

I lean into Sawyer's tall frame and beam up at him.

"I know that smile," he grouses.

He's been in such a state since his alt coin collapsed. Angry, moody, aggressive by turns. It has taken every ounce of energy to cajole him into doing the things he used to love. When your back is to the wall, you lash out at everyone, but I've grown tired of tiptoeing around because he wasn't diversified.

I've grown tired of a lot in this life with him.

"I want to show you my new intro," I say.

His eyes are hidden behind his sunglasses on this bright, bright morning, but I can't mistake the set of his jaw.

"You promised." I can hear the whine in the pitch of my voice and I hate myself for it.

He drops his chin to the top of my head and rests it there. "Of course. And then let's go spearfishing. Maybe catch something for the party?"

My spirits lift instantly. I'm already wondering if my GoPro is charged and what bikini will look best for underwater shots.

"Did I hear you on the radio earlier?" I ask.

"Yeah, Brendan called. Some local kids went out fishing yesterday—early—and haven't made it back. Some cruisers and locals are heading out to look for them."

I raise my head to look at him; he looks down at me, expression serious.

"They'll turn up," I reply.

"Or not." He shrugs. "Let's head toward Beacon's Reef so we don't run into search parties."

"But I love parties!" I pout. "You never take me anywhere."

"Very funny," he says, giving both my arms a squeeze. I scooch away from him as a skiff passes our boat. Locals with serious expressions. The one manning the outboard lifts a hand in greeting.

We rock in their wake.

Sawyer takes my chin in his hand, leans down, and puts his lips on mine.

His hand moves to the back of my head, strokes down my back. He wraps his arms around me and presses me against him. His hold quickly becomes suffocating. I stiffen, then force myself to relax, ignoring the pain that the pressure of his embrace brings to the bruises on my arm, a testament to how bad things have become out here. I'm not a quitter. I'm a fixer. And I still believe I can fix him. Us. This.

I muster a smile and lead him down the companionway.

CHAPTER

2

Serendipity

Sawyer Stone III

DANI AND I sit together at one end of the U-shaped banquette around the kitchen table as we wait for her thirteenth *Sailing with the Foxes* YouTube video to go live. Though the anchorage in the Exumas at Sand Dollar Beach is less rolly today than it has been the past few days, Dani reaches for her ginger tea, wrist wrapped in a gray anti-nausea acupressure bracelet.

I'm not prone to seasickness as Dani is; still, I try to minimize my time below deck as a rule. But it's too hard to see Dani's laptop screen in the light of day, so we've come down here. I'm not a Fox, I'm a Stone, but on screen, our reality is drowned in Dani's content creation. I barely managed to talk her out of calling it *Sailing with the Stone Cold Foxes*.

"Is it bad today, babe?" I ask, nodding at her wrist.

She shakes her head.

"You okay?"

This time she shrugs. I recognize the pout. My sigh is inaudible, but she looks up, her big blue eyes full of something I don't recognize. Disappointment? Regret?

"Look, I'm sorry. Okay? This isn't my thing. I hate being filmed. You know I don't like the whole idea of this channel."

"It's *work*," she replies. "You never appreciate anything I do anymore."

She's not wrong.

"I'm an ass." I sigh. "Where do we go from here, Dani?"

I don't know if I'm asking a geographical question or a relationship question. Both, I suppose. I don't wait for her to answer. "I love you and I'm not letting you go."

Her head tilts as she meets my gaze. "What is it you love, Sawyer? Because you don't even seem to like me anymore."

I answer as honestly as I can. "I love the look in your eyes when you surface with something on your spear that you caught four meters down free diving. I love that you swim every damn day but never to shore. I love that you can't figure out any of the basic sailing knots." I pull her into my lap; it's a tight squeeze. "Most of all I love that I can count on you to do whatever we need—to keep watch in a storm, to keep up appearances, to keep me in line."

She rests her head on my chest.

Minutes later I'm doomscrolling on my phone when she hits play and the first eleven seconds of "The Fox (What Does the Fox Say?)" come on. My hands curl into fists at those opening bars. I have begged her to change it to literally anything else, but she is the sound editor.

Averting my eyes from the screen, I microfocus on the years of dirt worn into the pebbled texture of the vinyl banquette cushions, so far embedded no amount of scrubbing will ever render it clean again. Like everything else on the *Serendipity*, it doesn't look bad from far away. It's only when you get close that you see the banquette is not off-white by design but due to deterioration and neglect.

Then, her voiceover.

"Hi, I'm Dani Fox, and this is Sawyer. Welcome to *Sailing with the Foxes*! We are cruisers, living our best life on an around-the-world adventure—join us!"

The footage shows a generic montage of turquoise waters, white sand beaches. Some of them are places I know I've never even seen before. B-roll stock footage. There are a few shots of Dani walking or swimming away from the camera. There are a few of us together, including me at the helm, and one of me raising the anchor. This is a fair representation of our life onboard: she does whatever her impulses require while I steer and anchor us.

Dani's disembodied voice continues: "If you've been watching our videos, you know that when I say we are cruisers, I'm not talking about the kind of cruising that regular people do, where you travel with thousands, like cattle, on a giant white boat, going to the most basic ports in the most obvious places." I wince at her words. What are the chances of winning over viewers while insulting major swaths of the population? It's not a great strategy.

"Our kind of cruising is totally *not* basic. We go wherever the wind takes us—like, literally. Imagine life free of mortgages and bosses and traffic and whatever crap regular people have to put up with."

Now the video shows a cacophony of urban images, and the quick jump edits create a sense of tension and stress. I can't help but be impressed by the quality of her editing, but I refuse to admit it to her.

"Cruisers like us live on their boats and are ready to pull up anchor and travel long distances to go anywhere in the world, all without the help of any paid crew. And if that sounds like a flex, that's because it is. We're out here doing everything for ourselves and have no one to rely on for our own safety but each other. Life on the open seas is not for the faint of heart—it is high-key dangerous. I'm not trying to scare anyone, just keeping it one hundred."

The visuals have switched to a quick tour of the boat. "This is our home, *Serendipity.* She's a 2007 Bavaria 42 Cruiser. The forty-two is a reference to how big she is—forty-two feet long. Forty-two feet, ten inches, to be precise.

Speaking of ten inches, this would be a perfect time to introduce *Serendipity*'s captain, and my own number one guy, Sawyer Stone."

I mentally acknowledge that she is rounding up here, but I keep all concessions to myself. The photos look candid, but our position in each is one hundred percent consciously constructed. I always hold the phone, because my arms are long enough to get the perfect angle, taking the picture from above, to maximize the impact of what she describes as her best feature, her superior bone structure.

I would argue that her best feature and the actual star of the channel is her ass, if you go by what's said in the comment section.

"Sawyer and I met the analog way—in a bar—and as soon as I saw him, it was kismet! We connected over a love of adventure, sailing, and travel. Sawyer grew up on the water, and he was sailing Lasers before he could walk—because he's bougie like that. I'm learning as we go. We haven't made it around the world yet, but it's all part of the grand plan. One thing you'll learn about us both is that we aren't dreamers, we're doers. I bet you're the type who likes to watch, so join us on our sailing adventures on this channel every week—like this video and hit the subscribe button! Like and subscribe!"

I examine the image of us standing on the bow, waving at the drone. She's clad in her favorite saffron bikini, smiling wide, exposing her bleached, perfectly aligned teeth. I'm unsmiling and shirtless in faded red board shorts and Tom Ford sunglasses. Smiling would've been a big ask as this was her fifteenth attempt to get the shot. Per her direction, the drone flies behind us, I wrap an arm around her, and we kiss. It's the kiss viewers want to see, passionate but not too long or intense. We pull back to look at each other as the sun sets behind us. I remember what my eyes promised her as we stared at each other, unblinking.

I'm not doing another goddamn take.

That's the end of the intro, so she shuts it off.

She's learned most of what she knows about video editing and YouTube channels over the past few months from our fellow cruiser Jim Marsh, who has his own semi-successful YouTube channel: *Aboat Time to Fish*.

Whenever I try to teach her anything about navigation, tacking, or comms equipment, her eyes glaze over. I tried to walk her through the operation of the Emergency Position Indicating Radio Beacon on board, a device that is marketed as being easy enough for a child to use, but she tells me it's too techie and when are we ever going to need it anyway. But when it comes to learning video editing from Jim, within twelve weeks she's Steven fucking Spielberg?

I'm itching to leave the Bahamas and go anywhere else—Panama, Cuba, Galapagos—but we're short on cash and Dani has fallen in love with this anchorage. I suspect it's more due to the reliable Wi-Fi than the scenery. On the plus side, the Bahamas is the stomping ground for some real crypto whales, so with a bit of luck I could land the connections I need to run the alt coin pump and dump that's going to get me out of the hole I'm in. I need the price of Soltana to rebound before I can swing the cash outlay reprovisioning would require. Even the cost of groceries can mount up fast when it comes to boat life, forget about fuel and maintenance and repairs. It's one thing breaking after another on this boat, and who knows how long it will take Soltana to recover in this Dogecoin world. The crypto market is full of idiots. If Soltana doesn't save us, it's going to have to be *Sailing with the Foxes* . . . and what would that even look like?

Dani shuts her laptop and looks at me expectantly.

"Intro looks amazing, babe," I tell her, but if she hadn't told me she redid it, I wouldn't have noticed. It looks pretty much the same to me.

"We're celebrating tonight. I hit my monetization marks for the channel finally, so now we're on track." Her smile is bright and genuine. "Now that these videos can actually generate money for us, maybe it's time to think about adding a baby to the mix."

I draw back. "There's already one anchor on this boat. We don't need another." She pouts and I gather her in my arms. "Let's table that idea for now, okay?"

I know I should congratulate her on monetizing our channel. I should do a lot of things to try to get us back to where we were.

I sailed *Serendipity* solo for six months before I met up with Dani.

Sailing solo sucks.

It's the sleep deprivation that gets you. There's no way to get enough uninterrupted sleep on passages without another person on watch. Reefing sails, making repairs on the fly, much of that is doable solo—but setting proximity alerts that go off frequently in well-trafficked seas is not conducive to rest. And when you're sailing at night things can get hairy.

So, despite Dani's "C-minus" deckhand rating, sailing is better with her.

Free diving, scuba diving, even snorkeling is better with her too. We share that passion. Diving is the adhesive that holds us together when things fall apart.

And things have fallen apart.

"How much money are we talking?" I ask.

"Well, pennies so far, but it's based on the number of views and we only just enabled monetization. Going forward all of our videos can earn money, if they get enough views."

"And how likely is that? Haven't all the people we've met who have tried and failed to get traction with sailing YouTube channels told you anything?" I ask.

"It's simply a matter of getting the right content out in the right way and getting those initial followers and watches. Trust me, babe, I've got the right assets to make our channel a success," she says, twerking in my direction, in case I missed her ham-fisted double-entendre.

I grimace. "Why not start an OnlyFans account and be done with it?"

This is a direct hit; her smile fades. "Someone has to make money around here," she says, biting back.

And she's got me.

"Until your crypto pays off," she says with the placating tone one would use to concede a point to a child.

"Crypto doesn't 'pay off.' It's not a slot machine."

"Fail videos are also popular," she says, examining her perfect, pearly white manicure.

Her nails attest to her limitations as a crew member. Actual working crew would chip and ruin a manicure within hours out here.

My body stiffens. "I'm not going to sabotage this boat so middle-aged losers can feel superior in the comments."

"Fine, but we need a hook. Our collective hotness, some travel porn, and maybe we add some drama, sailing into storms or something."

"I'm not sailing into bad weather on purpose, Dani. Did our Bermuda experience teach you nothing?"

"I'm giving you options, Sawyer. We need to generate some story arcs. Attempt a circumnavigation. Get caught in a storm. Stage some fails. I'm open to suggestions."

Whenever she talks like this, it makes me feel every minute of our eight-year age gap. "We have enough drama, Dani, without manufacturing it. I'm not down for having all my private stuff out there or coming off like an asshole."

My hand finds its way under her hair to her thin neck. I tighten my fingers.

She leans forward to shake me off. "What does it matter if viewers hate you? Strong feelings drive engagement. Hate is better than indifference. Feelings generate clicks, clicks generate money. Don't you want to keep living like this?"

I nod. "There's no other way to live."

"It's only content, Sawyer. Let's see where it takes us."

"No fails," I state.

"No fails," she agrees.

But we both know she can't be trusted.

"Listen, I don't want to spend money on groceries for the potluck tonight. Let's go catch something." I don't even attempt to keep the annoyance out of my tone.

She smiles. "Gimme two minutes to get ready."

It's been eighteen minutes and counting since Dani told me "two minutes" and went to her cabin to get ready. Yes, we have our own cabins. There's only a few hundred square feet on this boat and we value having our own spaces to retreat into. I've already gathered up the snorkeling and spearfishing gear into the dinghy.

The air is thick with moisture and the weather system says storms will come through tonight and bring at least temporary relief. I don't miss many creature comforts out here on the water—the diving and sunsets more than make up for them. My tolerance for bugs, heat, and humidity was forged in my childhood boating and camping on the Eastern Seaboard. But I fantasize about an air-conditioned cabin to sleep in the way other people fantasize about winning the lottery.

Finally, she clambers over the side of *Serendipity*. "Where are we off to this afternoon?"

I'm her fish concierge apparently. "I thought we'd head to the marine protected area around Exuma Cays."

"We'll never get back in time. I need a couple hours to get ready for the party. And going to a protected area is asking for a hassle from the marine police."

"But it's much faster to fish in a marine protected area. There's more fish there, that's the point."

"Somewhere closer, please."

And she gets her way again.

Scowling, I fire up the outboard and head us toward a secluded bay we'd been to before up the coast a ways. We only have one decent spearfishing gun so I opt to stay in the dinghy and give Dani first crack at the reef to see if there is anything around worth eating. Dani puts on fins and a mask, adjusts the GoPro attached to her head, grabs the gun, then sinks into the water from the side of the dinghy with a jaunty wave. The water visibility is fantastic. Her form is visible for several meters as she sets off for the reef, her white swimsuit blindingly bright on the surface, buoyed by the aquas of the Caribbean Sea.

It isn't long before she surfaces, beaming, holding the gun aloft, a good-sized fish skewered on the frog tip.

Dani's smile is triumphant. "Big enough?"

"Looks it. Guess I found the right spot."

She grunts in response as I boost her back into the dinghy with my one free arm. The snapper is still in full body twitch mode, speared cleanly in three places, as Dani lays it ceremoniously at my feet in the bottom of the dinghy.

"Do the ikejime, babe," she says, looking me dead in the eye.

Ikejime is the Japanese method of killing a fish favored by spearfishermen. Allegedly the fish tastes better, but I can't tell the difference.

I plunge my knife quickly right behind the snapper's eyes, straight into the brain. I know I've hit my mark precisely right as the snapper gives one last big twitch and dies instantly, its fins stretched out as though it's been startled to death.

Dani switches off the camera and removes it from her head.

"Let's go laze on a beach somewhere," I suggest. It's a pretty good vibe all around right now, and these moments have been few and far between lately. I crank up the outboard and head further up the coastline, drowning out any objections Dani might be voicing about needing the time to get dolled up.

I've got a place in mind, a tiny beach on a little cay past Beacon's Reef that is only accessible by boat. The kind that is a slice of heaven until some vlogger puts it on the map and it's overrun with influencers doing yoga and trying to angle their photos so as to crop out all the other influencers crowding the "secret" beach.

Just as I turn sharply to the rocky cove that hides our beach, there's a flash of something metallic against the base of a rocky outcropping far up the coastline that catches my eye. It's amazing how the smallest glimpse of something out of place will grab you when you're out on the water. It's a skill you need to captain any boat, to spot deadheads or other hazards in the water.

"Something up ahead. Going to check it out."

I rev the outboard to speed closer to whatever it is. It's a small aluminum boat, jacked up on the rocks in a way that looks decidedly unintentional.

"Looks like it ran aground," Dani shouts.

It's on an outcropping with steep jagged rocks that rise higher and higher the closer you get to land until it's pretty much a sheer rock face. There's no reason for anyone to stop here—you couldn't even get out to fish.

And looking at the position of the land jutting out into the channel, my captain sense tells me there's going to be some funky currents going on. There's a reason why this area remains so desolate among all the places in the Bahamas overrun by locals and tourists. Even from several meters away I can see some dangerous eddies roiling near the rocks.

"You think it's been stolen or gotten loose?" Dani asks.

"Weather's been pretty calm lately, so not likely to have been unmoored in a storm."

"Will it be dangerous for us to get in close?"

I pull alongside the jetty but a powerful current grabs hold of our dinghy, and it's taking all of my strength to keep us on a straight path.

I fight to keep us from getting run up onto the rocks. Now we're close enough to see that that is indeed what has happened to the other boat—there's a jagged hole in the hull, which is sticking up out of the water. The stern is anchored on the rocks below the waterline, and now I'm close enough to see the outboard is still attached.

I scan the coastline, looking for a washed-up person on the beach. Nothing.

We are closer to the wreck and now I'm half expecting to see a body pinned between the wreck and the rocks. Our dinghy starts to spin around backward, caught in another whirling current. I can't hold us stationary but I can see almost the whole wreck; the only thing of value is the outboard, and I'm not really in the mood for a fixer-upper project to rehabilitate a drowned motor. I've got enough shit to fix on my own boat. I'm not interested in salvage work.

"I've seen enough." The words are barely out of my mouth when above the sound of the engine and the churning tide, shouts come from the other side of the jetty.

Those missing locals. *Fuck.*

CHAPTER

3

Dani

"It's those missing kids!" I say.

Sawyer nods. "I thought they were last spotted by the Berries. Nowhere near here."

A boy tall enough to be a teen and a shorter child clamber up the pointy rocks to the ridge of the jetty, waving their arms as if about to take flight. They're hollering, and even from this distance the hoarseness of their voices is evident. They've been missing since yesterday morning, so they've probably been a while without water. The sun has been relentless today.

"There's no way to get our dinghy to shore here," Sawyer says. "It's too rough. Our boat will end up like theirs, and we don't have the money to replace it. Let's call someone. The Marine Unit can come out." He checks his phone. "Damn it. No signal."

We have yet to wave back acknowledging them.

"We're already here. They're probably terrified," I say. "Besides, think of the views we'll get on the video! It'll be a fail vid, but it's someone else's fail. Win-win. Move the dinghy away from the rocks and I'll do a swim rescue while you film me. We can be heroes!"

"Just for one day?" he asks.

"What?"

"Nothing." He maneuvers the boat out of the current and away from the jetty but it's as though we're mired in quicksand. The engine whines as he opens the throttle completely to try to move perpendicular to the eddy that is pulling us back toward the rocks. The waves are breaking rough here, atypical of Bahamian conditions. That's the ocean for you—even here in paradise, danger abounds.

The boys scramble frantically over the rocks toward us, yelling. But there's no way to communicate rescue plans with them above the sound of the surf and the strain of the engine.

The taller of the boys loses his footing, sliding a few feet down the rock face. I wince, knowing what that barnacled rock is doing to his backside.

Sawyer angles the boat again, and the current loses its hold. With a jerk we break free and move smoothly over the water.

We go ten meters before Sawyer drops the anchor. "Damn it," he mutters.

"What?"

He pulls up the anchor and tosses it out again. "We're dragging."

"So?" I don't see the problem. "You can stay with the boat."

"There are two of them, there are two of us, you need help getting them."

"I'll be fine. I did swim rescue training as a yachtie."

"The currents here are wild, Dani. I don't trust the dinghy anchor to hold and we don't even know if they can swim."

"You stay in the boat and film," I insist. I hand him my phone, then pull on flippers and mask and put the GoPro on my head.

Sawyer presses record on his phone.

"Dani here from *Sailing with the Foxes,* about to swim into very dangerous waters to rescue these two local boys who were lost . . . at . . . sea . . . yesterday." I keep my tone breathless and halting, as though I'm truly afraid of what I'm about to do. The truth is, I don't feel fear. Plenty of adrenaline. But I'm not afraid of death or pain. It's just not something I experience. I'm lucky that way.

"Sawyer and I went out searching for these sweet boys as soon as we heard, and it is an answered prayer to have found them. It's too dangerous to boat in—our outboard can't fight these currents—so I don't know what condition they're in yet. I'm going to have to swim them to safety. I don't know what my chances are. These are ultra red flag conditions. The waves are pounding; I hope I'm strong enough to pull this off. But I can't leave those children one more minute. They must be terrified, and I've got to get them to safety."

I put on my mask and fins, give a small wave, and drop over the side.

I've been in powerful riptides before, swimming on the diagonal to get to shore, but the currents off this jetty are unusual—they push and pull in different directions with what seems like every freestyle stroke I make. I kick hard and lift my head high out of the water to track my progress. The boys are whooping, progressing down the rocks toward my heading.

Despite my daily swims, I'm winded when I reach the outer rocks of the jetty. I hope I have the energy reserves to get them back to the dinghy. I hope to God they're decent swimmers.

The younger boy greets my arrival. "I knew someone would come! I knew it."

The teen is more reserved but his eyes well with tears. "Thank you. Thank you for finding us," he says, his breath hitching.

"Do you swim?" I ask.

The younger boy nods vigorously. "I'm Lucas. I'm a good swimmer. A very good swimmer." His face falls as he looks at the older boy. "Jacques is not so good." Terrific. Figures that the older, bigger boy with no appreciable body fat can't swim.

"Okay. This is how we're going to do this. Lucas, you are going to swim next to me. If you get tired, we rest. Jacques, I'm going to put you on your back, with my arm across your body. With the fins on my feet doing the work, we'll get to the boat. Your only job is to stay calm. Do you hear me?" I can see the terror in his eyes, but he nods. "We'll get through this."

Lucas jumps into the water. It's not the prettiest of free-style strokes, but it will do. I coax Jacques down the rocks. He slips and lands on his back with a cry of pain. He gets to his feet and half turns. He's given himself a good gash from a barnacle or something. "It's okay, keep coming, it's not bleeding. Just a scratch." Actually, it's bleeding pretty good. He's sliced it deep enough to warrant a few stitches but there's nothing I can do about it now, so I lie and continue to coax him into the water. His body is rigid with fear as I get him into the lifesaving position. Lucas is treading water next to me, grinning.

We get about fifteen feet from the jetty and I'm kicking against the current for all I'm worth, hauling Jacques's deadweight, when an errant wave crashes on us. I hold my breath and Jacques starts a panicked wriggling. Lucas has surfaced, sputtering, but I've lost my hold on Jacques. I tread water, searching for Jacques, when something grabs me from behind.

Jacques.

I suck in a breath, tuck my chin to my chest, and duck under the waves. Jacques releases me immediately. I take a few powerful strokes away, then a few more. I surface and see the older boy floundering.

"Jacques, don't panic."

I approach him—he lunges at me. I back away. "Calm down. I've got you." I dive down and swim, resurfacing behind him. His panic has brought fatigue. His head is barely above water.

"Lucas, you okay?" I shout.

"I'm okay," the boy says. I can see he's made progress; he's closer to the dinghy than we are.

"Keep swimming," I tell him.

"Jacques, I'm right here." He lunges at me but he's tired and it shows. "No, don't jump on me again." I kick away a foot. "You jump on me, I go underwater. Let me get you, okay? Trust me." We'd had a lot of fun as yachties practicing life saving techniques on each other—simulating just this kind of panicked swimmer situation. It's a lot less fun in an actual emergency.

I get Jacques in the hold again, my arm across his body. I grunt as I use my fins to kick us out of the current, toward the dinghy. As luck would have it the next current we hit takes us toward the open sea and the dinghy where Sawyer is, presumably, still filming.

Jacques's body has stilled. The water is calmer. I glance over my shoulder and see Sawyer hauling Lucas into the boat.

I've depleted every store of energy. My arms and legs are trembling. Damn this teenager and his zero buoyancy—no wonder he's not a swimmer.

I'm gasping as I reach for the dinghy, anchoring us with one hand. Jacques struggles out of my hold and reaches for Sawyer. I cling to the boat, incapable of hauling myself out. Sawyer reaches for me, but I wave him off. "Give me a second to catch my breath and then film me," I say. I wait until he does as I've asked before hauling myself out. I land in the bottom, next to my waterlogged compatriots.

Jacques is crying silently, covering his face with his hands.

"Thank you, rescuers," Lucas says solemnly.

Sawyer frames us in the camera: three exhausted people and one dead snapper.

"How did it look, babe? Did you like my suck, tuck, and duck?" I say.

"Is that what you did?"

I sit up and shake the ocean water out of my ear, then give the camera a brilliant smile. "If someone you're trying to rescue in the water jumps on you, all you have to do is suck, tuck, and duck. Suck in a breath, tuck your chin to your chest, and duck under water—trust me, they won't follow you down, the last place they want to be is underwater. Then try to talk them down from their panic. It's not easy, but it works."

Sawyer turns the phone to focus it on the lifejackets in the bottom of the boat. "If you're not a strong swimmer or the conditions are bad, consider tying a line to a flotation device. Throw, don't go."

I take the phone from him and continue to film the jetty, the boys' tired smiles. Lucas gives me a thumbs-up as Sawyer hands each of them a water from our cooler. Jacques avoids looking at the camera.

"You gave me a couple of bad moments," Sawyer whispers, handing me one of his beers.

I smile at him, thinking of the views soon to be rolling in on the channel.

CHAPTER 4

Sawyer

Serendipity

Hours later I'm trying to goad Dani into leaving *Serendipity* for Sonja's party. She complains that she hasn't had enough time to "contour," whatever that entails. Truth is, she looks fantastic despite the afternoon's rescue and the minor hoopla that greeted us on our return to shore with the children. I'd called in to the harbor to let them know what had transpired and the little George Town dock was teeming with relieved locals and cruisers showering us with accolades. She was in her element, primping for the cameras and posing with the rescued boys.

She tells me this little rescue could be YouTube gold.

"How do I look?" she asks, pirouetting to display her floral minidress.

"Amazing," I tell her, and it's the truth.

Her beauty is rather spectacular camouflage; few see past her miniature bombshell body—sure, her breasts have been enhanced, but mostly her figure is the byproduct of good genes and a fanatical commitment to improving what nature endowed with regular workouts.

"Who cares what a bunch of decrepit cruisers think of you, anyway?" I ask. I must not err on the side of too many compliments. Dani's ego is chronically inflated to maximum PSI.

I ready the dinghy that will take us to the Nilssons' fifty-two-foot Lagoon catamaran SV *Xanadu*, one of many boats in this anchorage I covet. It's large enough for a dozen people to party on, but given the size of this party, it's likely a few boats will be rafted together. Sonja, our host this evening, is one of those people who seems to have a connection to everyone and every place you could think of—a non-celeb version of Kevin Bacon. Every topic that comes up, Sonja knows someone who knows someone.

It's exhausting.

But it also means nearly every cruiser from every sailboat in the Bahamas is likely to represent at Sonja's birthday. Our little anchorage is teeming.

"Sawyer, they're not all old, and you know very well I don't care what anyone thinks of me—except you," she adds as an afterthought. I find myself wondering if she does care what I think of her. I'm not so sure.

I scan the immediate vicinity for a camera. I'm pretty sure I'm being filmed and recorded 24/7. Dani is obsessed with getting her footage—the good, the bad, the mundane. Her quest for content makes no allowance for my loathing of the experience of being filmed. I've told her I don't want to be filmed surreptitiously, but Dani's mantra is to beg for forgiveness instead of asking for permission.

Dani disappears with her laptop, and I do a more thorough check. I don't find any cameras but that doesn't mean they're not here. You'd think it would be hard to hide things in the handful of square feet that comprise our living space above and below deck, but that's not the case. Like any boat, *Serendipity* is designed to utilize every nook and cranny in every direction. Nearly every surface, vertical and horizontal, hides some other function, with storage space or an appliance or equipment panel. Lift a hinged square on the kitchen counter and pantry storage is revealed underneath.

Its ingenious design is thwarted, though, when someone as thoughtless as Dani leaves a trail of dirty dishes anywhere behind her that isn't the sink, clothes anywhere but in her room, and beauty products on every surface, which tip and spill and gunk up every surface when it's rolly—and it's nearly always rolly on a monohull.

Her behavior would be inconsiderate in any shared living space, but it's absolutely infuriating on a boat. How someone so perfectly put together when it comes to her own appearance can be such a slob in her environment is confounding. She reappears five minutes later with a red cooler containing our catch of the day, wearing a floral print one-shoulder minidress that would be more appropriate at a Biarritz billionaire yacht party than a cruiser party.

Cruiser parties are characterized by their haphazardness—there are no themes, unless potluck qualifies. Invariably they are "come as you are, bring what you've got." It's not good for the 'gram, as Dani would say, with most cruisers being Boomers or Xers versus Millennials or Gen Z. Everyone out here prioritizes function over form with sensible footwear and UV protection. Exactly the opposite of a one-shoulder minidress, full makeup, flat-ironed hair, and that impeccable mani-pedi.

I can't help smiling as she hands me the cooler.

She shivers as she gingerly steps barefoot into the boat. Unless we're planning a land excursion, she goes without shoes. The footwear acceptable to sailors is rubber-soled deck shoes, and Dani says they're too frumpy.

Serendipity is about four hundred meters from SV *Xanadu* but it's a choppy ride. Dani balances, keeping her dress dry against all odds. She raises her chin toward the west.

The storm is on the horizon.

I keep the dinghy against *Xanadu* as Dani climbs aboard, handing off the cooler containing our snapper to a cruiser manning the grill. The man opens the cooler and stares at the fish we caught earlier. He nudges the guy next to him. Their heads swivel to me, but I make myself busy tying up the dinghy, keeping them in my peripheral vision.

When I look back, they are having an animated discussion, portside.

The second man, red-faced, reaches into the cooler, lifts out our fresh red snapper, and throws it over the side.

The last time we brought fish to a party, everyone became ill. Cruisers are not inherently suspicious, but they do love to gossip, and my buddy Brendan made me aware they all blamed us for the whole mess, when it could've been any of the potluck sides at the gathering.

There are boats rafted on either side of *Xanadu*. The crowd looks like they've assembled to see a Jimmy Buffet tribute band, but it's BTS that's inexplicably blaring over the sizable Bluetooth speaker on deck. You never know what you'll get with the cruiser crowd.

Dani doesn't look back, melding into the throng of partygoers half-dancing and chatting in small clusters. Rod, one of the creepier sailors at this anchorage, follows closely behind Dani as she breezes her way through the crowd of partygoers. People stop her, effusively congratulating her on saving the local boys. Word travels fast out here.

I make my way to the stern, stopping to shake a few hands, reciprocate a few high fives, and accept congratulations for my role in the rescue, barely breaking stride. I head directly to the drink cooler. These cruiser gatherings have a potluck ethos, where everyone brings a dish, or fish to grill, but that communal spirit does not extend to the libations. It's considered offside to pluck someone else's beer from the ice without asking, but I never bring my own; it's easier—and cheaper—to swipe. Surveying the cooler contents in a single glance, I pick out a bottle of Island Pirate Ale for its higher alcohol content.

One of the largest groups out here is former exec types: accountants, lawyers, investment bankers, office drones for years, now living on a generous but fixed income from their investments as they catch up on all the gallivanting they missed while putting in eighty-hour work weeks on Wall Street/Bay Street/Lombard Street grinding numbers/cases/accounts. But it doesn't matter how long it's been since a cruiser of this ilk has left behind the workaday world, they still constantly think and talk about money. I've learned not to bring up crypto with this traditionalist crew. They can drone on for hours about cryptocurrency price manipulation, participants they've known who've been defrauded or exploited, and the assets they've seen stolen outright. I resent this whole visionless contingent.

"Sawyer! All hail the local hero!"

Brendan Weatherby makes his way toward me through the throng. I've only known him a few weeks, but growing up in Annapolis I went to prep school and college with many Brendan Weatherbys.

He slaps me on the back.

"It was all Dani," I say. "She rescued the kids, all I did was pull them into the boat."

Brendan leans down and opens the lid of a smaller cooler tucked farther behind the first, crammed full of the good stuff, local Bahamian beer. I grab another Pirate Republic ale. Brendan always has a bottle opener on him, so I hold out a hand while he fishes a keychain with a flotation device and bottle opener from his shorts pocket.

"I think you're taking the concept of a Pirate Republic a bit too far, ya bastard," he says. "I know you didn't bring those beers."

Anyone else leveling such a charge against me would probably find themselves on the receiving end of a swift uppercut. But I let it slide with Brendan because he doesn't take anything too seriously. He might call me out on something, but he isn't going to get all worked up about it. "Didn't you hear I saved some lives today? You would begrudge an actual real-life hero a couple of beers?"

Brendan laughs, a little too raucously. Judging by his flushed cheeks, whatever's in his Solo cup isn't his first tonight.

Everything about Brendan testifies to a life of too much sun and too much rum. His trust fund baby uniform is less pressed than you would find with his land-based compatriots, but all the components are there: the Vineyard Vines polo with a popped collar, rolled-up khakis, and Sperry Top Siders to not mark up the teak decks on their expensively finished boats, which Brendan will exhaustively inform you are more expensively finished than ever because of having to illegally import teak now thanks to overly ambitious European legislators who are trying to regulate something in . . . Myanmar? Even though Brendan is the most friend-like of my cruiser acquaintances, I still am not going to listen to every damn thing he says, especially on the subject of hardwoods. Bro, the "teak" on my deck is made out of PVC.

When Brendan and I met at our first Bahamian cruiser soiree, we swapped stories of our prep school glory days, soccer, lacrosse, sailing, and troublemaking. Our experiences growing up were almost identical, but now our respective prospects are entirely different. They say money never lasts three generations and that was certainly true for us Stones. Thanks to the enormous, unhealthy appetites of my father, the Stone Mustard millions the first Sawyer Stone made selling to Kraft in the 1950s had been completely squandered before I was out of high school. Growing up with money, but then not having any, is the absolute worst of both worlds. You know what you're missing.

Brendan's dad, a self-made man, had no such appetites. There was plenty of money left for the third generation since he kept all his offspring on the same fiscal leash he had been trained on. I have no idea how Brendan talked his dad into buying him a boat for a yearlong circumnavigation, but I admire his success. A decade later, Brendan hasn't left the

Caribbean, and his "career" consists of alcohol-fueled parties and running aground when not at anchor. It's possible Weatherby Senior regrets his largesse, but maybe it's for the best if the black sheep stays isolated from the Connecticut flock.

"Another day in paradise, eh?" This is Brendan's go-to comment, a placeholder for the next topic of conversation. The booze his words waft over is powerful.

"I don't know, man, if this was paradise, my engine wouldn't be leaking oil like a motherfucker," I reply.

"I told you, you gotta replace your main seal. You keep tryin' to jury-rig your way around when you need a new seal. You gotta quit jackin' around and shell out before you trash your engine. Shell out, don't cheap out." Brendan may be slurring his words, but he's right and I know it.

But replacing seals will run me at least three grand.

"Great idea, man, why didn't I think of that." Brendan misses my sarcasm. So deeply rooted is his trust fund perspective that he cannot fathom pecuniary distress so epic, repairs cannot be made.

I catch a glimpse of Dani on the port side of *Xanadu*, tossing her hair and laughing, surrounded by a clutch of admirers. Rod is standing silently behind her, his eyes boring into her.

Brendan follows my gaze. "Are you checking out Rod and Dani over there? Dude is a full-blown creeper. Last party we were at, he was wasted and offering to show me his live camera feed from the ladies' room at the Sand Bar. I couldn't get away from him fast enough. You ever notice how he follows Dani around, like, all the time? It's like she's a tennis ball and he's fucking Pete Sampras's Labrador retriever.

"Rod Zild is fucking Pete Sampras's Labrador retriever? Shocking." I take a swig of ale.

"He never takes his eyes off her."

I shrug. "I can't get worked up over every guy that ogles her. Dani knows better."

"Well sure, but Rod seems sketchy to me, man. I've heard the dude has to live on a sailboat because he's banned from coming within one hundred miles of a school."

It wouldn't surprise me if that was true. I know a full-fledged pervert when I encounter one.

"Dani can handle herself with the likes of Rod Zild, and if he gets out of line, she'll come to me and I'll handle it."

Dani is popular at these gatherings, and not only because she's young and blonde. Men, regardless of age, are attracted to her on a visceral level. She likes to inform me of the "better offers" she often receives from rich men with bigger boats. But I know her better than she knows herself. She'd never go for a retired CEO who only ever talks about his golf game. Ditto the Silicon Valley millionaire who cashed out and now wants to repopulate the planet Aryan-style. I expect her loyalty, but neither of us are interested in forever.

The wind kicks up. Thunder rolls in the distance.

"Sounds like we are going to see a show tonight, bro. Light it up!"

For once I share Brendan's enthusiasm. There's nothing quite like being out on the water, in the safety of a harbor, during an electrical storm. If your electronics get blown out by a lightning strike you can dinghy into shore easily. Sailing *into* weather is another matter entirely—out at sea you'd better know how to navigate with a sextant.

A few prudent people on *Xanadu* take the party below deck, but Brendan and I wait on the stern for the storm to rumble in.

CHAPTER

5

Xanadu

Dani

I CATCH SAWYER'S EYE on *Xanadu*'s stern.

He meets my gaze and my smile widens, but he turns his back with a scowl.

I shake off his bad mood and head down the companionway into the galley, grabbing a plate as Sonja comes down the stairs.

Sonja is the matriarch of this Bahamian outpost of the cruiser community. She's gone all out, her glitzy fuchsia shirt adorned with dyed-to-match feathers circling the neckline like a built-in boa going in for the kill. Judging by her zero-fucks-given sense of personal style, I would guess she is at least a decade past the "40!" on the plates, balloons, and napkins. I'm not dumb enough to ask which birthday we are actually celebrating. Besides, I overheard her demurring when someone else tried to ask the same question earlier: "Don't you try and pin me down, älskling!" I don't know from her tone if that's Swedish for *asshole* or *honey*.

"Well, if it isn't the rescuer of lost locals!" Sonja says, giving me a one-armed hug. "Good girl!"

"Your shirt, Sonja. I've never seen anything like it," I reply, trying not to inhale a feather.

"Thank you for noticing, honey! I had it made special for tonight."

It would be hard not to notice, with Sonja molting everywhere she went.

I nod in mock understanding. "You certainly wouldn't ever expect to see that available off-the-rack, would you?"

Sonja beams in response. "Do you think I look like snatch?"

"What?!"

Sonja explains it's slang her granddaughter taught her, that she had picked up on "the TikTok."

"You look snatched," I gently correct her, thereby breaking my minutes long no-lie streak. "Has your granddaughter ever mentioned the instant facelift skin tape that's all the rage on TikTok? You pull the skin around your eyes and forehead taut, and tape it in place at your hairline. Takes years off your appearance, for a few pennies."

Sonja snorts with laughter. "I think I saw that in Terry Gilliam's *Brazil*."

For some reason, she snorts even louder when I tell her that I've never been there.

My eyes narrow as my already limited enjoyment of our conversation disappears entirely. Nevertheless, I generate a warm smile for her benefit and lift my red cup of white wine to tap Sonja's own. "Happy birthday, dear friend."

She gives me a quick embrace. "I love your dress. I never look that perky in a strapless bra," she complains, staring at my chest.

"I'm not wearing a bra, silly, these are fake." I take her hand in mine and put it over my chest, giving my left breast a squeeze. "See? You should get some."

She makes a face and removes her hand. "Well, you look amazing. How is the channel going? Have you posted the next video?"

"Yes, and I redid the intro to all of them. I'm happy with it."

"I was going to load up a plate and make the rounds. Join me?"

"Of course. Listen, you said you'd lend me that sailor's cookbook." Availability of food is one of the most difficult aspects of boat life. A lot of the places you end up at as a cruiser have limited options when it comes to food, and there's just not enough room on a boat to store everything you would have access to on the mainland. I often find myself dreaming of well-stocked pantry shelves, with spices and condiments galore, the way others dream of sex.

She walks over to a shelf and pulls a book from it. She hands *The Galley Gourmand* to me. "It looks like rain, so why don't we leave it here and you can get it before you leave?"

I nod, put the book on the table, and watch as she loads a plate.

I raise the cup to my lips and take a fortifying swallow. "It's so nice without the men around," I say, with a glance up the companionway where things are increasingly raucous.

"Isn't it though?" Sonja replies. "We need to do a girls' weekend. Maybe one at a hotel on shore."

"Oh, yes, please! Sawyer will complain though. That's all he does lately."

"Why on earth would he complain?"

"Money," I say, rolling my eyes.

"We're only talking a few hundred dollars for a couple rooms on shore for a night or two. That won't break the bank."

"Plus, dinners out and—"

"Drinks," we say at the same time.

I giggle and Sonja raises her glass to me. I take it from her so she can finish loading her plate.

"It's always money with him—me spending it or him having to replace and fix things. I am telling you—our stuff breaks every damn day."

"Life on a boat." Sonja deposits a spoonful of ambrosia on her plate, sniffs it, and shrugs. I doubt they had it in Norway or Finland or wherever she's from, but the coconut, mandarin orange, pineapple, mini marshmallow, and whipped cream dish was a staple of my Florida childhood. "And anyway, so what if Sawyer complains? Anders complains all the time, girl, you learn to ignore it."

I take a long swallow, look down and play with the rim of the glass. "Sawyer isn't like Anders."

Sonja raises a brow.

I meet her stare. "He can get mad."

Her head tilts and her eyes narrow.

"Yesterday there was a blockage in the head . . ." I say.

"Gross. That's the worst!"

"I know, right? But Sawyer was so pissed. Crazy mad. Accused me of putting tampons in it—I had to go for a swim before he completely lost it with me again."

And it wasn't tampons, it was my makeup removal pads. Lesson learned.

"Lost it?" Sonja says, brows coming together. "Again?" She's finished loading sides on her plate and gives me her full attention.

I attempt a smile and shrug. "He has a temper. It's nothing. I think I can get him on board with the girls' weekend," I say. "I just have to time it right. Pick a moment when I haven't done anything to aggravate him in a while."

A flush heats my skin, and I press my lips together. My eyes sting so I blink rapidly to dissolve the tears. I am not ruining my smoky eye over Sawyer and how unreasonable he's being about every little thing right now.

"What's going on with Sawyer, Dani? Is he getting physical with you?" she asks, plate forgotten.

I stare at the table. The swell has picked up, or someone's dinghy has put off too much wake. The dishes creep back and forth as the table rocks. I lean forward to fix the angle, so her food doesn't dump on the floor. "No—well, I mean, he's great when he's sober," I say. "It's just lately. He's only drinking so much because he's stressed." I press my knuckles to my mouth to prevent anything else from spilling out.

"He hits you when he drinks?" Sonja's voice rises two octaves.

You cannot drop your guard for a second with people out here. Cruisers are bigger gossips than the entirety of the *Real Housewives* franchises put together.

"That's not what I'm saying. I shouldn't have said anything. Sawyer's under so much stress with our financial issues, and I know it's annoying that I'm so useless with the boat stuff. Everything falls on him and it all gets the better of him sometimes. It's not his fault." I reach out a hand; her fleshy forearm is tight beneath my fingers. "Please, Sonja, I swear to God, it's nothing."

"Dani, if you don't feel safe—"

"It's not like that. Please. Forget I said anything. Our problems are temporary. He's never been like this—so volatile." An involuntary shudder rips through me. "It's the stupid crypto—our savings. But things are bound to get better, we went free diving today and—"

"I know a little something about bad boyfriends, Dani," she interrupts, her gaze never leaving mine. "I had a lover who hit me, years ago. One time. I hit him back harder and we were done. You cannot put up with it. Not even once."

"Sonja—it's not like that. It's not a regular thing. He's so frustrated with everything that's happened. And we live in such a small space. It's enough to make anyone crazy." I hold her gaze. "He's a blue belt in jiu-jitsu. If he wanted to do damage he could. He rarely loses control." That used to be true. Once crypto crashed and took our savings along with it, his fuse became alarmingly short.

When I raise the glass to drain my drink, her stare goes to the purple fingerprint bruises on the side of my neck, bruises I thought well masked by my Dermaflage concealer. Heat rushes through me, my cheeks flaming from the humidity, wine, and shame. My hand moves involuntarily to my throat.

She inhales sharply. "Girl, that needs to stop."

"I'm not leaving him," I say in a hard voice. "Sawyer and I are in this together. As soon as we can provision, we're going to restart our circumnavigation. We've had a run of bad luck with our finances and boat issues, but we'll get back to sailing." But I'm no longer sure who I'm trying to convince.

Sonja leans forward and puts a consoling hand on my shoulder.

"Let's plan that weekend, okay?"

"We all have pressures, Dani. There is no excuse for using you as a punching bag."

"I know how to calm him down."

Sonja shakes her head. "You can't count on that. I'm worried about you, älskling."

"I'm a strong woman. You don't need to worry about me. I can take care of myself. And if I ever need anything—"

"You get me, you call me on the radio, you dinghy over, swim if you must. You hear me? You have brought out my mama bear side and I'm here for you. Promise me you will reach out for help."

"I promise." I squeeze the older woman's hand.

"I'm starving," I say, directing Sonja's attention back to her neglected dinner plate. "What's good?"

I leave Sonja and carefully pick my way across *Xanadu* to where *Nauti Buoy* is rafted alongside her starboard side. What is it about rich people that they will lay out hundreds of thousands of dollars on a boat and then name it after a pun so stupid you wouldn't even put it on a bumper sticker?

If I ever own a boat or salon, I will name it something bougie. *Bougie Nights* would be a great boat name. I wonder if Sawyer would ever change the name of *Serendipity*. I should have a say in what the boat is called if my channel is what ends up keeping us afloat. Sure, so far I haven't made enough to cover a cup of coffee, but now that I've received enough views, I can lengthen the videos and fit two ads in. Ad revenue plus YouTube views could bring in real money.

I look down at the dark water between the two boats. It's always a little dangerous moving between rafted boats, especially when alcohol is involved. It's too easy to hit one's head on the way down, and too hard to be rescued from the space in between the boats when they're so close together, separated by a couple of fenders. Of course, it doesn't help that I'm wearing a micromini, but this is how we suffer for fashion. The benefit of wearing bodycon clothes is that help is never far away.

Indeed, as soon as I am about to climb the rail, Jim Marsh appears to take my hand. I'm half surprised it's not Rod, that guy who shadows me incessantly. Rod is a certified creeper, but even pervs have their uses. Still, I'm glad when I manage to give him the slip for a while.

"Get you a drink?" Jim asks.

"No, thanks, I've already had two glasses of white and a ton of bean salad. It was the only somewhat healthy dish so I went to town on it. Polished off the whole bowl. Check this out." I turn and cradle my puffed-out stomach like a longed-for pregnancy. A group of cruisers a few feet away see my gesture and one calls out "Congratulations!" I smile and wave.

Now rumors will spread that I'm pregnant.

Fabulous.

Jim turns his head away and changes the subject. "Did you post the new video?"

"Yep."

"And?"

I share my first genuine smile of the night. "I hit my monetization marks, finally."

Jim laughs and gives me a high five. "That's wonderful! Congrats."

"Thanks to you and your idea for that crossover video! You were right, we seem to have overlap in our viewers." I owe Jim for doing this for me. His idea of having me on his channel spearfishing last week, and then having him on mine reel fishing was the thing that kicked up my channel views to meet the YouTube metrics for monetization.

"Men?" He winks at me. "We sure do."

I reach for his hand and thread my fingers through his.

He flushes.

"I appreciate you so much. I think fate put you in my path—you have taught me so much, you really have a gift for editing, and . . . well, all of it. I'm thankful for you. There is no one like you in this world, Jim, so gifted and willing to share some of that gift with me."

I release his hand, wondering how long it has been since someone has touched him with that kind of intimacy.

Jim clears his throat and takes a swallow of his diet soda. He's been sober for a dozen years. A feat out here. He doesn't talk much about his past, but from what I do know, it's dark and full of pain. Stints in jail, violence, divorces. I put Jim in the small but notable cruiser category of "Damaged Goods"—those who have such pain and trauma that they can't or won't maintain normal relationships. Cruiser life with a partner can be lonely enough. Sailing solo? That's Tom-Hanks-plus-volleyball-grade loneliness.

"Are you okay? You had a pretty crazy day with the rescue," he says, his eyes full of concern. He's clearly been thinking about me. "And Sawyer seems like he's in a mood. He didn't even say hello when I saw him tonight."

I laugh, but even to me it sounds bitter. "His moods change faster than the weather. I never know which version of Sawyer I'm going to get. One minute he's furious about our financial state, the next he wants to go free diving." I shake my head. "But what I know for sure is that whenever something goes wrong, he's going to blame me. I'm the scapegoat for all our failures—as if I control the price of crypto or sabotaged our engine seals! I'm constantly on eggshells." The words come out in a rush—Jim is the only one I've really confided in about the Sawyer stuff. He's the only one I trust. "And I can't stop thinking about what you told me last week. It's not going to stop and go back to the way it was before, is it?"

Jim shakes his head.

"Sawyer is only a small part of the channel," I say, thinking aloud. "I could do it without him . . ." My throat thickens and suddenly I'm fighting tears.

"Dani—"

I glance nervously over my shoulder, scanning for Sawyer.

I put a hand on Jim's chest, over his left pectoral muscle. His shirt is thin enough that my fingers pick up the increase in his heart rate. "No lecture tonight, please, Jim. I know what I need to do, but I want to enjoy the party, not mourn the demise of my relationship, okay?"

He looks up at the stars and I follow his gaze. Above us, the night sky is showing off, the Milky Way sprawling above us, a darker ribbon running down its middle, the place, I've been told, where new stars are being formed.

"I never knew how many there were. I thought I'd seen stars, but until you get out here, out at sea, you have no idea how many you miss living in civilization," I say. It's dizzying, overwhelming even, but it doesn't make me feel small or afraid. I love the thought of our universe constantly expanding. We're all truly living our best lives out here.

"You know, despite all our efforts, I'm still not sure we're ever going to be able to convey how amazing this life is to our landlocked friends. How liberating it is, real freedom," Jim says, reading my mind.

"At least you're able to convey it to fifty thousand followers. I'm pretty much talking to myself. This whole big universe out there, and yet I can't seem to gain more than a few hundred subscribers."

"Nonsense. Now that you hit four thousand views, the algorithm will kick in, you'll see. Traffic will pick up, and with today's rescue it sounds like you've found your foot."

I laugh.

During one of our editing lessons a few weeks back, Jim told me the key to his channel's success: "You only need a dash of real serendipity. You need to reel in a foot."

"A what?" I asked.

"A foot. That's how my channel was discovered. I had about a hundred followers, pre-foot."

"A foot. A human foot?"

"Yep, still in its shoe."

"Tell me," I ordered.

"Nothing much to tell. I was fishing a little ways offshore of Knight's Key in Florida. I was big game fishing, but I got more than I bargained for when I reeled in a running shoe. I netted it out of the water expecting to trash it and about jumped out of my skin when I saw there was still a foot inside. You can look on my channel for the footage and see my reaction. I always have my GoPro set up on deck to record when I'm fishing, so I'm sure to get good footage when I'm fighting a big sailfish and don't have a hand free to capture the action. So I got the exact moment I saw the foot inside the shoe. I'm not ashamed to tell you I yelped like a schoolgirl. It was the darnedest thing. I edited the reaction video to add in a goofy shot of me holding up the shoe in your typical catch of the day pose. I posted the video online and sure as you're born, it went viral. I got interviewed on the news and that got picked up as a national story."

"So cool!"

"Yep. They used my YouTube channel for the footage of reeling it in and voila. Twenty thousand subscribers, overnight. The algorithms kicked in and YouTube did the rest."

"Was it a dismembered murder victim?" I asked.

"Well, there was a lot of speculation on that. On how just a foot would end up in the ocean like that. There was about every theory you can imagine in the comment section: mob hits, shark indigestion, human trafficking, alien autopsy, serial killer with a foot fetish, I don't know what all. Everyone had a different theory, and they hashed it out in the comment section going around and around in circles with evidence and deduction and wild guesses. Every comment would be so convincing! And you'd read the next one and think, *Oh no, this must be it.*" He shrugged. "Maybe I'm just gullible, because it turned out they were all wrong. A bunch of scientists in a lab figured the foot out. Apparently, this is something that happens a lot, all over the world."

"Feet get discovered in the ocean? I've never heard of it."

"In the ocean, washed up on beaches. Whenever a body goes in the ocean with shoes on, all the bottom feeders scavenge the soft tissues, and you wouldn't think it, but ankles aren't so much bony as all soft with ligaments and such. So the crabs and lobsters and bottom fish eat all those soft tissues and off goes the foot. Pop! Nowadays, they make sneakers with a lot of air in the soles, so they're buoyant, and they'll rise up and catch the currents. There goes the foot, riding the ocean currents until it washes up somewhere, or in my case, gets reeled in."

"But how do they know the foot wasn't cut off?" I asked.

"Forensic people can tell if there are cut marks on the foot bones—there was no way it could've been some criminal dismemberment like some of the commenters on my channel thought. They were even digging up profiles of missing persons, trying to judge by the shoe size and location who it could be! I didn't ever post the scientific explanation for how the foot came to be, because I could tell that the arguing back and forth with all the different theories and no one having the answers, well, that's what kept people coming to my channel."

I sighed. "You are so lucky you happened upon the foot."

"They call that a driver of engagement," Jim said with a wink.

Thinking about it now, maybe Jim's right.

"Jim . . . my rescue today could be my driver of engagement."

He nods. "I was just thinking the same thing. You have your foot! You should get a lot of views from that."

"You should've named your boat *Something's Afoot*!" I reply.

Jim laughs, even though I'm not kidding. His boat is the *Aboat Time*, which to me is the corniest of the corny boat puns.

"But seriously, you could rebrand your boat. I bet you would sell a ton of T-shirts. *Something's Afoot*! Do it, Jim! Let's launch some merch."

"With my luck, whoever's foot it was would come limpin' after me, looking for a cut of the action," Jim says.

"I still can't believe the police can't figure it out with all that DNA technology."

"They can get DNA profiles from bones, but there has to be a match in the DNA database or it doesn't help. You know there are something like forty thousand unidentified bodies in the US alone? And with ocean currents involved, that foot could have come from anywhere. I doubt it will ever be known."

"Wow, that's a lot of unsolved crimes. So many bad people going unpunished," I say in my best pearl-clutching voice.

"Well that forty thousand is not only foul play. There are natural-cause deaths in there too. I'm not sure how many of each. Every one is a tragedy though. Every last one."

I have met enough people in my life to say, with conviction, that a substantial percentage of those forty thousand "souls" were no great loss. Criminals, lowlifes, basic nobodies. Literally, who cares. Still, I mirror Jim's facial expression.

"How sad," I murmur.

Sawyer appears, having made his own way over from *Xanadu* to the *Nauti Buoy*. Jim nods to Sawyer and gives me a wary look on his way out.

"Did you get some nice daddy-daughter time with old Jim-bo?" Sawyer asks.

I don't take his bait. He's always felt threatened by my relationship with Jim. There's nothing more to say about it.

We silently watch the stars wink out from west to east as they're covered by clouds. The celebratory carousing around us has quieted as we all await the storm. It's instinctive for this crowd to give Mother Nature our undivided attention. No matter the size of our liveaboards, we all are vulnerable to her vagaries out here.

I shiver as the wind gusts, knowing the rain will be close behind it. Sawyer loops an arm around me, holding me close to the furnace of his body. I've lost count of the dates, hook-ups I met on dating platforms and in bars, businesses, and coffee shops, all the came-befores. The moment I met Sawyer I recognized a kindred spirit.

Sawyer leads me back to *Xanadu.*

The first wind gust sends discarded red cups, plates, and napkins spiraling off surfaces, to be chased down by inebriated cruisers. Sonja hustles around with a garbage bag. In the time that passed while I was on *Nauti Buoy* talking with Jim, the tenor of the party shifted. We've moved into the "alcohol plus time equals bad decisions" part of the equation. I watch as one of the more party-hardy cruiser types gingerly makes his way down the mast to both cheers and admonitions of us assembled below. I pull out my iPhone, wishing I hadn't left the drone on *Serendipity.* There are high fives all around as the cruiser reaches the deck, triumphant post-dare. I'm mildly disappointed by his safe return. A slip and fall could've been the perfect dramatic event for a future *Sailing with the Foxes* episode.

Thunder fills the bay with echoing booms and strobe lighting.

Sawyer strips off his shirt. "Time it!" he calls to Brendan, then, to me: "Hold my beer."

I take his Pirate ale. Sonja looks from him to me, mouth agape. She's expecting me to say something, but I don't know what.

I avoid meeting her wide-eyed gaze and focus on recording footage with my phone.

"Sawyer, it isn't safe!" Sonja calls out, but the inebriated crowd is already chanting his name.

"Fuck safe," Sawyer replies.

Nearly everyone has crowded under awnings or in galleys of the three rafted boats, but we all watch Sawyer race up the structure.

He's at the top, framed against the lightning.

He releases one hand and leans back.

The skies open.

CHAPTER 6

Serendipity

Sawyer

The day after the party

I WAKE WITH A start, naked, atop a bed, with the immediate understanding that I've been beaten. Taking inventory of the damage is automatic, honed from years of playing full-contact sports and the occasional bar fight. I assess for fractures and organ damage by gingerly lifting and flexing areas of my body. The initial assessment indicates deep, aching soreness—not the sharp, stabbing pain of fractures or the radiating agony of internal injuries.

I turn my head.

I'm in a cabin.

My cabin.

I'm on *Serendipity.*

Relief floods in. Whatever happened last night, I am home.

More worrisome is the realization that I have no memory of how I came to be in this state.

Am I concussed?

Dread surfaces from my amygdala.

It's a sensation I'm unfamiliar with.

I squint and turn my head to view the sun coming through the starboard porthole but it's a weak, hazy glow. It's early but already steaming in this space. A stench permeates the room and it dawns on me that the foul odor isn't the tide, the head, or rotting food; it's emanating from my body, every pore leaking out toxins—beer and rum are those I can identify. The only parts of my body not in pain are the soles of my feet.

My head is so bad and my mouth so dry I barely notice the pain in my hands at first. I draw a breath, sifting through my memory banks, grasping for whatever the hell happened last night, but there's only a toxic, hissing emptiness.

I push through the stabbing pain in my head and reach for lucidity.

I remember arriving with Dani at the party on *Xanadu*. Having a beer and shooting the shit with Brendan.

Then . . . nothing.

Not a damn thing.

Have I been fighting? I stagger to my feet and call for Dani. She doesn't answer but I'm not very loud because of the stabbing pain behind my eyes, a tight band relentlessly squeezing my skull.

Nausea rises, forcing me up.

I stagger to the head.

Urinating brings a wave of back pain so severe my stomach flips. It hurts to move my eyes.

I've been putting off an offshore dump for most of a week—it was critical days ago, it's now at DEFCON 2. Motoring offshore to dump waste is the very last thing I want to do right now.

I call Dani again, but it comes out like a moan.

She's probably gone for her morning swim. She's like the fucking post office, neither rain, nor sleet, nor hail. Dani never skips a day.

I dry heave into the head a few times, which brings a whole new level of pain to my aching body.

And the dread is still there. I don't know what terrible thing I've done, but I can't shake the feeling that I have.

My sludgy brain is barely processing through the splintering agony.

I move to the galley to splash water on my face, cupping my damaged hands to drink.

I down the last of the pink Pepto, attempt a few swallows of a yellow sports drink, and toss down four ibuprofen.

I will it to stay down.

I glance at Dani's cabin.

The flimsy wooden door is closed, with a fist-sized hole, low, dead center.

What the hell happened here last night?

I knock once and enter.

"Dani?"

Nothing.

I can't think, I can't stay upright. I can't imagine how I got to this state, but I know one thing: I need sleep.

I stagger back to my cabin, holding the walls for support, and lie down.

It's much later when I wake again; the sun is no longer coming through the porthole but no air is coming through the cabin either and I have soaked the sheets with my noxious sweat. I stare at the ceiling for a full ten minutes.

Why can't I remember anything from last night? I've been blackout drunk exactly never in my life.

The nausea is still there but I fight it down.

Now that my brain is more operational, I must clean up, and dump waste.

Stat.

"Dani? You back?" I call out.

I call again but there's no response. I lie back down to gather my strength.

There's the sound of an outboard close to *Serendipity.* Not our outboard though—whatever is approaching is more powerful. It shuts off and seconds later, "Yoo hoo! Dani!"

Sonja. My brain helpfully names the accented voice but also changes the dread to panic.

I hurtle out of bed so fast the room spins, and I grab the door jamb to stay vertical. My heart thunders in my chest. If it's possible, my body hurts more now than it did when I first woke. I glance to my left. The door to Dani's cabin is open but she's still not in her room. She's not in the galley either.

I take the companionway stairs to the stern, breathing heavily, staring down at Sonja in her dinghy. I'm in such a rush I've forgotten my sunglasses.

The Caribbean sun is blinding. I squint until I can barely see but it doesn't help. The relentless light triggers a nauseating, pulsing, nightmarish throb from the base of my neck over the top of my head to my temples.

When she sees me, Sonja's lips twist. "I brought this cookbook for Dani. She forgot it last night."

"She's out," I say, making a shooing motion, clenching my teeth against the pain.

Sonja looks at our dinghy, still tied up, and raises an eyebrow.

"Someone picked her up, obviously," I say, desperate to get rid of her.

"Who?"

"None of your business."

"Did she swim this morning? I didn't see her."

"She swims every morning," I reply.

She scowls but stands in the dinghy and holds the side of my boat.

"She's not here," I enunciate. My tongue is thick in my mouth. I'm slurring.

Sonja peers around, suspicious. "How's your head?" she asks, her tone snide.

"Fine."

"You were a mess last night. You better not have laid a finger on that girl," she says.

What is she talking about?

She's never been this hostile.

"Adios, Sonja," I reply, putting the back of my hand to my mouth as I will my stomach to settle. My mouth fills with saliva and I know what that portends.

"Tell her to call me," she says, suspicion lacing her tone. "Tell her I'm here if she needs me." She hands the book to me.

When I reach for it, she grabs my hand and gasps.

"What did you do?" she asks, her voice quavering.

I pull my hand out of her grasp, without wincing.

"Your hands—" she says, moving as if to try to climb on board.

I block her way. "I will throw you into the water," I warn. No matter how badly my body aches or if I vomit doing it.

"Dani!" she tries again, louder.

"Still not here," I bite out.

My heart is crashing around in my chest, my hands shaking. If she doesn't leave, I will fall over.

She gives me a final scowl and pushes off, restarting her engine.

I make it down the companionway and collapse onto the banquette in the galley. My phone is at the end of the table.

I call Dani's cell.

A trill comes from her room.

I limp over to her cabin.

She's gone out on her own before but never without letting me know, and never, ever without her phone. Her laptop is here. Her GoPro. The drone. A king's ransom in camera equipment. Her backpack. Her ID and phone, her passport, vaccination card.

The room is trashed, but that fact is meaningless, her room is always trashed.

I down the rest of the yellow sports drink.

It takes me a good two hours to clean up the mess in the kitchen and dump everything into a garbage bag. It's a few hours before sunset when I get up to scrub the deck. I do a half-assed job there because I need to go motor offshore to dump my waste tanks.

I text Jim but no response.

Finally, I call his cell.

"Hey Jim, have you seen Dani?"

"This morning." The reception is terrible, and his voice comes through the line in pieces.

"You saw her this morning? Swimming?" I ask.

"Well, yeah—I helped her get you in the dinghy around one AM."

I'd argue that was last night, not this morning, but whatever. "Did she mention any plans for today?"

"Not that I remember."

"Okay, thanks."

"You get rough with her, son?" Jim says after a beat.

"No fucking way."

"You were pretty combative with everyone last night. Anders got between you and Dani and you took a swing at him but you missed. You were barely able to stand and pretty incoherent."

I shake my head. "No."

"What do you mean, no?"

"That didn't happen."

"Son—"

My teeth grind together, triggering the blinding ache in my skull. "Don't call me that."

"Sawyer, I was blackout drunk for two decades and did countless things I would never have done sober. I've seen the bruises. You have a problem. Get some help."

"If you hear from her, tell her to call me." I disconnect the call and stare at the phone in my hand.

I text Brendan. *Seen Dani?*

It takes a while, but he replies.

No, and then, *Bro you were so fucked up last night.*

Feeling it. How did I get home?

I can see the three dots indicating he's typing.

They vanish.

Then they return.

I was fucked up too. Don't remember much after the mast climb.

I close my eyes. There's something at the edge of my memory: black sky, lightning ripping across it.

I go down the companionway into the galley and through to her cabin.

I check for anything that might indicate where she went or what she's taken, but it's impossible to tell. Something red pokes out of the pile of clothing on her bed.

I toss the clothes aside.

There, atop the white fitted sheet, is the leather studded paddle not even the masochists can handle. Why is this out? Who was she here with last night?

Black rage fills me. I pick it up and break it in half with my damaged hands.

Where the hell is she?

CHAPTER

7

Royal Bahamas Police Headquarters, George Town

Inspector Knowles

Two days after the party

INSPECTOR VERONIQUE KNOWLES is taking her last sip of lukewarm Monday morning coffee when the rookie deferentially knocks on her half open door.

"Ma'am, there's a couple here to see you. A Swedish couple."

"Give me five minutes to finish this report, then you may send them in," Inspector Knowles says.

The report is finished, actually, but she requires more coffee. She refills her industrial-sized mug from the pot of coffee kept on the credenza behind her and sits back down at her orderly desk. Everything about Inspector Knowles is orderly, from her closely cropped black hair, kept too short to ever allow for disorder, to her uniform jacket, immaculately pressed. Even her teeth are evenly spaced. Her words come out the same way—orderly, measured.

She transferred from Nassau two months ago, and compared to the armed robberies, sexual assaults, and crime there, this is a sleepy outpost, and she's thankful for it. There's still some domestic violence, bar fights, and others behaving badly, but nothing in the Exumas comes close to Freeport or Nassau.

She takes out her notepad and reflexively pulls up the robbery reporting form.

She stands as a middle-aged white couple enters, the woman leading, her companion a few steps behind. "Inspector Knowles of the Royal Bahamas Police Force."

"Anders Nilsson, and this is my wife, Sonja."

She shakes their hands, indicates the seating area, and takes her own chair. "How can we help you?"

"Our friend is missing," Sonja says.

"Are you staying here in George Town?"

"No, we're anchored off Lee Stocking Island. We live aboard."

Ah. Cruisers. She hadn't encountered them as much in Nassau, where there were more cruise ships and yachters. But the Exumas are famous, or infamous, for attracting the live-aboard crowd. In peak season, there are thousands of them. She makes a note on her pad to contact the Maritime Authority. That would be the appropriate protocol to observe.

"Can you tell me the name of the missing individual?"

"Dani Fox."

"Does she live with you on—I'm sorry, what is the name of your sailing vessel?"

"We're on *Xanadu*, a catamaran—they're on *Serendipity*, a monohull."

Knowles raises a brow. "They?"

"She and her boyfriend, a guy named Sawyer Fox—" Anders begins.

"No, he's Sawyer Stone," his wife says. "Sawyer Stone the third." Scorn is evident in the accented English.

Keeping her expression impassive, Knowles makes a note of the animosity and catalogs the absence of the boyfriend in the making of the report. She prides herself in never influencing a witness report with leading questions or suggestive reactions the way her sloppy colleagues so frequently do. "Let me get some basic information," Knowles says. "Full name, date of birth . . ."

Anders and Sonja exchange glances.

"We only know her as Dani Fox."

"How old is she?"

Sonja shrugs. "Early to mid-twenties?"

"Citizenship?"

"American."

"Can you tell me when you last saw her?"

"Saturday night on *Xanadu*. It was my birthday and there were a lot of people on the boat," Sonja says. "The reason we're here is that we think—"

"*You* think," Anders interjects.

"*I* think her boyfriend may have hurt her."

Knowles looks up. "Why would you say that?"

"She told me he hits her, and has problems with rage and drinking. He was very drunk Saturday night. By the time they left our party, he was aggressive with some people on the boat. He looked beat up when I saw him on Sunday."

"You saw him yesterday?"

"I went by their boat to see Dani, to check up on her and give her a cookbook. He said she wasn't there—but he looked awful. His hands were red and swollen, with cuts on the knuckles like he'd beaten someone."

"Do they have weapons on the boat?" A physical fight can turn deadly with the presence of a gun.

Anders frowns. "We all have knives."

"Do they have a gun?" In Knowles's experience some of the larger yachts had an array of weapons—for security in case they were boarded or to protect their wealthy owners. The Bahamas has its share of rifles and shotguns; obtaining a handgun would be more challenging, but it would be easy for Americans to get guns back home and stash them on board. They had to know they could be boarded, the weapon confiscated, and face steep fines if discovered, but that rarely stopped them.

"Probably a speargun for fishing," Sonja says. "We all have those too. A flare gun for safety I would expect. But they wouldn't have a handgun, would they? Those are illegal."

Knowles didn't reply to that. "Have you asked her boyfriend where she is?"

"He said she's gone out."

Knowles nods. "Is there anyone they have a dispute with?"

Anders shrugs. "He was stumbling around and snarling by the end of the night, but I don't think he connected with anything he swung at when they were leaving. We had to physically help him into the boat—and he's a big guy, maybe a little over six feet, maybe one hundred and eighty pounds. I think he does some martial art—"

"Jiu-jitsu," Sonja says. "But to answer your question, Inspector, I don't think any of the other cruisers have ever had a problem with them."

"The Fenwicks did . . ." Anders says.

"That was nothing," Sonja says.

Knowles raises her eyebrows.

Sonja sighs. "One of the other cruisers had them on board a few weeks ago for dinner, there were a few guests, we weren't there. Anyway, Linda Fenwick's engagement ring went missing. There was a whole to-do about it. She'd left it on a ring holder by the sink and she discovered it missing halfway through the party. They knew the other couples well, so Linda accused Dani and Sawyer of stealing the ring and asked them to leave. Then the next day Linda found it in the pocket of the sweater she was wearing the night before," Sonja says.

"She said she didn't put it there," Anders says.

"What else is she going to say? Linda Fenwick is a fåne," Sonja says.

"I'm sorry?" Inspector Knowles asks.

"An idiot," her husband translates. "The Fenwicks left yesterday."

"Name of the vessel?"

"*Seaearthski.*"

Knowles writes it down. "Can you give me a physical description of Dani?"

Sonja obligingly pulls up a photo of a beautiful young woman striking a practiced pose with her dinner plate, like a game show model displaying a prize. Of course she's blonde. Dani appears in the photo as carefree, but Knowles doesn't put too much stock in appearances.

"She has a YouTube channel called *Sailing with the Foxes*, and she's on Instagram as SerendipiDani," Sonja presses on. "You can get all sorts of recent pictures there. And there's video of her with Sawyer, where she's talking about their relationship. You will see why I'm so worried."

Knowles makes a few notes to look up the two sites later.

"But she didn't post yesterday or today and no one has seen her swimming," Sonja says. "That's—what would you call it? A red flag."

"Swimming?" Knowles asks.

"She swims every morning for about an hour, usually before nine. Usually a straight line away from the boat, out to the channel and back," Anders says.

"There was a small craft advisory yesterday," Knowles says. "Her companion is not concerned?"

"Yesterday morning—Sunday—I asked Sawyer where she was and he said she'd gotten picked up and was ashore. But no one I've spoken to has seen her since late the night of the party—or I suppose it was early Sunday morning—when she took him back to their boat in that state. I wanted to board *Serendipity* to look for Dani, but Sawyer basically threatened me. He wouldn't let me even look around. I called out for her but no answer."

"And no one has seen her on their boat?"

"No, and we're anchored not far from them," Sonja says.

"Rod has binoculars, and he hasn't seen her," Anders says. "We don't see her swimming; we think something is wrong."

"Is that common, to look at other boats with binoculars?" Knowles asks.

Sonja frowns. "Rod is a bit—"

Anders says something under his breath.

Inspector Knowles gives him a pointed look.

"A pervert," his wife says.

"Last name?"

"Zild. Rod Zild. His boat is the *Zildgeist*."

"Is there anyone else who's taken an unusual interest in Ms. Fox, other than Mr. Zild?"

"Not an unusual interest, but Brendan Weatherby spends a fair amount of time with Sawyer and seems to be on friendly terms with Dani as well. Dani's also friends with Jim Marsh—his boat is the *Aboat Time*. He has his own YouTube channel too."

"Has anyone contacted him?"

Sonja shakes her head. "He planned to sail out last night or this morning. He goes off-grid, fishing, camping, all the time. He only stayed anchored with us so long because of the party. He spends most of his time farther south."

"If you can give me the cell phone numbers of these people, including her boyfriend, it would be helpful. And where off Lee Stocking are you anchored?"

"Sand Dollar Beach."

Inspector Knowles gets a bit more information from the cruisers, gives them her card, then ushers them out of her office.

She sits back down, calls the Maritime Authority, and asks for the supervisor.

"It seems we may have an American woman who has gone missing from her liveaboard vessel under suspicious circumstances," she says. "I'd like you to find the sailboat *Serendipity* anchored out off Sand Dollar and see if the woman,

Dani Fox, has returned. If she has not, please bring me Sawyer Stone, today."

Knowles's even keel extends to her own thoughts. There are enough red flags here to warrant taking this report seriously. Missing woman, hot-tempered partner is a well-worn trope for a reason. Even when the husband/boyfriend seemed like a great guy on paper, experience has taught Knowles to take the possibility of violence behind closed doors seriously. And this Sawyer Stone does not reach the good-guy-on-paper standard. Not when, if the Nilssons' report is true, he was drunk and combative prior to the disappearance of his girlfriend. Inspector Knowles will investigate as thoroughly as resources permit, even though her mind is still generating all the innocuous explanations for a person to be "missing" for a day. The timeline is still well within the realm of sleeping it off.

Knowles took note of Sonja's propensity to slide into hyperbole in their interview, but on the face of it, this report is cause for concern. A member of an itinerant population disappeared. But that's what itinerant people do best: they disappear.

Knowles's naturally dialectical thought processes continue, analyzing all the possibilities and keeping her from the investigative trap of jumping to conclusions first and then searching only for the evidence that will support that theory.

But as she turns over the details from the short interview with the Nordic cruisers, Knowles's thoughts keep coming back to the description of Dani's daily swim. What kind of person would consistently eschew such a basic safety principle as sticking near the coastline? Why head for open water? Any person with experience knows how quickly weather can change, swells can come up. Stick near the coast, in shallow water, don't swim alone. Is that some subliminal desire for escape being expressed?

Knowles firmly believes that all actions have underlying meaning and evidentiary value.

She pulls up the SerendipiDani Instagram page and clicks through the photos. Dani in a red bikini, Dani topless from behind, Dani and her boyfriend Sawyer Stone III, she presumes, rolling around in the surf. Dani topless on the bow with blonde hair covering her breasts, Dani topless on shore with a grinning Sawyer behind her, his large hands reaching around to cover her breasts. Dani swimming away from the camera with a speargun and fins wearing . . . nothing? No, there's the barest hint of a light brown thong, matching her tanned skin so well as to give the illusion of total nudity.

Knowles looks skyward and blows out a breath. She's out of her depth in the social media realm, and not being unduly hampered by ego, her reflexive instinct is to assemble a team with the skills needed to shore up her own shortcomings. Officer Walter impressed her on previous assignments. While Walter's jocular nature is seen by some of the other senior officers as impudence, Vero sees it only as evidence of a sharp mind. And Walter has the added benefit of proximity—his desk is right outside Knowles's door.

"What are the nudity rules here anyway?" she calls out to Officer Walter.

Walter instantly appears in her door frame. "In this office, ma'am? My recollection from recruit training is that there is very little leeway on nudity in the station itself, with a temporary exception being allotted for the duration of the annual office Christmas party."

"On Instagram. I am reviewing the postings of the missing woman."

"You know what platform is a thousand times better than Instagram, boss? Instakilogram. Oh, I'm sorry boss, I just can't help myself." Walter laughs heartily at his own joke, and does not seem to mind that he's laughing alone. "Nudity rules on Instagram, off the top of my head: Women can't display their nipples—because it's a site for twelve and up. You can post nude breasts if you blur the nipples or paint them or put stickers over them. You can't show male or female genitalia but you can show some ass . . . excuse me, buttocks, but not close up or anything."

Knowles stares at him. "Evidently this is your area," she says dryly. "How exactly did you acquire this encyclopedic knowledge, Walter?"

His cheeks flush and he looks down.

"Perhaps I spend a little too much time on social media. 'Terminally online' is the diagnosis, you might say."

"I wouldn't say that. I don't know what that means. I defer to your demonstrated expertise. Come and have a look at this account."

Officer Walter comes around her desk, peers at her computer, and groans theatrically at the images displayed on Knowles's screen.

She shoots him a quelling look.

"Sorry boss, but those are all thirst traps," he says. Seeing her look of puzzlement, he adds, "Seductive pictures, ma'am."

"Is that what you call it? In my day we called it narcissism."

CHAPTER

8

Royal Bahamas Police Headquarters

Sawyer

Day 3

THIS IS NOT my first time being questioned by the police. It's not even my first time being questioned by the police in a foreign country. The interview room is dim, cramped, and humid. There's no window to put an air conditioning unit in and the ceiling vent is barely puffing out enough air to flutter the gray paint peeling on the wall.

"This is Officer Walter, he'll be assisting with the investigation," Inspector Knowles says, taking her seat next to Walter. "Thank you for coming in to talk with us today, Mr. Stone. Can you give your passport to Officer Walter? We want to check some things."

I hand over my passport and sit on the rusty folding chair. It's not a great feeling; it seems like the first small step down a path of ever-increasing restraints on my personal liberty.

"Mr. Stone, the reason we requested you come in is that we've had some individuals express concern regarding the whereabouts of your girlfriend. We were hoping you could shed some light on the matter."

"I wish I could. The last time I saw her was Saturday night."

"Not Sunday?"

"I was pretty wasted late Saturday and early Sunday. I don't remember much of anything. People tell me Dani got me into the dinghy and back to *Serendipity.* I woke up in my own bed, Sunday morning, ill. That's all I know."

"Is this a common occurrence for you? Blacking out? Drinking excessively?"

Her tone is neutral, but I bristle. "No. It's not even a rare occurrence. It never happens."

"Apart from Saturday. So, tell me what you remember from Saturday night, from the party on"—she checks her notes—"*Xanadu*?"

"I remember getting to the party. I had a few drinks. Talked to a few people. After that, nothing."

"Is Dani the type of person to leave without letting you know where she's going? Could she have left you? We have reports of a physical altercation."

I know where this is going. I lean back in my chair.

"No, she's not the type to disappear, no, she didn't leave me, and no, we didn't have a physical altercation or fight of any kind."

"But you're not sure about that last one, correct? Because you don't remember." Inspector Knowles is harder to read than most cops. I'm not sure what she's thinking, so I'll go straight to the most damaging possibility and address it before Knowles does.

"I have never raised a hand to a woman and anyone who says I did is a liar."

Knowles's eyes narrow. "Are you concerned that she is missing?"

"Yes, I'm concerned. Mostly because she swims every morning and I worry she may have run into trouble. Or maybe she left with friends. I have no idea."

"Are there any of her personal items missing as well? A suitcase?"

"I haven't noticed anything missing. Her phone, wallet, computer, everything she would need to travel is still on the boat." Obviously, this is hugely important information, as it argues against a whole subset of innocuous explanations for Dani's absence. I watch Knowles's face as she takes in this information and see no change of expression. I wonder if she's going through the motions here. Some island cops are disinterested in getting involved in the business of tourists and foreigners because it's almost always messy.

She hands me a paper. "Could you complete this missing person checklist?" she asks.

I skim it. "I don't think I can answer all of this. Dani and I are close but we value our privacy—and we don't talk about our past. We live in the moment."

Knowles's lips purse. "That's fine, answer what you can."

Basic information about the missing person:

Full name: Dani Fox
Date of birth: 01/02/2001
Birthplace: Florida?
Nicknames: None
Current and previous addresses: *Serendipity*, Sand Dollar Beach, Bahamas, at anchor
Current and former employers: Unknown
Relatives: Mother dead, father unknown, Uncle Anthony maybe in California
Height: 5'3"
Weight: 105 lbs.
Age: 23
Hair color/length/texture: Blonde, medium length, straight
Eye color: Blue

Markings (tattoos, birthmarks, scars, etc.): Some scars—chin, back, inner right arm, breast implants

Social media of the missing person: SerendipiDani on Instagram, *Sailing with the Foxes* on YouTube

Does the person smoke? If yes, what brand of cigarettes? No

Does the person drink alcohol? Rarely

Does the person use recreational drugs? No

Does the person chew gum? Never

What types of recreation or activities does the person engage in, including hobbies? Swimming, aquatic fitness, running, strength training

Does the person have particular banking habits? No

Is the person religious? No

What level of education or training does the person have? Some college

Overall health and condition of the missing person: Excellent

Clothing that the person was wearing the last time seen: Dress with flowers

Type of footwear: None

The time and location of where he/she was last seen: Saturday evening, SV *Xanadu*

Was the missing person concerned about anything before he/she went missing? No

Physical condition: Excellent

Any known medical problems: No

Any psychological problems: No

Any medications: No

Any addictions: No

Provide the name of the missing person's family physician and their health card number, if possible: N/A

Provide the name of the missing person's main dentist, if possible: Unknown

I hand back the form.

"Sonja Nilsson is very concerned about your girlfriend," Knowles says.

I roll my eyes. "Sonja is not my biggest fan—I would expect she would assert the obvious, that I've had something to do with Dani's disappearance. I'm the missing person's romantic partner. It's the twenty-first century equivalent of saying the butler did it. Which is to say, trite and shallow. Exactly the quality of insight I would expect from Sonja," I say.

Preempting someone's accusation and characterizing it as facile is an effective rhetorical technique I picked up in Debate Club at my prep school. It's funny how much emphasis elite schools put on developing the capacity of their students to sell bullshit. My classmates have put their Advanced Bullshittery skills to good use in selling IPOs and congressional testimony. For me it comes in handy during police interrogations.

"Intimate partner violence is a problem that affects millions of women regardless of age, economic status, race, sexual orientation, or education," Knowles intones. "Did anyone see Dani with you Sunday?"

"I don't know."

"Where do you think Dani is, Mr. Stone?"

"No idea." I frown. "Dani has gone her own way before—to resupply, visit friends, shop, whatever. We're not joined at the hip."

"So you *aren't* concerned?"

I lean forward. "I wasn't initially but I am now. It's been two days and she hasn't contacted me. Wherever she went, she didn't bring her phone or her passport—which is out of character. I mean, I could see if she went to stay with a friend—"

"Does she stay with *friends* often?" the detective asks.

There's an emphasis on the word *friends* I don't care for.

I lean back and stare her down. "Look, we live in a very small space. Although we enjoy each other's company, sometimes one or the other of us will want to leave, get off the boat, go to someone else's boat, go ashore. Whatever. We're independent people and I am not her keeper."

"Do you think she could've . . . gone off . . . with someone?"

There it is again. That implication that Dani's left me for someone else.

I keep my voice level. "As I said, I could see her going to the shops or meeting up with friends or even staying with a friend on a boat, but not for this long, not without contacting me, and not without her gear."

"What gear?"

"Computer, phone, drone, camera, ID, all of it."

"We spoke with her friend Sonja—"

A laugh sputters out of me. "Sonja is not her friend."

"She says she's a friend of your girlfriend."

I shake my head. "I'm telling you she's not. Dani was nice to her, but she wasn't a friend."

"Apparently Dani told Sonja you'd been violent."

My breath halts mid-exhale. "She's lying. That's utter bullshit. I would never hurt Dani."

"Now see, we've considered that. Sometimes people like to get overly involved, insert themselves into the investigation, jump to conclusions, but she showed us some texts she sent to your girlfriend Saturday night and Sunday morning—where she appears to be checking up on her after a discussion they had about your violent temper, at the party."

I laugh and it's genuine. "Sonja's got the wrong end of the stick. Dani had the short fuse, not me."

"Had?"

"What?"

"You said Dani *had* a short fuse?"

"No, I said she has a short fuse."

The detective gives a sidelong glance at the police officer sitting next to her.

"Sir, you said had," the officer says.

I clench my fists under the table. "I misspoke. Rather than police my grammar, what I'd like you to do is your actual police *jobs*. Investigate. Find Dani." The charm offensive is over. They're not buying it and I don't have to be here. I stand.

"We've seen your channel," Inspector Knowles says, fingers clacking on her laptop keyboard.

I sit back down. "What, her YouTube channel?"

"Yes, *Sailing with the Foxes*."

"You and about five other people," I say. "We've been at sea for most of a year and she's posted a dozen videos."

"She has several thousand followers," the inspector says, turning her computer screen to face me.

"Several *thousand*?" I echo.

She'd made noise about hitting monetization targets or something, but I haven't paid much attention.

I squint at the laptop and see an unfamiliar thumbnail on her YouTube page. "She put a new video up *today*?" I lean forward. "Did she actually post it today or was it pre-scheduled?"

"We were hoping you could tell us that," Knowles says. "On this page it says they're going to post every Monday."

"Cool," I say, stifling a yawn. "She's said with the algorithms you have to try to post weekly. Which makes it tough for us since we're sometimes not in places where we're able to upload the videos—no signal."

The detective hits play on the new post and turns the sound up. "Do you remember filming this?"

I nod. It's a mashup of our time in the Florida Keys and the passage to the Bahamas. "It's old footage."

"Is that common for these videos? Using old footage?"

"I wouldn't know. The video stuff is all her. My part is holding the camera occasionally and making sure I show her best angles." I smile broadly at the male police officer, Walter, who stares back at me, unsmiling. Apparently these two don't ascribe to the good cop bad cop method of establishing rapport. "She's been putting a lot of time into these. At least that's what she says."

"Well, Mr. Stone, this is the part that we found most interesting." Knowles swipes the bar at the bottom of the video to get close to the end, then hits play again.

Dani is alone in our galley. Her eyes are bloodshot and tearful and she's in full makeup. It's what I think of as her "natural" look but takes as long to produce as her more dramatic looks. "It's not going all that well. I know you all tune in to see the magical paradise we live in. And most of the time it is a paradise. But lately, Sawyer has been . . . upset," Dani says in a voice barely above a whisper. The camera is so close I can see her pores.

I'm frozen in my chair.

Dani darts a wide-eyed, frightened glance over her shoulder. "He's worried about our dream coming apart and I am too." She stares straight into the camera, lips trembling. "I have to go." There's a noise behind her, the feed shuts off.

I stare at the screen with its closing photo of her swimming away from the camera with a speargun and fins. The *Like! Subscribe!* buttons are above her butt.

Inspector Knowles is staring at me. So is the cop seated next to her.

"What the actual fuck." I rub a hand over my face.

"Mr. Stone, can you tell me why your wife—"

"Girlfriend."

"Why did your girlfriend seem so afraid?" the inspector asks.

Why indeed. What the fuck was that?

"She wasn't. I don't know what that even was. Things have been more stressful lately, we've had some issues with the boat, but she wasn't *afraid.*" I stand. "If you need me, you know where to find me, out looking for my girl." Get me the fuck out of here.

Knowles slides my passport back to me. "Sir," she says, as I pocket it. "Please don't leave the Bahamas."

I fix my gaze on her. "With Dani missing? No chance in hell."

Serendipity

Sawyer

This ends now.

I pull up our YouTube account.

Wrong password. Try again.

I try again.

Wrong password. Try again.

I sit back, staring at the screen.

Someone has changed the password and didn't tell me.

I pull up the new video again.

8,000 views. 2,560 subscribers.

Holy hell.

It's evident from the YouTube comments that someone has shared the link for our channel in an online cruiser forum. It doesn't take me long to find the culprit.

The original poster in the CruiserLife forum is OlivijaNJ. What a poor alias for the owners of *Xanadu.*

Attention cruisers! We're missing one of our own! Dani Fox of Serendipity disappeared sometime Sunday evening or Monday morning near Lee Stocking Island in the Exumas. Police are investigating the suspicious circumstances surrounding her disappearance. If you see or hear from Dani, or have any information, please notify the Royal Bahamas Police Force in George

Town via their website linked below. I've also posted a link to her YouTube channel.

capnbeachbruh25 I know them IRL. She was even hotter in person. They were both super cool, fun cruisers. There didn't seem to be anything wrong with their relationship whatsoever.

cruiseraspen281 We all know how this ends—with her body washing up somewhere and the dude in prison.

skipperjonesey my issue with this bro's behavior is that there is not one thing that is normal about it. if you love someone and they disappear, sound the alarm, go to the police. WTF bro?

H20geezer Did he or didn't he? This is as bad as the monohull vs. catamaran debate!

BTfan7688 This all going down in the Bermuda Triangle, folks. We all know anything can happen there.

rowrip77 What excuse could the boyfriend possibly have for not going to the police right away? Observing the sabbath? He doesn't SEEM like the churchgoing type. Wanted in surgery? Oh wait he's not a doctor. Binge watching Season 5 of *Stranger Things* before getting spoiled? Oh wait it's not out yet. Dog ate this guy's alibi I guess. GUILTY 👏 AS 👏 CHARGED 👏

CHAPTER

9

Royal Bahamas Police Headquarters

Inspector Knowles

Day 4

BEFORE KNOWLES GETS to the door of the police station, Officer Walter comes out.

"Boss, you didn't happen to advertise a happy hour with half-priced drinks here at the station this morning, did you? Because there is an absolute gaggle of cruisers waiting in the lobby. Standing room only. Here's the sign-in sheet."

"You know I did no such thing," Knowles replies.

"I know, boss, but you have to admit that it's pretty remarkable to have even one cruiser worried about anything at all, let alone three cruisers worried about the same thing. That's got to be some kind of record for the *don't worry, be happy* crowd living their best lives. They want to give statements about the missing woman."

There's not enough coffee on the island for her to deal with all these cruisers today.

"Join me for these interviews, Walter. I will need your eyes and ears."

Knowles pulls open the door, strides through, and nods to each of the three people standing in the small room. "I'll be with you momentarily."

She continues through to her office, deposits her extra-large travel mug on the credenza, and pulls out her notebook.

She calls Walter to bring in Brendan Weatherby first. Sonja had mentioned that Weatherby was the closest thing to a friend that Sawyer had in their community.

"Have a seat," she says.

"Brendan Weatherby." He extends his hand.

Knowles is unsurprised by the flaccidity of the handshake. "Inspector Veronique Knowles."

"Veronique? You don't often hear French names around these parts," Weatherby says, seemingly more at ease than most are while making a police report. Knowles feels no need to respond. Part of her interview technique is to allow long silences, discomfit for people to reveal themselves. She sits, clicking through some files on her desktop, surreptitiously observing the man in front of her. He's a ruddy white man with a prematurely receding hairline. His leg bounces on his knee and, despite the spearmint gum he's chewing, Bahamian rum fumes waft over. She can almost identify the brand from what is leaching out of his pores. Finally, she clicks her computer monitor off, and takes out a pen and notepad.

"Thank you for coming in today, Mr. Weatherby."

"I figured I had to come when you've got this lot planning a visit."

"Which lot is that?"

"Darcey and Sonja—couple of Karens who don't much care for Sawyer. Figured he needed someone to vouch for him, so here I am—up much too early."

Knowles nods. "When was the last time you saw Dani Fox?"

"Saturday night, at a boat party on *Xanadu*."

"Did everything seem normal the last time you saw her? Was there anything unusual or odd about the party or Dani and Sawyer?"

He frowns. "Sawyer got astoundingly smashed, which was quite odd. I'd never seen him that drunk before. We all drink, but not like that. Boats aren't the best place for getting blackout drunk, if you catch my drift. Turns out he's one of those combative drunks. There are the gregarious drunks and then there are the ones who are aggro and probably a million types in between."

Knowles doesn't respond. She's learned over the years to let people talk, not to interject with questions or the small noises to indicate listening. Some people will do anything to fill an uncomfortable silence. She's seen a few talk themselves straight into self-incrimination over the years. Officer Walter has the good sense to follow her lead. Most rookies would interpret the silence as an invitation to insert themselves into the interview. Despite his immature wisecracking, Walter is showing good instincts.

"Anyway, nothing unusual happened. Well, Sawyer at one point climbed the main mast in the middle of an electrical storm."

Seems Dani and Sawyer are a matched pair. She swims straight out to sea every day and he launches himself up metal objects in a thunderstorm on the water. It's a wonder they've survived this long. "I believe that would qualify as unusual," Knowles says dryly. "How did the mast climbing come about?"

"I don't know. I wasn't privy to that decision-making process. I expect it was some manifestation of drunken male peacocking. One of the cruisers had shimmied right up the pole like it was nothing a few minutes prior. But that was before the thunder broke out. You'd think that would put an end to mast climbing contests, but no, I think that's what got Sawyer going. He's always one to take a dare to the next level. Someone jumps off a cliff into the ocean, he will do the same but add a backflip."

"But he's not a habitual drinker?" Knowles asks.

"Oh, he's a habitual drinker in the sense that he enjoys a beer or two whenever there's a cruiser meetup, but never to excess, and never to lose control of his faculties."

"How about Dani? Is she known to overindulge?"

"I wouldn't say so. She has a glass or two of wine or champagne or an Aperol spritz on occasion, but I wouldn't say I've ever seen her intoxicated. Maybe a little tipsy sometimes? It's hard to tell, she has one of those flirty personalities. She always seems a wee bit tipsy."

"Have you spent a lot of time with Sawyer and Dani as a couple?"

"Eh, yes and no. We cruisers can put in a lot of hours together, as no one works a regular job, where your hours belong to someone else. We will sometimes fish together or laze about together, do a deserted beach meetup or hit the bar and hours roll by without real note of it being made. But I would say that there's not deep friendships. With Dani and Sawyer we spend time together, and cross paths over and over again as we both drift about, but it's a potluck party level of knowing someone. There's something of a culture among cruisers, keep the conversation in the present. Live in the moment. We don't talk about where people came from, or what they did when they lived the landlocked life. I've spent a lot of time in the company of Dani and Sawyer, but I wouldn't say that I know them, in the intimate sense, at all."

Weatherby is warmed up now and waxing philosophical. Knowles weighs whether more time interviewing him will reveal anything worthwhile.

"Were you drinking to excess that night, sir?"

He tips his head and doesn't respond.

"The reason I ask is, alcohol can impair one's memory."

"No more than usual, and I can hold my liquor," he replies. "I didn't see them leave. I was on the Madrigals' *Nauti Buoy* most of the night. They have an extra cabin so I crashed there instead of going back to my boat."

"When did you last see Dani?"

"Probably ten PM? I'm not totally sure, but it was after the storm rolled through."

Knowles writes the time down. "What can you tell me about Dani Fox?" she asks.

"She's nice, always asking a lot of questions. How are you, whatcha been up to, that kind of thing. I don't know if she's all that smart, but she's sexy as all hell."

"Did you have any kind of romantic relationship with Dani?"

Weatherby throws his hands up. "Hell no! Sawyer is a friend."

"Okay," Knowles says, making a note in her book.

"Dani didn't have a lot of friends among the cruisers," he continues.

"Why not?"

"They haven't been here long. Then there's the fact that most of the women don't like her. Probably because she's younger and hotter. Guys generally dig her. Rod Zild is obsessed with her."

There was that name again. "In what way?"

"He's always trying to flirt with her, touch her and stuff. Once he went out swimming with her, but she left him in the dust," he says with a chuckle.

"Did that make him mad?"

"I don't know about mad, he's a pretty wimpy guy. Very soft. In a fight with Zild, my money would be on Dani. She seems like she could hold her own."

"Regarding Rod, can you give me any specifics about his 'obsession'?" Knowles says with what she hopes is patience.

"He watches her, with binoculars. That's not cool. All of us cruisers value our privacy out here. Someone told me he had night vision goggles, which is super creepy. I told all of this to Sawyer a while back, hoping he'd do something about it."

"Did he?"

"Not as far as I know."

"Did Dani ever mention Sawyer being abusive?"

"Nah. She loved the guy. They're a great couple. Super friendly. Everyone likes them."

"Except for all the women cruisers."

Weatherby frowns. "Yeah, well. I told you why. Some of the women like her. Sonja does. Those two were tight."

Knowles makes a note in her book as this doesn't jive with Sawyer's account of the relationship between the two women.

"There was something a while back with a missing ring that people thought Dani took, and it turned up on their boat so she didn't take it—you'd think they'd apologize but instead she kept insisting it was Dani. They were assholes, the Fenwicks; I was glad when they headed out." He leans forward conspiratorially. "You see Darcey sitting out there? She doesn't like Dani and she's made it obvious—uncomfortably obvious. She and her crew are oddballs, I mean besides the throuple thing, they're odd. And one of them, I don't know if it's the guy or the girl, hit on Dani two weeks ago. Darcey is still pissed about it."

Knowles searches her memory for the definition of a throuple. A threesome with commitment is the best her brain can come up with. With her track record of two failed marriages, she was certainly in no position to throw stones, but there is something disorderly about the idea of a three-way commitment. The asymmetry of it bothers her. She isn't a prude, exactly, but when things veer outside the mainstream of human behavior, it always unsettles her. In some respects, the comfort Knowles finds in conformity helps her investigations. When something is out of place, not as it should be, Knowles notices.

She appreciates the tip on the bad blood, but as her doctor once told her after an abnormal blood test: When you hear hoofbeats, look for horses, not zebras. Same with police work. Ninety-nine times out of a hundred, things are exactly what they appear to be.

Which is why she needs to steer the conversation back on course. "You never saw Sawyer be abusive to Dani?"

Brendan shakes his head. "Nope. And I know Sawyer, he's a nice guy. Short on cash with the crypto thing, but a good dude."

Knowles tilts her heard. "What crypto thing?"

"He had a bunch of money in Soltana and it tanked. I told him it was unreliable as hell—my dad is a money guy, and he told me that the value of crypto comes from 'the greater fool.' That's the idea that some stupid investments can be profitable so long as there's another fool stupider than you who will buy when you're ready to sell. It's like musical chairs, and sooner or later the music stops. The market runs out of fools and the bubble pops, whether it's tulips or Pets.com. I told Sawyer this, many times, but gamblers gonna gamble."

Knowles has spent too much time in Nassau and Freeport not to follow that up. "He's a gambler?"

"Not with cards, with crypto. He laid all his eggs in the Soltana basket. I mean, I guess it's not surprising that a guy who will climb up a mast in a lightning storm for shits and giggles doesn't have a diversified stock portfolio. But Soltana? It's an altcoin, for god's sake."

"An altcoin?" Inspector Knowles asks, although she knows all about cryptocurrencies. After all, a Bahamian law enforcement team arrested and then extradited the disgraced founder of the largest cryptocurrency scheme. Crypto brought big business to their tiny nation before it went bust. Bahamians lost millions of dollars and hundreds of jobs when it collapsed. But in her investigative experience, it's often illuminating to ask a man to explain something she knows more about than he does.

"That means it's not one of the two main cryptocurrencies, Ethereum and Bitcoin. You're at one level of risk for being in a cryptocurrency rather than a traditional stock/bond/mutual fund type investment, but then you take it even further by passing up the mainstream coins to go out on a limb with an altcoin. There're hundreds, maybe thousands, of altcoins, each with their alleged use cases, white papers about their technological superiority and all that, but it's pretty impossible to tell what their price is going to do. It's a complete crapshoot. A given altcoin could be worth a fraction of a cent, but then some billionaire or celebrity tweets about it, and the price rockets up. But all that is to say, it's not investing so much as walking into a casino. And the problem with Sawyer is, it wasn't his retirement fund he was playing roulette with, it was the money he and Dani were supposed to be living on. Now basically the money that should be in their checking account to pay for food and gas and marina fees is locked up in cryptocurrency and he's well underwater with the investments, so it's not like he can simply sell."

Knowles's eyes narrow. "So, Sawyer has money troubles?"

"Oh yeah, big time."

"And that's not causing stress?"

"You'd think so, right? But they're both so chill about it."

"Have they asked you for funds?" Knowles asks.

He looks sheepish. "Not Dani. Sawyer has hinted at it once or twice, but I don't lend anyone money. Neither a borrower nor a lender be, am I right?" He smiles conspiratorially and Knowles refrains from asking where his money came from. Where any of the money these young people had come from, that they don't have to work and can go sailing for the rest of their lives. "Living their best life" seems to be this generation's mantra. It's so far removed from her own hardscrabble existence that continues to this day.

"You should definitely check out Rod Zild," Weatherby says.

Zild has been thrown in her face by these cruisers one too many times. Weatherby is protecting someone. Is it himself or his friend Sawyer? She checks her notes from the Nilsson interview.

"What about Jim Marsh?"

"Jim is a great guy. He and Dani were tight."

Knowles perks up. "What does that mean?"

"Oh nothin' weird, he was old—past forty. They were friends because they both have channels they work on. Anyway, he took off days ago."

"So he wasn't at the party?"

"If he was, I didn't see him. He doesn't party—he hasn't had a drink in twenty years or something. And he's got something, heart disease or diabetes someone said. All he ever talks about is fish. Man, I don't even like to eat fish, much less talk about it twenty-four seven."

Sensing that Weatherby has little else of value to add, Knowles wraps up his interview. "Thank you for your time, Mr. Weatherby. Please take my card—if you remember anything, even something small that could be significant, please contact me."

"Okay—are you going to start dragging the area or organize a search?"

"Why would we do that?"

"Maybe a shark got her, on one of her swims."

"We're still investigating, but fatal shark attacks in the Bahamas are quite rare." She doesn't elaborate that of course a run-of-the-mill drowning would be much more likely, but it's not as though they're going to start dragging the ocean. If she drowned without human intervention, she will wash ashore eventually. Probably. In some form.

While Walter escorts Weatherby out of the office, Inspector Knowles switches on the overhead fan in her office. This room will bake later in the day when the sun gets good and high. Fans are a poor substitute for the air-conditioned, windowless, open space of her last office in Nassau, but you can't beat the view from her window. The waters of Exuma harbor are looking impossibly still today. No wonder the office feels so stifling; there's no wind at all.

Officer Walter clears his throat as he reenters her office. "This is Darcey Michaels, boss," Walter announces, ushering in a zaftig, middle-aged woman with brassy, thinning hair. She looks to be in her sixties, but she may be much younger. Her skin is leathery, a testament to the great amount of time she has spent on the water, as well as having grown up in an era when baby oil and tinfoil were considered a legitimate skin care routine.

Walter pulls out a chair in front of Knowles's desk for her, and Darcey sits on the very edge of it, poker straight and ready to assist in the investigation. Knowles's suspicion that Darcey must be American is confirmed with her effusive greeting. "Hello! You're a woman. My word! I honestly wasn't expecting to be meeting with a woman today. I haven't seen that many lady police officers in the Caribbean, and I have spent a lot of time around these islands, more years than you probably would think possible. And let me tell you, honey, I am observant. That's why I said to myself, 'Self, you need to get in and tell those police officers everything you know about Dani Fox.'"

Knowles deflects Darcey's commentary. "Thank you for your time, Ms. Michaels. We appreciate your assistance." Knowles starts with her standard questions, careful to keep Darcey from getting too far off track with her replies, before getting to the line of questioning that Weatherby had brought up.

"We've heard Dani wasn't well liked among the cruisers, especially among the women."

Darcey scowls. "Who said that?"

Knowles doesn't respond.

"She came off saccharine sweet, but then she'd compliment you in this backhanded way. Every time she sees me, she says, 'That suit looks great on you, it's so slimming.' It's true. That's why I bought it in different colors. But it's a microaggression, you know? And she flirted with everyone, mostly men, but sometimes women. It was gross. She's a total 'pick me' girl."

"She flirted with your husband?" Knowles asks.

"My wife, my husband, a sea cucumber, anything. She's that type. There were rumors that she did more than flirt. I heard from a friend of a friend who knew them in the Keys that they were swingers. I don't think they were doing that here—at least, if they were, we didn't hear about it. Dani, she's supposedly fanatical about what she put in her mouth, right? Talks endlessly about cruelty-free cooking and lentils, right? But my husband saw her eating a cheeseburger in George Town two weeks ago. A cheeseburger! And they go spearfishing all the time. I ask you, what kind of a vegan spearfishes?"

Knowles closes her eyes and takes a deep breath. "Perhaps she's a pescatarian," Knowles says mildly.

"Well, if she is she should say that. Dani didn't talk a lot, but when she did it was about her swims, her workouts, and her channel," Darcey says. "She was always smiling and acting like she didn't have a care in the world. Completely vapid or fake as hell. Take your pick."

"I think I'm getting a clearer picture," Knowles says.

"There were other things too. She was a terrible cook. In this community we do a lot of fish bakes and potlucks and stuff. Sawyer would turn up with fish sometimes and Dani would bring healthy stuff—which I don't mind. I've had plenty of fantastic vegan meals but the stuff that she brought could be considered lentil abuse."

Knowles stifles a sigh. For a moment, just one moment, she misses Nassau.

The woman is gorgeous, and a terrible cook, and other men were attracted to her. How many of these interviews is she going to have to do with these cruisers?

She makes a note. *Bad cook.*

"I don't mean not to my taste. I'm not talking about mushroom tacos or whatever. I mean stuffed with ghost peppers, or so much salt you had to spit it out. No one is that bad a cook—I think she got some evil pleasure out of making us gag."

Knowles makes another note next to her bad cook note: *too salty, too spicy.*

"But she's not the one who poisoned us. I think that was Sawyer."

Knowles's body stills. She looks directly at Darcey. "He what now?"

"He brought a yellowfin to a fish bake that was old or something. I think there was an issue with their freezer maybe. I'm not sure, but somehow the fish was toxic and we all got scombroid poisoning."

"I haven't heard of that," Knowles admits.

"Well, it's nasty. Once the fish has it, some issue with the cold chain or something, it doesn't matter how long you cook it—it's riddled with histamines. We all recovered but we were sick. Sawyer tried to tell people it wasn't his fish, but it totally was."

"Were Dani and Sawyer ill?"

"No—that's suspicious, right?"

"This was a mild illness?" Knowles asks, making a note to look up scombroid poisoning.

"I turned purple—probably because I'm so fair. It looked like we all had a bad, bad sunburn, our bodies were on fire. Then some of us were dizzy—a few people were throwing up and then the diarrhea started. Which was bad because we were partying on a deserted cay."

Knowles grimaces. "Sounds awful. Are you sure it was their fish?"

"We were pretty sure. The only other fish was Jim's, but that was a big skipjack he'd caught that morning."

"Did anyone speak to them about it? Bringing bad fish?"

"I don't think anyone held it against them, except maybe Henry because he was sick for a few days. He wouldn't take Benadryl like the rest of us. Can you imagine the dumbassery of refusing medication after a poisoning? Said he wouldn't put anything unnatural into his body. They sure put plenty of unnatural stuff into him when he had to go to the clinic with breathing trouble. Anyway, the rest of us improved a lot after the antihistamine. We were lucky someone at the fish bake was a retired emergency room doctor and figured it out and we were especially lucky Lena had the stuff. You know, that's someone you should talk to."

"Lena?" Knowles feels a moment's irritation at how many cruiser characters keep popping up in these interviews.

How she longs for an Agatha Christie type murder mystery of the sort she read as a child, with a limited number of suspects trapped on a train or some such. So orderly.

Real murder investigations sprawl.

"No, Jim. Jim was friends with them. He helped Sawyer on the boat. I think, and Ms. Vegan with her channel—they were having major issues with *Serendipity*'s engine and some other stuff. Like a lot was going wrong. Anyway, he'd be worth talking to if you can find him."

"Is he still in the Bahamas?"

"Who knows. I think he headed out on a fishing expedition. He finds some out of the way places—sometimes he'll leave his boat and go camp on an island and fish. You might find more on his channel. My husband and wife follow it religiously."

"He has a YouTube channel?"

"*Aboat Time to Reef Fish* or something. Kind of boring if you ask me. I mean, who wants to watch someone sit around with a reel or swim around after fish? He has tutorials on cleaning fish and tools, equipment—all that."

"What's Jim's last name?"

"Mars? March? Something like that. Last names don't often come up in the cruising lifestyle."

Knowles makes a note, then asks, "Do you have any idea where Dani might be?"

"Sorry, no."

"Anyone she was particularly close to? Anyone who had a"—she catches herself before using the word *beef*—"grudge or an issue with her."

"She probably took off with someone with a bigger boat."

Knowles stands and hands over her card. "If you hear anything about her whereabouts or anything that might be useful to the investigation, please call."

"That's it?" Darcey says.

Knowles nods. "We'll be in touch."

It's shaping up to be a bad week.

And it's only going to get worse.

CHAPTER

10

Xanadu

Sonja Nilsson

Day 4

SONJA SITS AT the table in her galley on *Xanadu* working furiously on her laptop, her decades-old marketing degree finally put to good use. She finishes creating a Fox Finders website for Dani and sets up a private Fox Finders Facebook group and makes herself the admin. Then she sets up an X account, @FoxFinders, and starts liberally using the hashtags #FoxFinders and #FindDaniFox in her posts on X, Threads, and Facebook. She creates a Fox Finders Instagram profile too, even though she isn't herself on the platform; there is simply too much quasi-nudity.

Marketing and communications have changed a lot since Sonja was in the workforce, but she still remembers the branding principle of consistency and repetition.

Even though there are dozens of gorgeous pictures of Dani available online, Sonja uses an image from her own photo library. It's one of the most conservative pictures she could find of the young woman. Anders had taken the shot of

Sonja and Dani on their dinghy after a scuba dive. Dani's wearing a long-sleeve T-shirt over her bikini top in deference to the windy ride back to Sand Dollar. She looks happy and fresh-faced.

Sonja crops herself out of the image and posts the photo everywhere, using only the two hashtags. She wants people to be forced to remember.

TikTok is a bridge too far for her social media capabilities so she messages Anemone, a lovely girl who works as crew for an Australian couple. Anemone is nineteen and obsessed with TikTok so she sends the images, links, and hashtags and asks her to create something. Anemone isn't Dani's biggest fan, but a few minutes later the girl texts her that she'll set it up and update Sonja with any news.

Sonja posts her two-sentence explainer in the comments section of every *Sailing with the Foxes* video, all fourteen, to spread the word. She shares the same information in the cruiser forum. Within minutes she's inundated with comments, much of it speculation about Sawyer.

She spends a few hours answering the people messaging her on various platforms. It's heartwarming how concerned people are for the well-being of a stranger. Some offer their paid services—psychics, detectives, even search party management consulting. Most state the obvious: it's the boyfriend, it's always the boyfriend.

Then there are the sightings. "I saw someone fitting this description at a café in Nassau," or "I saw her on the streets of Kansas City, Missouri." One man swears he saw her in a truck stop restroom on the I-30. But the crème de la DM crème are the sex trafficking trackers. They propose Dani has been abducted and proceed to explain that she'll be moved over state lines, from motel to motel, and advertised for sale on the internet like a piece of secondhand furniture.

Sonja doesn't take the time to respond to the sex trafficking conspiracists that this doesn't fit the typical sex trafficking profile. She simply cuts and pastes a reply acknowledging receipt of the information and asking the sender to keep vigilant for new information to pass along. It's a lot to wade through.

Anders comes into the galley. "Come outside. It's a perfect Exumas day." He moves behind her, examining her screen and all the tabs open in her browser, and groans. "Sonja, enough already."

"How can you say that? My friend is missing!"

"Aren't you going to be embarrassed when she shows up?"

"If she shows up it will be parts of her washing up on a beach somewhere, mark my words."

"Gode Gud, Sonja, do you believe that?" Anders says.

"Yes, Anders. I really do. Sawyer did something to her, I'm sure of it after seeing her video."

"A few days ago, you liked him."

"I said he was okay, then Dani told me he beats her, then he got drunk and aggressive with people at my party, and then she posted a video that she was scared of him. This is not a difficult disappearance to solve with all those clues."

Anders rubs his face.

"So this what you're doing now? Starting a search party? Becoming an internet detective?"

"Oh my God, internet sleuths! Thank you, Anders." Sonja leaps to her feet to kiss him.

Anders kisses her back, mumbles something about jumping to conclusions, and goes up to the cockpit.

Sonja searches the web for internet sleuths. The largest site tells her to immediately take pictures, video, and notes of anything pertinent like evidence or phone calls/voicemails or dates. She hunts through three drawers for a notebook before she finds what she needs to make notes of what she discussed with Dani and when, dates of outings, and parties.

She adds boats that left the anchorage after the party. She takes screenshots of all her messages with Dani and emails them to herself in case law enforcement needs her phone.

Another suggestion the website makes is for individuals to work together. She's already posted in the cruiser forum. Many have started following the Facebook group. What else can they do? She searches around a few different sites.

A search party!

Sonja sends a group message to all the cruisers in the vicinity asking them to do some beachcombing for clues. She doesn't want to consider that Dani may have been killed by Sawyer, drowned, or been eaten by a shark, but she's a pragmatic person.

The final step the website recommends is checking the Royal Bahamas Police Force website. She pulls it up and gasps when she sees the number of people on their missing persons page. Some of them look old enough to have wandered off, unable to find their way home due to dementia or some medical issue, but there are plenty of young people on the site too. The Exumas are known to be a safe haven, but there is crime everywhere, particularly in the larger cities with the mega hotels. The missing persons page on the Royal Bahamas Police Force site is a very sad place to find oneself.

The website recommends downloading the P3 app for tips, so she does. The P3 platform allows the public to share information anonymously with Crime Stoppers programs, law enforcement entities, schools, and large corporations around the world. Apparently one can submit a tip via the web page or the P3 tips app with full anonymity. Sonja downloads the app and updates the communities with where to send tips.

Finally, Sonja emails the George Town Police Inspector Knowles with all the links to the Fox Finders and Dani's YouTube page and Instagram. In her email to Inspector Knowles she recommends putting Dani's face up on the missing persons page. Sonja considers alerting the FBI in the United States but decides to make that recommendation in the email.

She also mentions what little she knows about Dani's family—an uncle in California, a childhood spent in Florida. The missing persons website she's been following said it's not necessary to loop in law enforcement because it may not be appreciated, but the inspector seems like a reasonable person and may need the tips coming in. Sonja closes her laptop.

She never should have let Dani get in the dinghy with Sawyer, not with what she knew about him, not given the enraged state Sawyer was in that night.

She puts her head in her hands and weeps.

CHAPTER 11

Serendipity

Sawyer

Day 6

I AWAKEN WITH THE remnants of a dream so vivid it could be a memory. A naked Dani, clad only in a weighted dive belt, floating on her back. Her right wrist is wrapped in a fuzzy purple handcuff, the other cuff connected to the base of Serendipity's anchor chain on the seafloor. She drifts there, her wide-open eyes cloudy and accusatory.

I'm tempted to put on my fins and mask and go take a look.

Instead I get out of bed, pull on board shorts, and head to the galley to make coffee. Thirty minutes later I hear some commotion outside and emerge from the cabin onto the deck, squinting in the bright sunshine. A police boat, blue and white lights flashing, approaches *Serendipity.* Every cruiser anchored at Sand Dollar Beach is alerted to the late morning arrival of the police by a bullhorn.

I put on my sunglasses.

"Mr. Stone, this is the Bahamian Maritime Authority and the Royal Bahamas Police Force."

They can see me, outside, standing on the deck, enjoying my second cup of coffee, and they need to use the bullhorn? Because it's exciting, that's why. George Town is a sleepy little outpost in the Exumas, where nothing much ever happens.

Missing women! Murderous boyfriends!

They're in the big time now and the big time means the bullhorn.

I considered fleeing, but the weather window to go north isn't great and I don't have the money to fill my tanks. Low on fuel, short on cash, and bad weather is one too many negatives for me—and I'm not exactly risk averse. Leaving now isn't an option. Refusing to let them search the boat isn't much of an option either. I've already taken the boat apart to look for incriminating items. Police officers aren't exactly the most formidable of opponents. I am not afraid of going head-to-head with them.

Even if I could get money from Brendan, thanks to Sonja, every cruiser in the Bahamas would be on the lookout for my boat and my AIS signal. They'd rat me out in a second if I tried to flee. There are too damn many cruisers.

I pull my phone out of my pocket and text Brendan *They're here*, which is redundant as he would've heard them anyway. Everyone knows everyone's business out here. He texts back, telling me people are wondering why I didn't join the body part scavenger hunt on Lee Stocking Island this morning. I know that they'll be inferring the worst from my unwillingness to look, but I'm equally sure that if I did take part, that would be criticized as well. I wouldn't look sad enough, which would mean I wasn't missing her, or I'd look too sad, and that would be interpreted as play-acting. There is no upside for me in the beachcombing-for-clues game.

Where the hell is she?

I'm thankful I dumped most of my garbage in the George Town dumpster last Sunday but it's reasonable odds they'll search every dumpster in dinghy distance.

I considered dumping her cell phone. God only knows what messages she's kept and what her phone reveals about our lives. Besides, it's password protected and I can't access it. It's not that I don't think she's careful; she's conniving as all hell. But what she's kept on her phone can't be worse than what she posted on YouTube, and I think they'll be able to access the messages even without the physical device. I already told the police Dani's phone had been left behind, and Knowles had made a note of it in her little book.

I recognize one individual in a police uniform as Officer Walter. He's scowling at the bullhorn operator.

"May we come aboard, sir?" Walter shouts.

"Of course."

I'm a little surprised the FBI from the Barbados legal attaché office hasn't shown up, but I know it's only a matter of time.

Dead American tourists, missing American tourists, even seriously injured American tourists are likely to bring out the legal attaché assigned to the region.

But lucky for me, the FBI, in their wisdom, has split up the Caribbean.

I give permission for the search and it's very crowded on *Serendipity* with all these people.

Officer Walter asks if I'd like to go back to George Town with him while they conduct their search, but I'd rather not spend any more time than I have to in a police station.

"I have a friend coming to get me, we're going to go have lunch at the Sand Bar," I tell them.

Brendan waves from his dinghy. I offer my cell number to Officer Walter but he already has it.

I climb aboard Weatherby's dinghy, and we make our way to the island bar.

It's too noisy to talk over the engine and he probably needs the hair of the dog, judging by his pallor.

We don't speak until he's downed his first triple rum punch.

"I don't know how you can look so casual, man, you're getting crucified online—and now the police are tossing your boat."

"Are they tossing it?" I ask, wiggling my eyebrows.

He laughs. "Whatever, bruh. You must have ice in your veins. I dig it."

"I didn't *do* anything."

Brendan ducks his head and looks over his sunglasses at me. "That's not how this works. You're the boyfriend." He ticks off his pinkie finger. "The last one to see her alive." He touches his ring finger. "And you don't remember anything from that night." Now all three fingers are raised—pinkie, index and middle. "That's three strikes, brother. Haven't you ever heard a true crime podcast?"

"No, that was more Dani's thing. Have you?"

"Nah, but I've seen *20/20* a bunch of times and it is always the husband or boyfriend who goes down for it. It's even worse in countries dependent on tourist dollars. They want it solved, and fast, so they don't scare any visitors away. They'll put more energy into framing you than investigating. You need a good lawyer."

"She'll turn up," I reply. I also have a rum punch. Probably the first I've ever had before noon.

"Like, parts of her, on a beach? That's what Sonja seems to be hoping for," Weatherby says.

"If a shark had the unfortunate idea to attack Dani, my money would be on shark parts washing up on the beach. Shark fin soup on the menu. Dani is a badass," I say.

"Dani? A badass? Are we talking about the same person?"

I shrug. "It never ceases to amaze how you all write her off as a bimbo because she's bangin'. She is smart and strong as fuck."

"Nah, man. She seems like a softie to me. Besides, you know how strong you'd have to be to fight off a shark in the open ocean? Like, you'd have to be Ronda Rousey to fight off a shark. I'd lose a fist-to-fin fight with a shark too. On land maybe I'd have a chance, but how would that come about?"

I think that's a rhetorical question and judging by the way Brendan fixates on fighting sharks, he's halfway drunk already.

"Where do you think she got to?" he asks.

Even if I did know, I wouldn't tell Brendan Weatherby, who is likely to overindulge and repeat everything I say to anyone who will listen. For these parts he's a harmless gossip, but the stakes here are high.

A couple of young women in bikinis finish playing volleyball and are looking for a table. We're at a four top so I beckon them over. They come, so they haven't heard. They're not cruisers then, just tourists. That's good for me.

"Come, sit." I gesture at the chairs expansively. "First round is on Weatherby." Up close they are not quite as young or as pretty as they looked a hundred feet away, but they keep us entertained for the afternoon, until I can go back to my boat and hope to God the luminol doesn't light her up like a damned SpaceX barge.

Brendan is the only one of the cruising set still on speaking terms with me. Everyone else has convicted me.

It occurs to me that Brendan has been pretty cavalier about the prospect of Dani being dead. He's treating it like an interesting thought experiment but doesn't seem to be considering the possibility that I may have something to do with it.

I'm his best wingman. He's probably not willing to give that up. I don't know if that's because he's an alcoholic or a sociopath.

I don't much care, one way or the other.

Bored by Kaylee and Brendan's broad hints about taking the party back to his boat, and semi-aroused by Bree's hand playing in my lap for the last ten minutes, I stand up. I raise my eyebrows to Bree and nod toward the bar. She follows me around the building to one of two bathrooms. I open the door for her and lock it behind me, then I scan the area.

Behind the door is a window with a new cube tissue box—suspiciously clean in this dusty, dirty bathroom—angled at the toilet. I suspect Zild's handiwork so I knock it to the ground. I pull Bree over to the tile wall next to the toilet, pushing her up against it. I hold her in place with my forearm against her throat. Her eyes are half lidded and glassy; she holds on to my arm as I slide my hand into her bikini bottoms. I don't have to rub long before she's writhing against the wall, coming in my hand. I pull my arm away and she slides to a sitting position on the floor, giggling. I unbutton and unzip, then reach down and thread my fingers through her hair, pulling her up. She takes me in her mouth, wrapping her arms around my ass, pulling me tight. My grip on her hair tightens and my hips pick up the pace. She tries to turn her head, but my grip is too tight. She's making little noises in her throat, her hands frantically pushing my hips away, and I throw my head back and come silently.

I release her and offer my hand to help her up. Ignoring it, she stands, wiping her mouth. She's out the door without looking at me.

I shrug, wash my hands, relock the door, then lean against the wall with the camera-containing cube tissue box in hand. Another ten minutes goes by before I unlock the door. Zild should've had time to motor over from the *Zildgeist* by now.

Moments later, it opens and a man steps in.

Rod Zild.

Right on time.

I yank him all the way inside, relock the door, and stand in front of it.

He pales when he sees me and the tissue box and puts up both hands.

"What did you tell the police?" I demand.

"Nothing. I swear to God. They're trying to pin this thing on me. They're searching *my* boat." Rod is anchored at Sand Dollar supposedly searching for crew for a passage to Grenada, but we've been hearing that for weeks.

"Maybe if you hadn't made your interest in my girlfriend so obvious, they wouldn't be."

He hangs his head. "I think they'll take my gear," he says. "All of it. The night vision goggles, the Phantom."

"They should."

"I never filmed you, not after that one time when you caught my drone over your boat. I told you I would never do it again and I haven't. I swear to God."

I stare at him.

His lower lip trembles.

"And?"

"What?" he asks.

"What did Dani ask you to do?"

"Nothing. I swear—"

I scoff. "I know, I know, you swear to God." I drop the tissue box, take his hand in mine, and put it in position.

"What are you doing?" he asks, trying to tug away, but I have him pinned against the wall.

"I'm going to dislocate your thumb. It will make sailing difficult for some time. Maybe forever."

His mouth opens and closes a few times. "Please, please don't. I don't know anything. I don't know what you did . . ."

"What *I* did?"

"Whatever you did to her. I didn't see it."

I'm so surprised I release his hand. "What are you talking about?"

"I didn't send the drone after you all that night. After all I did for her, she threatened me. Said if I didn't leave her alone, she'd . . . she'd dump my stuff overboard. And I helped her, man."

"What did you help her with?"

"She wanted me to get footage."

I have a knot developing in the pit of my stomach. "What footage?"

"Of you, and her, on the boat, and on shore," he says.

I take his hand again and he squeals.

"She had you film us?"

"I never saw it. She had me set up some cameras with audio. They fed to her, not me."

"Where is it?"

An oily lock of hair falls over his eye. "She has it all. I didn't even look."

"And the cameras?"

"She had me take them out last week."

"You have a hidden camera detector?"

Zild is the kind of creep who has all the spy gadgets, legal and illegal.

"Two, but—"

"Drop it off with me after the police leave."

"They'll probably keep it," he says, color draining from his face.

"I want everything you recorded."

"I told you, she has it. She wouldn't let me keep it."

"Bullshit."

"She said if I didn't fuck with her feed, and I didn't, she'd give me something . . ."

"What? Money?"

"No, a video."

"Let me see it."

"She said I could have it. I had to promise not to show it to anyone. And not to send any of the footage to myself. I believed her. She's scary." He avoids eye contact with me, but that's not unusual.

"Show me."

"I only have this file on my phone. I had to delete the one on my computer because they came to search it."

"Show it to me."

"She gave it to *me*," he says, his voice quavering.

I take his trembling hand back and put almost enough pressure on his thumb to dislocate it.

He yelps. "Okay, okay." He holds his hand to his mouth and reaches into his pocket for his iPhone.

He finds the file and starts the clip.

I remember that night; it was shortly after we arrived in the Bahamas. A very vanilla foursome. She was a former dancer and very flexible; he was a voyeur.

They left our anchorage the next day.

"Delete it," I say.

His eyes tear up.

I'm barely able to refrain from punching him in the throat.

We all have our vices, but Rod is a worm. I doubt he's capable of kidnapping or killing anyone, but he does fit some of the criteria—creepy loner with resources. And he is completely obsessed with Dani.

He doesn't need to be told a third time; he deletes the video.

"Show me what you have, from the night she went missing."

He opens the camera app, scrolls to the video, and hits play. It's immediately evident that I'm barely able to stand. I'm muttering something but it's inaudible from where he's filming. Sonja and Anders maneuver me from the sugar scoop into the dinghy. Dani looks up at the camera and, presumably, Rod behind it. Her face changes. He's right. She is almost scary when she looks like that. I may need that video for my defense, to show my state of mind or inability to stand. I take his phone, send the video to myself, save it as a password protected file, then delete the video from his phone and my email and empty his email trash.

Is it possible that Rod, seeing that I was incapacitated, followed Dani to our boat under the guise of helping? Did he zap her with a stun gun, restrain her, and stash her nearby?

Would he be here if he had Dani captive? But with the police searching his boat, it stands to reason he'd be careful.

I hand the phone back to him and grasp the front of his shirt. He cowers and won't meet my eyes. "Do you know where Dani is?"

"No! I swear to God."

I release him. "Take your cameras out of the bathrooms," I say.

He shakes his head. "I don't know what you're talking about."

I am tempted to break his thumb and find them myself but I'm being investigated and don't need the trouble.

I shrug and lift a foot over the box containing his camera.

He drops to the floor and picks it up, clutching it tightly to his chest as he stands.

I use the collar of his polo shirt to pull him close to me.

"If you don't take your hidden cameras out of the bathrooms and keep them out, I will not only dump your gear, I will set your boat on fire once you're asleep. And I will enjoy watching it, and you, burn."

He can't get out of the bathroom fast enough.

CHAPTER

12

Serendipity

Inspector Knowles

Day 6

KNOWLES SNIFFS THE air. There's a faint hint of bleach, which doesn't quite cover the smell of mildew.

The luminol lights up in the kitchen, including the galley ceiling—which is not a great finding, as it could be from spurting arterial blood. But Knowles is already considering alternate explanations, especially on a boat with a ceiling so low. Most of what they find is in the kitchen, but there's some in Dani's room, on her broken door. Knowles makes her way to Sawyer's cabin where Walter is opening a drawer under the bed. It's full to the brim with an assortment of leather bondage gear and a sea of rubber sex toys in every imaginable color.

"Geez," the novice officer says. "Look at all that."

Knowles shrugs. "We've had reports they had a very active sex life."

The young police officer takes a second pair of gloves out of his pocket and puts them on without a word.

Walter crouches down and reaches into the drawer with a gloved hand, pulling out a green vibrator. "Looks like the charges in this case will include sexual battery," he quips, waving it around.

Knowles shoots him a quelling look and leaves Sawyer's cabin to poke around Dani's—sailboats are a poor place for people with a hoarding disorder and that's what this resembles. It's not simply the clutter. There's trash, food, dirty laundry, and a sock that smells suspiciously like urine. They may have a pest problem on board judging by the softness of some of the wood. It's a small space but it's quite disgusting—and very different from Sawyer's everything-in-its-proper-place kitchen and cabin. She pulls something blonde from under the covers—hair extensions by the looks of them. Her mess could damn well be motive, especially when you contrast it with his neatness. She'd seen people homicidal over less. Could this be a junk room and they share the other? No, everything in here is hers. Everything in the other cabin is his. How could anyone live with someone like this, and in 200 square feet?

"Boss," Walter calls from the galley.

Most of the drawers in the kitchen have been searched, indicated by the blue painter's tape, but one is pulled out.

Walter is taking photos of something in the drawer from all angles. He hands the camera to the officer standing behind him and pulls something gently from the partially opened drawer.

Walter's eyebrows are nearly at his hairline.

The probationary officer observing lets out a low whistle.

A floral, blood-soaked minidress.

Truth be told, there's not much to soak. The bodycon dress, made of some flimsy material, is tiny. Walter holds it over the evidence bag.

"Hold up," she says. "What's the tag say?"

Walter handles it gingerly. "Coby for Neiman Marcus. Size 2. Dry clean only. Silk/spandex," he reads.

Knowles nods and he bags it.

Knowles texts Sonja Nilsson and asks her to send any photos she has of Dani from that night.

Her cell phone beeps not three minutes later. There are a dozen photos with Dani in the dress that's now in the bag held by Walter.

"Continue," Knowles says.

Royal Bahamas Police Headquarters

Inspector Knowles

Day 7

Inspector Knowles absently picks up her ringing phone. "Knowles."

"What the hell is going on there in George Town?" an irate voice at the other end asks.

"I'm sorry?"

"This is Assistant Commissioner Taylor, Knowles."

Knowles sits up straighter in her chair. "Yes sir, sorry sir. What are you calling about?"

"The missing American. Where are we on that?"

"Well, she hasn't turned up."

"I know that, Knowles. I'm getting inquiries from the press all over the world about the case."

"What?"

"The damned thing has gone viral."

All the blood drains from Knowles's head. There is no protocol for this, no procedure to run to navigate the unrelenting force of interference from the internet. This wasn't covered in criminal investigator training.

She leans over in her chair, getting her face as close to her knees as she can, and takes deep, calming breaths, phone mouthpiece at her neck to muffle her panicked breathing.

"Haven't you seen them? Organizing searches, putting up fliers, I've got oceanic current experts from Florida State offering to figure out the search area if we can tell when the body was dumped and where."

"Ah, she's missing, sir. We have no evidence that she was killed and dumped."

"What have you got?"

She searches frantically for her notes. "A bloody dress, likely what she was wearing at the party according to the incident report and photos from the night in question. We found it stuffed in a drawer in the galley on *Serendipity.* As far as the boat, luminol lit up areas in the kitchen and head, cabin, and deck. We haven't told Mr. Stone about the dress, but the blood on the boat he says came from an accident with fileting a fish—there were some indications of spatter, we took samples and have sent DNA. His behavior, lack of concern, delay in reporting are all suspect. There is one report that he was physically abusive to Ms. Fox. He's cooperative, to a point. He did motor out on Sunday early evening according to some cruiser accounts, he says to dump waste. We've requested information on both from the Americans, but we don't have access and they haven't responded yet. There are a number of messages coming in on this case, more than we're accustomed to with a missing person."

He sighs heavily. "Yes, missing white woman syndrome. We have pages of our own Bahamians missing—kids, women, elderly, yet all those cases combined haven't generated the interest we've had on this one missing a week."

This is bad. This is really bad. "Yes, sir."

"Get her photo on the website. I'm going to get a dedicated line set up. I'll send it to you by this evening. The American agent is on their way from the US Embassy in Barbados."

"Maybe they can help me access background."

"Have you looked at social media?"

"I was sent some links by one of the cruisers, Sonja Nilsson, on Thursday, but I haven't had a chance to give it a thorough look, sir. We searched the boat yesterday. I'm using the regular channels."

"Well, it may behoove you to put someone on following up information coming out of the Facebook group."

"Sir?"

"We've got allegations pouring in on the pair of them."

"But sir, that's . . . is that going to be, I mean, has the information on social media been verified?"

"The FBI legat can help sort it. But you need more personnel. I do not want this to get out of control."

"Yes, sir."

"I have faith in you, Inspector. I know you are a very effective and experienced officer, but please let me know if you can't get people on this round the clock. We don't want a Natalee Holloway situation."

"Yes, sir. I mean no, sir. No, we don't."

"You tell me what you need as far as resources, personnel, and I will get it for you."

"Yes. Thank you, sir."

"I'm going to email you my personal numbers. Together, we'll figure this out, Inspector."

Knowles hangs up the phone with a shaking hand.

Viral? Every law enforcement officer's worst nightmare.

Knowles clicks through the links Sonja sent. There are now thousands of comments in the Facebook group, hundreds in the internet sleuth forum, and pages upon pages in the cruiser forum.

She's going to be here all night and so is the rest of her staff. She starts making calls.

Inspector Knowles had just finished ordering lunch to be delivered for her staff working overtime when Officer Tanner hails her.

"Boss, you gotta come see this. It just posted."

He has up the Fox Finders Facebook group that had been assigned to him. The first page of the yellow legal pad next to him is full of notes.

"There's a lot of information here posted by Sonja Nilsson."

"We've interviewed her twice."

"But look at this."

Jaden Blecker, who claimed to know Sawyer Stone in New York, posted that Sawyer's first wife died in a suspicious accident.

Five minutes later, user Biloxi Adams posted a snip from an obituary.

Emily Penelope Standish Stone, 27, New York City, died Saturday from injuries sustained in a scuba diving accident in Punta Cana in the Dominican Republic.

Emily was born Dec. 14, 1994, in Greenwich, Connecticut. She received a BA in English from Colgate University and received a JD from Columbia University Law School. She was a second-year associate at Graham Edwards LLP. Emily was an avid runner and cyclist.

She is survived by her husband, Sawyer Stone III of New York City; her mother and father, Julie and Matthew Standish of Greenwich, Connecticut; and sister Courtney Elizabeth of New York City. She is preceded in death by her grandparents, Joseph and Leigh Lawson, and Kenneth and Evelyn Llewelyn Standish.

Services will be held at 10 AM, *Friday, March 20, at the Montgomery Funeral Home. Burial will be in the Oak Street Cemetery.*

Friends may call at the Montgomery Funeral Home, Greenwich, from 11 AM *to 9* PM *Tuesday, and the family will receive friends from 7 to 9* PM.

Contributions in memory of Emily may be made to World Kitchen, c/o Montgomery Funeral Home.

Inspector Knowles whistles. "I'll be damned. Verify that, please."

Knowles looks up as a tall, dark-skinned woman in a burgundy pantsuit enters the room carrying a briefcase and rolling a silver suitcase. The woman puts down her belongings. "You all are only finding out about the first wife now?" she says.

Inspector Knowles walks over and offers her hand. "Inspector Veronique Knowles of the Royal Bahamas Police Force."

"Michelle James, FBI, legal attaché. I've just arrived from Barbados."

Finally the FBI has sent their legat.

"We've been stymied, I'm afraid," Knowles says.

"I'm here to help," James replies.

Knowles sets James up at the miniature desk in the corner of the room. "Coffee's there," Knowles points at the credenza behind her workspace. "Want me to brew a pot?"

"Nah, I'm a Diet Coke addict and bring my own supply. I stopped at the market on my way in." She taps her suitcase.

"Fridge is down the hall."

Knowles resettles herself behind her own desk and clicks on the CyberSleuth page. She squints at it—someone posted a local news piece from the Dominican Republic.

An American woman has died after being pulled unconscious from the ocean in Punta Cana. The woman was scuba diving with her husband and another woman on Wednesday morning when she got into difficulty.

The comments have exploded.

Knowles studies the page, reading through the responses.

"Walter?"

Walter appears in the doorway. "Yes, boss?"

"We better find this girl before these white people start a podcast."

CYBERSLEUTH MODERATOR: THIS THREAD IS CLOSED TEMPORARILY FOR A CLEANUP OF NUMEROUS BLATANT VIOLATIONS OF CYBERSLEUTH'S TERMS OF SERVICE.

To avoid having your post flagged and removed and risk losing posting privileges:

- remember that Dani, her family, and her friends, including her BF, are considered VICTIMS, and protected by our victim-friendly policy
- don't accuse someone of being guilty of a crime (unless LE has)
- don't post anything as fact without an MSM link
- don't use derogatory names
- the ONLY SM links allowed right now are those belonging to the missing person Dani Fox, OR MSM and LE sites
- don't sleuth anyone except Dani

CHAPTER

13

Serendipity

Sawyer

Day 9

THE *SAILING WITH the Foxes* video drops promptly at eleven AM. The sun is merciless so I'm hiding out in the galley, toggling between threads about Dani's disappearance on CyberSleuth and CruiserLife. Brendan texted me a link to a Facebook group but I don't have the stomach for it.

Apparently, I'm to be tortured weekly.

The new video is a homage to our life together on *Serendipity.* Well, the PG version, at any rate.

My stomach churns. The video starts off showing me in my best light. How kind I am when she's seasick. How we work together as a team with the sails, dropping and lifting anchor. Attempting to fix the engine, with me in the hole and Dani holding the flashlight with one hand and the GoPro with the other.

There's a lot more smiling than I remember.

There are montages of us swimming with eagle rays near Nassau. There are parties with other cruisers, bonfires. The two of us making out in the surf, *From Here to Eternity* style. I remember how hard it was to get the right angle with the surf coming in and messing with the tripod.

But my jaw is clenched, and my heart is racing.

The last clip is drone footage of us on a beach.

I close my eyes.

Not this.

When I open my eyes, I am watching myself shouting and shaking her by the arms while she shrinks from me, crying. Three weeks ago, Dani had failed to tie up the dinghy correctly after visiting Jim. It vanished. We were looking for it on Lee Stocking while Jim and a few other cruisers pitched in to search. Eventually it was found, still adrift.

The video is courtesy of Rod Zild, no doubt. I hadn't even heard his damned stealth drone. It's bad. There's no context. Viewers don't know that she did something so stupid, something I had warned her about a hundred times. We can't function without a dinghy, and they cost upwards of a thousand dollars to replace. This, at a time when we can barely afford groceries. I know how it looks. It looks like I've gone off the rails for no reason. But if I hadn't given her a shake, it might have not registered with her at all. And then where would we be?

When I check the same video again at the end of the day to see if anyone has commented, I am well and truly shocked. I refresh the page and stare at the numbers.

Views:

6 million 5 million 5 million 5 million 10 million
Subscribers to *Sailing with the Foxes*: 4 million.
There are thousands of comments to wade through.

fredumisntfre The boyfriend is controlling as hell in all the videos! He watches over her in a controlling manner and on occasion she will look back at him for approval. Check out the 4th video, at 3:15

bealziebubadvocateforu Devil's advocate here, but if the BF DID do something to her wouldn't it be likely that he would GTFO in his sailboat? Staying where she disappeared seems like a NOT guilty thing to do. Giving him the benefit of the doubt, it seems more likely that they split up and she got lost or some harm befell her apart from him and now he's facing a shit storm.

theoristaprilmay22 My theory: she went out for a swim and had a cramp or got caught in an undertow or got eaten by a shark and then was run over in the shipping lanes. Hard to find a dead body in the ocean. No body, no crime.

jvennyla she'd have taken her phone! She's fully addicted to posting on IG on the daily! How is she able to keep uploading videos if she's missing? SM might help to crack this case and lead to answers.

geecraquers73 she was probably kidnapped or trafficked. that happens to good looking girls in foreign countries all the time. bf prolly panicked, worried about being accused of her disappearance and facing the hell that goes along with it.

Massmrderlvr10 2 women were recently killed in the Tortugas around the same time. maybe it's a serial killer going after girls on vacay.

I'm fucked.

CHAPTER

14

New York, NY

Courtney Standish

Day 9

I DON'T WANT TO go to the happy hour after the all-hands meeting. But I've flaked on so many of them before, and not only in this job.

I shrug on my jacket, staring out the window of my office in the International Plaza building, overlooking the intersection of 59th and Lex. It's a very unsatisfying view, too high up to see passersby on the street in any detail but too low to have any bucolic views of the East River.

Everything in my life feels like this: it's all simultaneously too much and not enough. My job itself—director of business development at Epsilon Capital, your local neighborhood hedge fund—is not important enough to keep me interested, but it carries too much responsibility to completely skive off from.

My father got me this job, which is fitting, as basically all it requires is to monetize one's personal connections into a milkable client list for the firm. Step one on the path to getting my job? Be rich. The ironic part is that being rich is also the very thing that keeps me from working very hard. What people don't understand about rich kids with trust funds is that we lack motivation to work because the interest our money generates each day exceeds what we can earn in the same timeframe. So why work at all?

The only answer I can come up with is to avoid Dad's odious lectures about the importance of hard work that he feels compelled to deliver whenever I lose another job. This lecture, which I've almost learned by rote, is particularly insufferable because this doesn't even reflect my father's beliefs. He doesn't value hard work in and of itself. It has to be the right kind of work, with the right kind of people.

This is the most important thing to understand about having family money, lest you become jealous of us Haves: family money always, *always* comes with strings attached. They control you by controlling "your" money. They put the money in a trust to parcel it out based on age, or, worse, some subjective measure of maturity that they define.

The other thing regular people don't realize is that in very wealthy families, everything is always, ultimately, about money. How much they have, how much it's earning, how much things cost. And, of course, the constant war between their peer-driven, competitive conspicuous consumption and their innate stinginess. Wealthy people in general, inherited or self-made, have extremely fucked up priorities. Granted, it's not poverty or PTSD or trauma or cycles of abuse or neglect. In wealthy families it's about control. My parents happily paid a half a million dollars for my prep school education and college. But gift me a tenth of that amount, to, I don't know, invest or start a business or travel or have any real independence? Never.

Now that I'm the sole surviving child, the heir is dead, they fear estrangement more than anything else. Healthy is the last word I'd use to describe my relationship with anyone in my family—living or dead.

Two years ago, death brought my life to a screeching halt. I filled my days with TikTok and Insta, interspersed with hours of reality television, podcasts, and murder shows to avoid the guilt and grief that besieged me.

Six months ago, my parents and therapist had an intervention.

Post-intervention, I acquired my cat Peaches, an antidepressant, and a personal trainer, and I consented to the removal of all social media apps from my phone. Depression soon turned to boredom, so my dad cajoled someone into offering me this job. The novelty of working in Midtown, consorting with billionaires on the regular, was fun for a while. My coworkers are decent people, my boss isn't awful, but I can feel the ennui creeping in around the edges. I've struggled to get up in the morning and have started missing work.

But today, for whatever reason, Peyton, the office manager, has convinced me to stop by the happy hour.

I head to the microbrewery next door and take a quick look at the specialty drinks list.

Charcoal malt lager.

Cinnamon coffee stout with blueberry notes.

I order a gin and tonic.

Gin was our favorite.

Inching my way through the happy hour crowd I find Peyton. She's bright eyed and waving her hands with a fluidity that indicates she's a drink or edible ahead of everyone else. Her deep and abiding love for Negronis may spell death for her role in the company sometime in the not-too-distant future. Water cooler gossip has odds on her expulsion every week, after every softly repeated exploit.

I stir my drink and lean in.

"She's dead. Have you seen the way he treated her? He probably tossed her over the side."

"I think she might've left his ass."

"Ghosted him?"

"My money's on her turning up with another cruiser—"

"I'm sorry, a what?" I interrupt.

"A cruiser—people who live on their boats and sail around. You don't watch the *Give Me Liberty* channel? Or *SV Boob Barge* on YouTube?"

"I get seasick easily," I reply.

A few people oblige me with a laugh.

"We were talking about the missing girl—that YouTuber. Dani something. You know, the one who went missing last week in the Caribbean."

"Never heard of her."

"Courtney—seriously? It's leading the news. You must've seen her channel."

I shake my head.

My social media ban makes me akin to a Mennonite with my peers. I never have any idea what friends and coworkers are talking about.

Three drinks and several hours later I'm floating on a cloud of gin, riding a barstool next to Peyton, who is chatting up the married finance guy. I'm making some heavy eye contact with the bartender but my heart's not in it.

All these steps my therapist and I have taken dig me out of my hole, but it's no chemical imbalance I suffer from. I'm grieving, with a side order of crushing guilt.

The financial guy's wife hauls him off with a deadly glare and Peyton spins in her chair, nearly losing her balance into me.

"It's weird, you know? Watching all that."

I have no idea what she's talking about, as my blank expression reveals.

"Dani? The missing woman?" she says.

"Are you still obsessing over that?."

The crowd has thinned. I'm starving and don't want to end up as Peyton's dinner date. I'm not feeling it with the bartender either. Time to go home. Back to Peaches. Clichés are clichés because they reflect some universal truth, and a lonely woman loving a cat is where I am right now.

"I mean, he comes off like a sweetheart of a guy, Mr. Fixit, spearfishing, making bonfires, partying. Super into her. But then . . . ho boy. Sawyer gets angry. I mean, I wonder if he threw her off the *Sherendipity*." Peyton's slurring now but I barely notice.

An electric shock travels my spine, turning my fingers nerveless. My tumbler falls to the lacquered wooden surface of the bar as a river of gin, ice, lime, and precious little tonic travels both directions.

"Courtney!" Peyton grabs her handbag from the bar top, moments too late. "Goddamn it!"

"Sorry," I mumble, scooting back.

The bartender is already on the way over with a rag.

"She's cut off," Peyton says, jerking her thumb in my direction.

The bartender gives me a practiced smile. "No worries."

"Can I cash out?" I ask, pulling out my wallet.

He nodded and hands across a device. I slide in my card, tip, sign, and stand.

I take a deep breath. "Lemme see."

"See what?"

"See the pictures of these people you've been talking about."

Peyton, recovered from the spill, waves her phone in my direction.

I take it from her and see SerendipiDani's Instagram page is loaded.

"See? Weren't they so cute?" she says, leaning toward me.

I squint at the photo of the couple, then tap my finger on it. There he is. In front of a sailboat, arms wrapped around a blond girl my age. Only she has perfect skin, fake boobs, and an ass worthy of Sir Mix-a-Lot.

My heart skips two beats.

Sawyer Stone III.

The third.

The one.

Social media ban be damned. I've reloaded all my apps in the Uber, long before I arrive at my apartment.

Courtney

Day 10

I stretch out my plush king-sized bed that I refused to part with despite my therapist's concerns that I spend way too much time in it. And it's true, I've called in sick to work the last two days—but not because I'm depressed and can't get out of it. Because I've decamped to it.

My phone is ringing and I check the number. It's my therapist's fifth call—he's probably worried since I've canceled an appointment via text. I text him that any further calls I will consider harassment and I block him. He was my parents' idea, and though he may have gotten me through the rough few months after everything went to hell, I don't need him anymore and I don't want him in my head.

Things are different now.

I've found Sawyer, and, after spending nearly every minute on the cruiser forums, Fox Finders Facebook group, Instagram, Threads, X, Reddit, YouTube, and the CyberSleuth site, I'm caught up with the investigation. I know the world's prime suspect in the disappearance of Dani Fox is her boyfriend, Sawyer Stone III. And despite all the scary headlines, I know he did not do this thing.

He *does* have some terribly bad luck with women.

This morning I can barely contain my nervous anxiety. I've arranged to meet with one of the lead investigators in the Reddit Bureau of Investigation forum to discuss the disappearance of this Dani Fox woman.

It's all a little cloak and dagger—he won't tell me his full name, only his first name, Allan, which is probably made up. And I don't like that the first meeting place he proposed was an expensive uptown hotel restaurant that my friends and I have been to countless times. A little discretion is advisable.

He tells me he'll be wearing a black baseball cap.

He doesn't tell me it will have *Investigator* emblazoned in white above the bill.

He's a white male in his late forties, with the pallor that comes from spending too much time online and a gut that tells me his diet is probably atrocious, confirmed by his double bacon, two waffle order already on the table in front of him. I remember all the times some internet busybody told me I needed to touch grass and think with a lot of self-satisfaction how much more applicable that meme would have been to Allan than it ever would have been to me. I contacted RBI—the Reddit Bureau of Investigation—a community of hundreds of thousands of amateur cyber sleuths who work together to solve real world mysteries. At times, they work miracles with their crowdsourced approach, but sometimes it is pure buffoonery. I wonder which outcome is in store for me.

I'm twenty minutes early to our meeting. This may be a first for me, a reflection of the intensity of my interest.

"Before we get started, let me give you my bona fides," Allan says. "I've done crime reporting as a freelancer. I've self-published a book on crime investigation and I've started blogs for several missing women—cold cases. You know, the ones the police don't care enough about to pursue. I was active on both the CyberSleuth site and RBI until recently, when I had a conflict with the moderators about some information I had gathered. I haven't been on CyberSleuth for twenty-three days."

I'm not sure how to respond to that, so I nod.

"Before we talk about the case," he continues, "I need to rule you and your family out as suspects—"

"I'm sorry, what?"

"I like to rule out the person I'm meeting with as someone with a motive to kill. The killer often tries to inject themselves into the investigation. We all think this is a clear-cut uxoricide, but I want to rule out sororicide."

"I didn't kill Dani Fox," I say. "I don't even know her."

"I'm not talking about Dani. I'm talking about your sister."

My eyes widen but I keep my mouth from falling open. "My sister died in an accident."

"A highly suspicious accident that was more likely murder," he replies. "Given what's happened to poor Dani Fox."

"What are you talking about? There's no evidence—"

"This is my area and that's exactly my point." He's not shouting but he's got a loud voice and a few people in neighboring booths turn around. "No evidence." He stabs the table with his index finger. "No equipment." Stab. "Missing witnesses." Stab. "The boat operator was never located. It's all very suspicious. Now, did you have any reason to want your sister dead?"

I press my lips together and shake my head. It doesn't seem like the time to mention that I'm the beneficiary of my sister's trust fund—once I come into my own, hers will be added.

He narrows his eyes. "From the digging I did, your family has money."

I swallow. "We do okay," I say at last.

"And how much did Sawyer inherit when your sister died?"

"Nothing—at least, not Standish money. They had a prenup."

He lurched back in the booth. "He didn't get any money? My God. He does it for pleasure then."

"It was a scuba accident," I say, far too loudly.

I slump down on the Naugahyde bench.

"No money at all?" His scowl lines are so prominent I think I could stick a penny in the groove in his forehead.

"She may have had some life insurance through work, but nothing much," I offer.

His eyes light up, and he leans forward. "The typical policy for a person whose company provides life insurance through work is a year's salary," he says. "My cousin works in insurance."

"That's probably what he got."

"So, fifty K, a hundred thou? She had recently graduated from law school, right?"

"She was a second-year associate at Graham Edwards."

"Sounds white-shoe. What did she make?"

I shrug. "Not more than a hundred fifty thousand or so."

"Bingo! There's your motive. That's money worth killing for. People have done it for less and I'll bet my life he used it to buy that boat."

I shift in my seat. I am definitely not going to tell him what I inherited.

I'm starting to think this was a mistake.

He's obsessed with what happened to Emily.

"Why didn't your parents go down there and do their own investigation?"

"I'm sorry?"

"It's a foreign country. By definition their investigation was going to be sub-par, especially in an island nation that is tourism dependent. They'll call everything an accident. Murder hurts tourism."

"We did go down there, all of us, to talk to the police and Sawyer and bring her home," I say quietly.

He waves his hands and scowls. "That's not what I'm talking about. I'm talking about doing your own investigation! Should have hired an investigator." He starts stabbing the table again.

I'm not staying for this. I haven't ordered, other than the coffee, so I quietly pull a bill out of my wallet to throw on the table.

"You should have paid to find the boat operator and the equipment. Should have made investigators find the witness, the woman diving with them. These were critical steps to take then, but it isn't too late now."

"Where is Sawyer now?" I ask. The Bahamas is a huge chain of islands and "the Exumas" doesn't narrow it down much for me.

"Our intel says he's anchored off George Town. So will you do it?"

"What, go there?"

"Go to the Dominican Republic and launch an investigation into what happened to Emily."

"Now? It's been two years."

His bushy eyebrows come together. "Of course now. How many more women have to die by his hand?"

"My sister's death was an accident," I insist. "There's no way Sawyer killed anybody."

No one knows Sawyer better than I do.

"Keep telling yourself that if it helps you sleep better at night. Meanwhile, he'll keep murdering wives and girlfriends. That's what serials do."

He stands and tosses money on the table. He's out of the restaurant before I realize he's left five one-dollar bills. Barely enough to cover the tip so I'll be stuck paying for his waffles with extra bacon on the side. "Go touch grass, Allan," I call out, too softly for him to hear. I feel the satisfaction of insulting him without having caused a scene.

Sawyer needs help clearing his name.

I have travel plans to make and parents to avoid.

But first, I need to see what's happening on CyberSleuth.

trixieliv reports from people on social media they saw Dani at ports or bars in the Caribbean and they are cooperating with detectives. one person put up a photo of her from a sex work website.

karenkk389 I bet they did drugs on that boat party and she fell off and drowned. he may have passed out, freaked out and left. One of her friends on the Find Dani Fox page says she was a very, very free spirt, which is code for a drug addicted skank.

lawyerup87 As a criminal defense investigator, I would advise him to refuse to answer any questions and lawyer up. exercising your right to remain silent doesn't make you uncooperative. But in the court of public opinion, this guy is guilty as sin.

dudeskeptik I'm interested in how their relationship "really" was. I've seen countless people creating a false impression on how their life is and how great their relationships are through SM but in real life it's not rainbows and unicorns. Boats are holes in the water that you pour money into.

SonjaN He was abusive to Dani. She told me so herself. And he looked like he'd been in a fight the day after she disappeared. The police need to arrest him before he flees.

CHAPTER 15

Royal Bahamas Police Headquarters

Sawyer

Day 12

I'M SURPRISED IT'S taken so long for the police to call me back in. Getting all their ducks in a row, I suppose. It's the same interrogation room in George Town that they had me in before. Airless and humid, conjuring images of unseen mold infestations and incipient lung infections. Suffocating. By now they know about Emily. And they've seen that video on the beach with Dani.

I'm convinced that the dinghy disappearance was a setup to trigger me. Dani had preternatural instincts when it came to button pushing. Has, I remind myself. *Has* preternatural instincts. She knew that letting the dinghy get away would get me going. She probably had Rod stash it nearby. She knew we couldn't afford a new dinghy. She knew I'd be in a rage.

I stand as Inspector Knowles and another woman enter the small room. The slim younger woman clad in a tailored charcoal pantsuit introduces herself as Michelle James with the FBI, Legal Attaché's office assisting the Royal Bahamas Police Force with this case. I offer my hand.

I know who she is and why she's here.

They know I've been in this situation before.

We all know it's not a good look.

One dead lover is a tragedy, a second is a pattern. This is too firm a line, if you ask me. It should take three to get to pattern. Two could still be bad luck.

"Mr. Stone," Agent James says, opening her file and fixing her gaze on me. "We understand that your first wife died during a scuba diving accident in the Dominican Republic two years ago."

We're right into it then.

"My first wife? My only wife, and yes, she ran into trouble during a dive and drowned."

"And who was with you on the dive?"

The Dominican Republic letterhead is evident on the papers in front of her. She has access to all this information, but this is how they want to play it.

"A woman we met there, Ella, I don't recall her last name, and the boat captain. Conditions weren't great. Looks like you have the report." I nod to the papers spilling from the file.

James looked at her notes. "Yes, Captain Marcos Reyes, I believe?"

"Yeah, that sounds right."

"Dominican Republic law enforcement identified him as Marcos Reyes," Inspector Knowles says. "He disappeared after the incident."

I shrug.

We go through all of it again. What I know, what I don't know, several times.

They want to see if my story has changed.

It hasn't.

"Let's move on to the videos posted on your YouTube channel, *Sailing with the Foxes*."

"Her channel."

"I'm sorry?"

"It's her channel. I don't have access to it."

"Were you aware the videos had been queued up to post automatically, weekly?"

"No. She discussed doing that, because sometimes we're in places without internet access and we can't upload. In those instances it makes sense; here, it doesn't."

"Why doesn't it?"

"Because this area, George Town, Lee Stocking, has excellent access—I've heard it can get slow in the peak season, but right now it's fine."

"So might she have uploaded the videos this way as . . . breadcrumbs, if you will, in the event of her disappearance?"

I stifle a yawn.

"Was your relationship . . . difficult?" James asks.

"No."

"Did it ever get physical?"

"No, other than what you saw on the video, me grabbing her by the arms." If they can be direct, so can I.

"You shook her," Knowles says.

I meet her stare with my own, unblinking.

"That's the only time? So when we ask some of the cruisers, or people who knew you both in the US, they're not going to tell us you got rough with her on occasion?"

"I've seen the websites," I say.

"What websites?" Inspector Knowles asks.

I give her a sardonic look.

"All of them. You people have a mountain of garbage to sift through. They've doxxed me. Slandered me. I'll have a helluva lawsuit against dozens of people when this is all over. There's so much chum in the water, and so many sharks feeding, you can't see a damned thing. Here's my statement. I didn't hurt Dani Fox. I didn't kill Dani Fox. I don't know where Dani Fox is."

I stand.

Agent James stands too. "Care to explain this?"

I don't even need to look down. She's had it peeking out of her file the whole time we've been talking.

My voice is level, almost bored, when I say, "It's a life insurance policy Dani took out for one million dollars, naming me as the beneficiary."

"Care to explain why she would do that?"

"She wants a baby. I think that's something people do when they're planning to get pregnant."

"Homicide is the leading cause of death for pregnant women in the United States," Agent James says.

"Is it? Well, we aren't in the United States, are we? Couple of things I happen to know about life insurance policies: First, you need a body. Second, the killer can't inherit." I lean back in my chair.

The women took at each other. Knowles makes a note in her open file.

"Is she pregnant?" Agent James asks.

"No."

"Are you sure?" Knowles meets my eyes. "Someone at the *Xanadu* party mentioned she looked as though she might be preg—"

I burst out laughing.

"Dani? Look pregnant? That's hilarious. There is practically naked footage of her on nearly every social media platform."

"But you said yourself, it's not recent."

"I said some of the footage wasn't recent. She wasn't—isn't—pregnant. She's a size zero, for God's sake."

Knowles reaches down into the bag beside her chair and puts a clear plastic bag on the table. "Size two."

I stare at the dress in the bag. It can't be. Oh, God. It's the one she was wearing on the night of the *Xanadu* party. Only now it has reddish-brown stains all over it. My brain has turned to sludge and for a few beats I can't comprehend what this means.

"Holy shit," I breathe, taking my seat again. "Did she wash up somewhere? Damn."

Both women are staring at me, expressionless.

I run my hands through my hair, then reach for the bag. James drags it out of my reach.

I drop my hands and clench my fists.

I know I'm supposed to feel something. Dani and I were good together. She was finally getting everything she wanted.

But I'm shocked. Numb. Disbelieving.

My mind goes back to that night, but there is only emptiness.

Dani might be the only person on this planet I wouldn't kill. But maybe we did have a fight . . . maybe she did, finally, push me too far.

Or did something happen to her on one of her swims?

I put my head in my hands. "She's dead?" I mumble.

"You tell us," Agent James says. Her expression is icy.

I lift my head. I can't take my eyes off the dress. It's a lot of blood.

"How did the blood get on the dress?" Agent James asks.

I draw back. "No fucking idea. Why, wait, how would I know? I don't understand."

"Where is she, Sawyer?" Knowles says.

"What? Wasn't her . . . body in the dress?"

The inspector and the agent exchange glances—this expression I can read. They are perplexed.

I've been dropped into the Upside Down.

"So—you *only* have the dress," I say, putting things together. "Because if you had her body, you'd know she wasn't pregnant."

There's an emotion rising up now but it's not grief or sadness.

It's rage.

My jaw clenches. "Tell me what happened to her."

"We found the dress on your boat, Mr. Stone," Agent James says.

I blink. "*Serendipity*? The hell you did." I had been through that goddamn boat, even her pigsty of a room. I would've found it.

"It was stuffed in a drawer—in the galley."

My mouth opens, closes, then opens. Then snaps shut.

I know exactly what drawer she's talking about.

The drawer we've never been able to open because it's so warped.

Apparently someone got it open and stuffed her dress inside. As what? A taunt? Proof of life?

Brendan was right.

I need a lawyer.

I stand and push my chair in. The metal legs scrape the floor, the sound echoing in the small, stuffy, windowless room. The Bahamas has constitutional protections not unlike the United States. "If you have any more questions for me, you can talk to my lawyer." I hope they don't ask me for a name. I don't have one, but I know who will be able to recommend someone.

"Did you think lightning would strike twice, Sawyer Stone?" Agent James calls after me, but I'm already out the door.

kaylashinessobrite on Instagram they don't seem in love to me. totes obvi he's bored by her. He's way too hot for her. That kind of imbalance never works for couples. He probably moved on. JMO

murderphile12 men disappear their partners all the time and stay in the same house where they killed the partner. They do it because it is the least suspicious thing to do and they don't have a conscience. Continuing to live on the boat is less suspicious than going on the run.

brandonfitnessquest890 DF decided to break it off with SS and she went off with friends they met along the way. She told SS to keep the boat. SS stayed at anchor with a broken heart. he lawyered up because he knows they'll be coming at him hard.

killerqueen17 this reminds me of the Jenna Dwyer case. Her BF Magnus Upton took her on a vacation to BVI. he claimed she went missing while they were snorkeling off Treasure beach. he was arrested and jailed for two months but they never found her so he was released. U need a body to convict.

KJonesl24 I feel like we have seen this movie before.

justaskingtheq Did she have mental health issues? Some YouTube clips show her sad or wistful. Maybe she suicided?

alttheoryenby What if she found out she was sick with cancer. Didn't tell her parents because she knew it would create such sadness. Wanted to be with her boyfriend and really experience what the world has to offer, explore, live freely, not be tied to anything. Decided at some point she would end it. Young love, nothing tying them down, and they both know it's for limited time. The plan was that once she was no longer with us, he was to sail off into the sunset. I don't think he hurt her. I think it's going to turn out to be something very different from all the sad cases we read about so often.

financialdude22 Who owns the boat? How did he pay for the boat? How can anyone afford to sail around with no job? Where are their families?

CYBERSLEUTH ADMIN NOTE:

Sawyer Stone has been officially named by Bahamas LE to be a POI in this case which is still a missing persons case. He may be sleuthed.

Speculation that the victim was somehow responsible for her own disappearance will not be tolerated. Negative speculation on a victim is not allowed. Such posts will be removed.

Warnings, time-outs, or suspensions will be issued for members who violate our Victim Friendly policy.

PART II

CHAPTER

16

Somewhere in the Bahamas

Dani

Day 2

I'M NOT A victim.

I'm not chum.

I'm a YouTube phenomenon. An influencer.

I am my own creation. Or I will be, anyway—I need to stay gone for a couple of weeks first.

I lie back in the beanbag chair on the stern and smile at Jim Marsh over my book. It's cloudy and humid but there's a breeze. It's a perfect day and I am content to read, doze, and watch him fish. Fishing is the most interesting thing Jim does. Let that sink in. Dropping a line in the water and waiting endlessly for some living thing, any living thing, to pick up what you are putting down, sometimes for hours on end with nothing to show for it. That is how Jim chooses to spend his time, day in, day out. That, more than any description I could come up with, tells you all you need to know about Jim Marsh. He's not a bad guy, just laughably predictable. He's giving me my space to recover from all the "abuse." I think the way Jim treats me is equivalent to letting a fish run, and I like it. He leaves me be, under his sphere of protection. He's my champion, my knight, my rescuer keeping me safe from the scary Sawyer Stone.

Come to think of it, Sawyer might be pretty scary right about now.

The plan is to sail to an outer cay in the Bahamas where the fish are plentiful and other cruisers nonexistent. Jim does not like this plan. He wants to go to the authorities and have me press charges, but I've told him I needed time to process and plan my Sawyer Stone–less future.

Jim loves playing the role of wise father figure almost as much as he loves fishing. I don't mind addicts in the throes nearly as much as I mind how sanctimonious they are in recovery.

We are off grid, having ditched our phones and switched off the boat's AIS transponder, putting us into stealth mode. Of course, we run the risk of other ships colliding with us, so we have to keep watch round the clock.

The incriminating videos are queued up to post weekly for the next three weeks. The first video goes live today. I'm working on edits now for the first video I plan to post upon my return—the rescue of the two Bahamian boys—since I have nothing but time. The rescue video could go viral once it's posted, but really, my plan has been in motion since long before that day. Sawyer has always had a propensity for violence; it's not huge leap to imagine him angry enough to kill. The last time we argued, really argued, he shoved me into the galley cabinet hard enough for the cabinet handle to bruise my back—and apparently my kidney beneath. I couldn't get comfortable for a week.

Something I learned a long time ago is that anytime someone is violent toward you, you have three options: go, stay, or make them fucking pay.

But it was the van girl who really inspired me—all those views when she went missing. Her channel was a little nothing and she was a little nobody, filming her little national park excursions with her reluctant boyfriend, and then BOOM! National news coverage, millions of channel likes. She would've been rolling in dough if the reluctant boyfriend hadn't turned homicidal-raging-maniac boyfriend. She never lived to see the success of her channel. That's a damned tragedy.

My plan is win-win. Sawyer pays the price for hurting me and losing our money; I acquire millions of views, followers, and YouTube revenue and maybe even launch my influencer empire.

I have heaps of footage: drone, phone, underwater, boat, party, bedroom, and bathroom. Stellar editing can elicit drama when there's none to be found. Reality television taught me that.

Nudity. Sex. Partying. Infidelity. People they love to hate. Sawyer has the villain-in-a-teen movie, fraternity bro vibe. His prep school diction, vocabulary, and confidence are rage catnip for a segment of the population who watch our channel and comment. There are plenty of people you'll love to hate in the cruising world.

Pre-Sawyer I fooled around with the cam girl thing, which led me to start a Pornvue channel. Talk about a hard market to crack. Porn is crowded and getting enough views to make money is near impossible. Sawyer thinks I learned everything I know about video editing from Jim Marsh in a few weeks, which, unbeknownst to Sawyer, would make me a savant. The reality is, my Pornvue channel, now defunct, is where I earned my chops with storyline editing, accurate metadata, ad optimizing, testing, analysis, community involvement, and the importance of views, ratings, CTR, and sales. I uploaded videos to nearly every category on that site, from "step-sister" to "BDSM," before I embarked on this sailing journey. But those videos never produced much revenue and frankly, sex videos are excruciatingly boring to act in and film. There are only so many holes, positions, and settings in rotation. Out here, in this life of cruisers, I'm a hot blonde commodity—easily a ten. In that world, I'm your average PAWG (phat ass white girl).

On *Sailing with the Foxes*, or any channel, drama and bad behavior are critical components for success. There isn't enough real-life drama, even out here, not for one episode per week. So start inciting. Faking is easy too; editing people's looks or remarks completely out of context does the trick nicely. Dropping a rumor here or a fib there and voila, instant drama.

But you could nail all of the above and still not have a successful channel.

Why?

Discoverability. This is the main reason Sawyer is always telling me I will fail. There's so much noise now.

So how can your signal cut through the noise?

Ask yourself two questions:

What do people *always* tune in to?

How can I do that?

Serendipity

Dani

After the party

It isn't easy to get Sawyer's 185-pound body from our dinghy onto *Serendipity*, even with Jim Marsh's help. Sawyer isn't fully unconscious but he's so uncoordinated he may as well be. Worse than deadweight, this unpredictable spasmodic movement puts us in danger of capsizing the dinghy as Sawyer goes from inert to lurching in an instant. He's muttering things that only made sense to his Rohypnol-addled brain. Every so often I catch my name. I'm proud he recognizes my hand in it.

"Jim, you're a lifesaver," I tell him as we drag Sawyer down the narrow hall to his cabin.

He grunts.

We dump Sawyer's body on top of the sheets, and he murmurs the word "bitch."

Jim draws back, alarmed.

I press my lips together to keep from smiling, widen my eyes, and try to echo the expression he's making.

I walk around the cramped cabin and hug Jim. He wraps shaking arms around me. I'm shaking too, not with nerves, but because Sawyer is damned heavy and all the Pilates workouts in the world don't prepare you for dragging a large adult male human around.

If I'd had to create an ad on Indeed for this project it would've read: *WANTED: male, older, gullible, pathetically grateful for female attention, wannabe mentor in less-than-optimal health, sketchy past, good video equipment, experienced with YouTube channel content creation, editing, and sound.*

Most people would think that it would be completely unreasonable to expect to find someone with such a laundry list of unlikely attributes, but I manifested it. I've got lots of crystals in my collection, but you don't even need them. Formulate your desires, be in tune with the harmonics, and your needs will be met.

Over the past several weeks, I painted Jim a picture of my life with Sawyer—a tableau of emotional and physical abuse. It was kind of fun. I'd take an aspect of my actual relationship with Sawyer, and shade it slightly to make him look as bad as possible, to look jealous and controlling. It wasn't that hard, especially after the crypto crash when Sawyer became increasingly volatile, but whenever I needed additional inspiration I'd draw upon experiences from my childhood but recast Sawyer in my mother Josey's role.

Josey was trailer park comely, her home-bleached hair in an endless battle with her dark roots and a temper to match. She always had on a ton of jewelry, and to this day I can clearly remember the soft wind-chime-like jangle of her bangles that would precede her slaps by like a microsecond. Men were attracted to her toned and curvy body but repelled by her gnawing, endless, bottomless need for approval, validation, and attention that nothing and no one could ever satisfy. Not her god, not her boyfriends, not her child. The only real gift my mother gave me, other than squeezing me into existence, was illustrating to me that playing the victim is an excellent, highly underrated technique for getting what you want.

There was no constant in my life, in case you are wondering what it is like to be raised by a roulette wheel of random responses to stimuli. Smiling at her one day might remind her to hug me, and the next earn me a smack on the ear. But growing up on eggshells honed my people-reading skills to a razor-sharp edge.

I haven't put it like that to Jim. Saviors don't want to hear the ways your suffering has made you stronger. I sometimes think of what a spineless nobody I'd be if I'd been raised by one of those loving moms, with honey highlighted hair and a fan of smile lines at the corner of her eyes. But that's not how stars are born. Stars are forged.

When I hit puberty, Josey farmed me out to her sister in Bakersfield, California. She didn't want to compete with my burgeoning curves.

And that's how I came to live with the Diazes. It wasn't exactly a TV family, but they were tolerable for sure, a few steps up the socio-economic ladder, with no significant downsides. I knew those extra rungs would be easier for me to get what I needed to launch myself.

They gave me the cover of family, and the infrastructure of the middle class. Beyond that, I neither wanted nor expected anything from them. I knew I would have to figure out how to get what I wanted myself, as we all do. And what I wanted was freedom, fame, and fortune. Not necessarily in that order.

Men are a means to an end, but my mother always forgot that part. I am not like her or any other girls. Men sense this. "You're so different," they whisper to me after orgasm.

I elevate your status with coworkers, employees, and friends. I love everything you love—how amazing, what a coincidence! I'm not psychic; you have everything out there on social media. You think it's locked down, but I've gotten you drunk or high or drugged (relax, it's usually simply a few doses of diphenhydramine and alcohol) and use your face to open your electronic storehouse of secrets. I know when you stop texting your exes and you have no more need for booty calls. I know what you're getting up to in your emails. I take what I can use, then I play *Far Cry*, cheer on our sports teams, crush you during Catan, and make your parents and friends love me. I drink beer, or bourbon, or craft cocktails (whatever *you* like) without getting wrecked, and then reenact your favorite porn scene. (Why don't people clear their browser history?) You are an open book to me. I don't do lesbian stuff for *you*; I'm bisexual, so I enjoy it. I'm the best sex you ever had. I'm the hottest girl you've ever been with. I'm the only one who gets you. And when it's over, as it inevitably will be within days or weeks, I'm the one that crushed your spirit, ruined your plans, destroyed you for other women. I'm the fugu sushi chef, but instead of carefully removing the liver and ovaries of the pufferfish where the lethal toxins are housed, my superpower is finding and spilling those toxic sacs.

You will still think of me and remember how you almost had it all, never realizing our relationship was a mirror. You projected what you needed and I reflected it back to you. I am the universe for you, but only for a while.

What do *I* like, read, aspire to, dream about?

You didn't know, care, or ask.

I take what I want—money, chaos, status—and depart.

I've suffered emotional abuse and sexual abuse and physical pain, but it doesn't fester, and I don't poke around in it.

Sometimes I think I should teach a seminar on how to get over shit.

A long time ago, when I was still leading that landlocked life, I was roofied in a bar. It was a textbook, by the numbers roofie-ing, nothing inspired or creative about it. I was alone in a hotel bar, a low-end Hilton in one of those Ohio C-cities, let's say Cincinnati. Some collegiate-looking Ted Bundy type came into the bar and chatted me up. He was passably fit with an average build, dark haired, overall not very memorable but not objectionable either.

So Roofie Guy opened with some pickup line that I didn't quite catch. I think it may have been math based if you can believe it. Something about finding x to solve for why? I didn't even hear it. I was in the mood to get fucked and he would do. He bought me a glass of wine, and we chatted about Cleveland or Cincinnati or Columbus or wherever we were. I never left my bar stool so I don't know when he managed to slip something into my vodka Celsius. It wasn't long before I started to feel the effects. I grew unsteady on my stool, the scope of my vision narrowed, with darkness creeping in from the perimeter until I could see less and less of what was in front of me.

I remember my own voice saying, "I don't feel well?" but sounding so weak and upturned in that questioning way, as if I didn't believe the reality of my own feelings. Then there were a few brief impressions, the expression on his face, caring and concerned. And an impression of the bar stool as impossibly unstable and tall. And then it was like the whole scene cut to a commercial.

I remember nothing from that bar stool onward, until I woke up in my own hotel room, naked and splayed, with Roofie Guy on top of me, caressing my body in the most solicitous way imaginable. That was a real mind fuck right there, his strange gentleness.

Have you ever driven yourself to work or school, a route you've been many times, and then one day, you arrive without any recollection of the journey at all? Where it's like your mind has been on autopilot and traced the route from muscle memory without any input from your conscious mind, and you arrive and snap back into the reality that you have been operating heavy machinery without giving it any conscious thought. That's what it was like when I came to bed with my assailant. There was no slow reversal of the bar stool fadeout; it was an immediate switch on. Like the hypnotist has snapped his fingers and I have woken up, to find myself acting like a chicken, debasing myself on stage for the entertainment of others.

And in that awakening moment, I realize many things in an instant. *I have been drugged. I've lost time. I have been raped.* My anger flared, my indignation. I'd been going to sleep with him anyway. Why would he be so stupid? It dawned on me, of course—*this* was his jam. I lay there, passive, until he got up to use the restroom. Then I rifled through his pants pockets, found his drug stash—it turned out to be Rohypnol—and appropriated the whole bag. I figured it would come in handy at some point.

There are many ways to get what you want in this life if you have no qualms about how you get it. Roofie Guy ensured he got what he wanted by removing the possibility that I might reject him. I was the variable he removed from the equation. I didn't much care for it being done to me, but that made me realize how potent I could be if I did the same thing.

As soon as I was done with the high school/living with the Diaz family iteration of my life, I decided to move to Florida to become a yacht girl. I had read about yachtie life in an expose I saw in a *Vanity Fair* magazine I was flipping through while waiting to pay for groceries. So many important life realizations I have had in checkout lines.

The yacht girl exposé revealed how vulnerable girls were working as stewardesses on the yachts of the mega rich. The kind of people who holiday on yachts are the kind of people who don't believe the rules apply to them. My kind of people.

You'd be hard-pressed to think of a way to get more intimate contact with the ultra-wealthy than yachting, and if the only downside is putting up with some yacht guests playing grab ass with me? Sign me up. Which I did—they make you basically sign your life away in nondisclosures, which was the thing that kept me from starting a *Hottie Yachtie* YouTube channel. But that wasn't the only reason I kept quiet about my time on the mega yachts. Many of the owners or guests were bona fide criminals. I'm not talking white collar stuff. In the United States we tend to think of billionaire yacht owners as sniveling Silicon Valley types, but in much of the world, the people who have that kind of money are war criminals, psychopaths, felons, murderers, and actual mobsters, none of whom would hesitate to send someone over the side of a boat under sail. But the tips were off the charts.

Having some familiarity with boating life was the only requisite for getting a job as a yacht girl, considering that I'd already checked the "Must Be Impossibly Hot" box. I submitted a full-body, pinup-style 8x10 glossy with my first application, and no one seemed to care that I had no experience. I got hired as a third stew within days of my arrival to Florida.

My first gig, sailing out of Palm Beach, was on a fifty-meter yacht called *Prudence*. With room for ten guests and twelve crew, it boasted a grand piano in the main salon and a Hefner grotto-sized hot tub on the top deck. Not that I spent much time on deck. I was assigned to the laundry, with minimal guest contact. I don't understand the point of hiring hotties if you aren't going to let them see the light of day. I sure got good at pressing and folding though.

I'd never known how little space there was on a boat. You never see the crew quarters in the luxury magazine spreads. We were stacked three high in bunks in postage-stamp-sized crew cabins, airless and windowless below deck. It made our old single wide trailer seem like Cinderella's castle by comparison. Like the movie *Parasite*, but at sea. The only thing that kept me going were the many, many routes I could see to make my way topside, and eventually I did.

The tips were glorious. I remember after my very first charter, my chief stew nonchalantly handed me a wad of cash: $2,700 for tips for the three-day charter we completed. It was an ordinary amount, typical for a charter of this length, but for me it was a revelation. Josey never earned that kind of money in three days. But here I was, holding this thick stack of well-worn $20 bills, fingering each one individually over and over. They felt so dirty and I loved it. I fell asleep that night in the middle bunk, clutching my money in a death grip even in sleep. It was the closest I ever came to sleeping with a teddy bear.

But working is no way to get rich, as any working person will tell you. It's how you get by, and getting by is not good enough for me.

Back in the Florida Keys, I met Sawyer. Once again, the universe delivered exactly what I needed. I jumped at the chance when he proposed I crew with him.

He bought a boat with the insurance payout he got after his wife died. I remember him telling me he'd named her *Serendipity*, and I asked if that was because *I'm Glad My Wife Died* was already taken.

He laughed in response and offered me the job of first mate.

Sawyer and I work. We can go for days without speaking and no one gets offended. We play the same games. I read and cook. He fixes stuff. He loves to do it, so I will periodically sabotage something just so he can feel needed. He lives by the same rules I do. It's not a traditional relationship and our combined impulsivity occasionally creates trouble, but the beauty of this life is the ability to pick up anchor at will and flee to the next port. I knew I could find my story with Sawyer. He would never impede my freedom, which is my number one priority. Well, that, and staying out of prison.

My number one rule: no cell.

Otherwise, anything goes.

Sawyer Stone III is the first person I've ever been able to be truly myself with and I've never had more fun. I'm not angry about the crypto losses. What's the point? Pragmatists don't get mad; they create a new plan. I'm not going to tell him what's coming next. I have my life and he has his. But one of us had to come up with something to save our lifestyle and that someone was me.

It's not easy to fake angst. "Sawyer is mean to me" generated puzzled stares from Sonja and Jim so I went on the internet to borrow a few lines. I added "maybe I'm too sensitive" and "maybe he's the only person who will ever care about me" and "maybe I *am* crazy/stupid/ugly," sprinkling these into conversations with Jim Marsh weekly, the way you would spice in a sauce.

I knew Sonja was hundreds of times easier than Jim, so I was careful not to reveal my "truth" to her too soon or she'd blow it with an intervention or confrontation. One conversation on *Xanadu* and she jumped on the line and I reeled her in. Landing Jim took skill, patience, and time. Jim had been both abused and abuser in the years before he got sober. People in recovery are better than most at sniffing out my bullshit, but eventually Jim had the hook in his mouth too.

Sawyer won't appreciate the genius of the plan—not at first. That's the first mover advantage. He would never get the jump on me. He'd probably kill me if he knew what was coming and that's not hyperbole.

Within hours or days Sonja will alert the cruiser community. How can I know this? She alerts the message board when she farts. She is hardwired for gossip. She couldn't keep a juicy item like my disappearance to herself any more than she could stop herself from drawing breath. She'll definitely tell them I'm missing; she'll alert law enforcement. I can only hope she'll be effective. I'm hoping for van girl coverage.

Missing white woman syndrome is media ratings gold.

I like my chances here. Not only am I white, but I'm hot and blonde to boot.

Which means keeping us hidden for a little at some god-forsaken tiny island in the middle of the Bahamas chain wiped out by one hurricane after another until everyone packed it up. I've told Jim enough stories about Sawyer's violent temper, abuse, jealous rages, how he's arranged at least one deadly accident and how he'll follow us to the ends of the earth given half the chance.

People will believe anything about Sawyer. He's got that kind of face.

Once we've offloaded Sawyer to his bed to sleep it off, Marsh comes into my cabin on *Serendipity* where he sees my disaster.

"Holy hell," he whispers.

"He's so destructive," I whisper back. "Can you load up these two tubs in your dinghy? I'll be out in ten minutes." He picks up one of the tubs. They're big and heavy and if he knew what was in them, he would reconsider everything he's been doing for me—but he would never violate my privacy that way.

Once he's gone, I change into my black cotton joggers and black tank top and tuck my hair into my brown hoodie for the dinghy ride to *Aboat Time.* I use a razor to slice the top of my scalp. I use my floral dress to absorb it. Scalp wounds bleed prodigiously. After a couple of minutes, I grab the styptic pen to slow the bleeding and toss the razor blade into the second tub. I take the blood-soaked dress into the galley and shove it into a drawer, then wipe my prints off the handle. Sawyer will never open it. He's complained about the damn drawer being stuck since we've lived on the boat. I managed to get it open by lubing the bottom. It still requires some heft to pull out, it's so warped. I know it's a long shot that the police will discover it, but maybe the Bahamians will surprise me. Anything to feed the narrative.

I wipe my bloody hands on the ceiling, in his cabin and in the bathroom.

Jim comes back for the second tub and sees the blood on my forehead.

"Dani—your head."

I reach above my forehead. "Goddamn it. I hit it on the cabinet. Is it bleeding?"

"Let's get a Band-Aid."

"No time," I whisper. "I'll deal with it on *Aboat Time.*"

He reluctantly agrees and grabs the second tub.

"Jim, please remember to turn off your transponder," I remind him when he comes back. "I'm sorry. I'm so afraid."

"Don't worry," he says, struggling up the stairs with the last of my gear.

"I'm going to take a quick look around, okay? I'll be right out," I tell him.

I head back to Sawyer's cabin to find the spiked leather paddle in the under-the-bed pull out drawer beneath him, stuffed with all the other instruments of pain and pleasure we've acquired and used in our travels. We're not sadists, but we give the people what they want and sometimes they want a beating. Sometimes you want to feel something.

I don't want to break any bones, but I need to feed my narrative of the abusive boyfriend for the police and bystanders and I'm the kind of woman who hits back—ask anyone. I strip him naked and use the paddle with gusto, enough to bruise the hell out of him but not break the skin—bringing his blood into the mix will confuse the narrative. I concentrate on his hands and random other areas of his body but leave his gorgeous face alone. He's in the fetal position by the time I'm ready to go.

I leave through the galley and I can't help myself. I toss around a few of his neatly stored canned items, dump rice on the counter. In the midst of this high-stakes gambit, I take no small amount of pleasure in knowing how much this disorder will irritate him. He's so goddamn sanctimonious about how neat he is and how messy I am.

Over top of the rice, pasta, and cereal I spill one of his sports drinks. He'll be uncovering sticky spots for weeks. My work here is done.

I've kept Jim waiting long enough.

CHAPTER 17

New York, NY

Courtney

Day 15

I'VE SPENT THE morning in bed, making futile attempts to contact Sawyer, booking a flight to Nassau and then another on a tiny puddle jumper to George Town, and avoiding calls from my parents and therapist. There are now photos online of *Serendipity* anchored off Lee Stocking Island. I'll swim to it if I must.

On the cluttered nightstand next to my sleep mask, mouth guard, calming lavender oil, and white noise machine, my phone vibrates an alert. I check the number. Under normal circumstances, I would never answer a blocked call, but today it's what I've been waiting for. I pick up, hoping against hope that it's him.

"Hello?"

"This is Allan," a man's voice on the other end of the phone says.

I frown. "I'm sorry, who?"

"Allan of RBI."

"Oh, Allan of CyberSleuth." Not this guy again.

"Not CyberSleuth. I already told you, I've been banned for the past thirty-two days. I'm with the RBI—the Reddit—"

"Bureau of Investigation. Yes. I remember our meeting. Is there new information?"

"Yes, the new information is we found another person with a motive to kill your sister."

My grip on the phone tightens. "Who?"

"You!" Allan says.

"Me? Are you insane?"

"I *asked* you if you had any reason to want your sister dead."

"I recall you asked that, and I didn't—don't!"

"You were the beneficiary of her trust fund."

This stops me cold. How is he getting this information? I'm grinding my teeth. I don't think I've ever done that while awake before.

"You aren't denying it," Allan says. "That's motive."

"I didn't kill my sister." I articulate each word as if trying to overcome a faulty connection.

"Oh, no one thinks you killed her. We think you paid Sawyer to kill her."

"What?" The way Allan is talking, he's channeling Perry Mason on cross-examination. Every ludicrous conclusion is pronounced with an a-*ha*! intonation, as if his allegation had inexorably been proved.

"How much did you inherit from her?" he asks.

"I have my own money, my own trust. I don't need hers!" Why am I even still talking to this guy?

"There's two things you can never have enough of: money and bandwidth."

I should never have contacted this clown. I know that now that I've bitten my nails down to the quick.

"You lied when I asked you if you had a reason to want your sister dead," Allan insists.

"I didn't lie. I loved my sister and didn't want her dead!" I'm almost shouting now. At the best of times, I get overwhelmed easily. Being accused of wanting to kill my sister has sent me around the bend.

"That wasn't the question. I asked if you had a reason or benefited from her death."

"You are insane," I say.

"By all accounts you didn't like your sister."

"Bullshit. I loved her."

"Loved her? So much you were hooking up with her *husband*?"

I blink.

Who has he been talking to?

"That's not true," I say, but even I can hear the hesitation in my response. "And none of this is any of your goddamn business."

"We have sources telling us you hated your sister and were jealous of her relationship with Sawyer. We have photographic evidence."

"Sources? Photos? What are you even *talking* about?" It comes out as a wail.

"One of our sleuths found photos of you and Sawyer. We see you, Courtney. We know you and Sawyer had a relationship."

My heart races. How much do they know? How did this spin out of control so quickly? My heart skips a beat. Is it possible for agitation to throw one's heart out of rhythm? I'm sure I am in AFib. I cannot hyperventilate again.

"You're talking about my brother-in-law," I say meekly.

"You're not even denying it. What happened? Did he dump you for Dani?"

My fingertips are tingling, and my legs give out. I fall to the couch and grab my laptop. I resist my first impulse to check out my symptoms on WebMD.

Instead, I click the browser bar, where Dani Fox's web sleuth missing page is bookmarked.

"Oh my God."

It's that horrible photo from the worst day of my life. The day the only man I ever loved married my sister. I was in a bad way that day. The party was almost over and I'd had a few fortifying drinks when Sawyer asked me to dance. He said something funny about my tangerine bridesmaid dress and I laughed. The photographer had snapped the photo seconds later with us still grinning at each other like fools. God help me, it looks intimate. I love and hate that photo—it hints at what eventually developed between us.

There are other photos on the sleuth page—photos of us hugging after the funeral, another one of me holding his hand a few weeks later at some family event, comforting him. Most damning of all is the photo of the kiss. It was a cheek kiss—well, corner of the mouth, but it was right before his lips touched me. My eyes are open and reveal everything I spent so much effort hiding when Emily was alive.

I begged my former best friend not to put that photo on her Facebook page, but of course she had.

My feelings for Sawyer had been innocent—until they weren't.

"We have hundreds of thousands of people combing through social media and other information, we've had people coming forward to tell us what they know. We are going to show how you and Sawyer conspired to kill Emily, and we're going to nail him for Dani's murder."

I hang up and throw the phone across the room.

I pick up the bottle of gin and glug for as long as I can stand.

My parents are going to freak out.

I must get to the Bahamas. I wonder if putting my weighted blanket in my suitcase will put it over the limit. Do I have time to fill a prescription? I'm going to the airport first thing tomorrow, but it will all be so much easier if I can take some benzos. I'm a nervous flier at the best of times. These are not the best of times.

CHAPTER 18

Somewhere in the Bahamas

Dani

Day 15

I EMERGE FROM THE tepid ocean after a swim and am swarmed by bugs. We've been at this abandoned little island for nine days now. We're anchored far enough offshore that the insects aren't a problem but here, on these untreated deserted isles, the whine of the mosquitos is constant. I hurry through my workout—lunges, squats, pushups, leg lifts—made exponentially more difficult in the soft sand. Sand workouts are one of the keys to a bangin' booty—something every SEAL knows. I should develop a sandbox for adults to sell to gyms for people to up their workout game.

I spit into my mask and rinse it with seawater to prevent it from fogging up. I get the long fins on my feet with some difficulty, my thigh muscles still trembling from exertion. The swim back to the boat is a few hundred meters. I'd love more time alone, but I don't want to end up with dengue, Zika, or chikungunya. A few years back, exploring off the beaten path in Nusa Lembongan as a yachtie, I had the misfortune of encountering someone suffering from dengue hemorrhagic fever. They were bleeding from every orifice. You think you've seen a few things, but then you encounter someone bleeding from the eyeballs. I held my breath and beat a quick escape out of that place. Ever since, I've been hypervigilant when it comes to mosquitos.

I'm probably condemning myself to developing some terrible cancer down the road, slathering myself with DEET every time I turn around while the ghost of Rachel Carson spins in her grave. Cancer is tomorrow's problem and there is too much going on today to worry about nascent tumors. The populated islands do a good job controlling the mosquitos, but on these deserted enclaves, I'm lunch for the world's most dangerous creature. One more reason I find myself ready to cut this process short. Time to bug out, if you will.

Living with Jim for the past two weeks has been challenging. He goes to bed soon after the sun sets and is up to fish before dawn. Sometimes he casts off the boat, other times he takes the dinghy out into deeper waters, and rarely, he goes ashore. He's finally stopped asking me to do any of these activities with him.

I've adjusted my schedule to spend as few waking hours with him as I can—bed at two AM, up when he leaves, and a nap in the afternoon. The time we spend together seems to get more awkward every day. I think the inspiring feeling of being my savior is wearing thin for Jim. An occasional grimace flits across his face every now and again. He never says anything, but I've detected an arch look a few times when he's had to move my dirty dishes to make room to prepare our meals. Is it that big a deal to push some dirty glasses over to the side of the sink? It takes about a millisecond.

Considering the friction, I do my best to steer clear. Mostly I squirrel away and read anything I can get my hands on—I've read about twenty books so far and have been forced to hunt through Jim's shelves, which are barren other than the Caribbean travel books, fishing books, and recovery books interspersed with the occasional Clancy, Child, or Grisham.

Every day I marvel at how much time has been freed up in my day-to-day now that I can't access social media. I'm surprised how much I miss looking at pictures of people my own age. I never stop noticing how old Jim is. There are places on his body where his skin looks like actual leather—and not some luxurious soft calfskin worthy of a designer purse, either, but weathered hide. He is fit enough, but it doesn't look as good on an old person. Sometimes I can see him moving with stiffness when he gets up from a crouch, or I'll see him reflexively put a hand on the small of his own back to stretch it out. I feel disdain for his decrepitude, but he is the only game in town, so sometimes I amuse myself by imagining what it would be like to make a TikTok dance video with him. The ridiculous difference of his beat-down self with my energetic youth might be enough to make it go viral. Like those endearing exploitation videos created by college boys and their grandmothers.

It's hard to go cold turkey. Fifteen days with no Instagram, no Snapchat, no YouTube, no nothing. It's impossible not to wonder what DMs I must be missing, especially under the circumstances. I'm left with reality: me and my old man, alone and bored on *Aboat Time.*

I can't wait until it's *Aboat Time* to get off. So I swim. I've always loved swimming for exercise, each stroke harnessing the healing power of the ocean, lengthening my muscles, expelling toxicity with every released breath, amping up my serotonin. I stay in my swimsuit all day on Jim's boat. I never know when I might need to dive in and escape—even though Jim complains that my diving off the boat scares the fish. What would he suggest I dive off then? His very presence is aggravating. I swim multiple times a day, and this session now has been an extra-long one. If I'm not careful, I'll lose weight.

When I get back to the boat and rinse off, he's there, waiting for me with poached eggs and toast.

"Is anything wrong?" He asks me this every goddamn day.

I've tried every response, from "I need to come to terms with the end of my relationship" to "I'm tired today" to "I'm sorry I'm such poor company. I have my period." Nothing works for long.

He expects me to talk about it. The abuse, Sawyer, whatever. I should have realized this from the recovery and self-help books he keeps. So I share a little about my mother and my childhood. Poor little Dani. Victimized by a teacher, her family, her mom's boyfriends, relatives, coworkers, Roofie Guy. It's a tale I've trotted out in various iterations over the years. Part truth, part after-school special, part true crime. Jim responds by sharing a few of his own tales of woe, which center mostly around wrecked cars and obliterated relationships. I make all the right sympathetic noises but wonder, why would anyone get married three times? That's the definition of insanity right there. I had a friend in elementary school whose mom and dad had to move from Kentucky to Florida because in Kentucky, it's illegal to remarry the same person four times. At least Jim married different women. Why marry at all—unless to improve your financial status?

So far, I've held off seducing Jim and keep letting him play the role of father figure—not because it's easier, but because I anticipate any physical intimacy will lead to more intense questioning.

I decide to pull out the response that usually gets me out of these circumstances while generating the most empathy.

"Jim, I was diagnosed as on the spectrum as a kid," I blurt out. It is not actually a lie. In my tween years one idiot therapist did spout off that diagnosis.

There have been a dozen others I've heard over the years.

There it is—the explanation that makes people comfortable. They can line up some of my behaviors: misunderstanding or ignoring social cues, dislike of emotional intimacy, and all the rest with what they understand about neuroatypicals and treat me with compassion while simultaneously lowering expectations. You'd be hard-pressed to identify a type of a behavior that couldn't be considered a sign of ASD. Talk too much? Misreading of social cues—ASD. Don't talk enough? Communication deficiency—ASD.

Jim comes over instinctively to hug me, but stops a foot away as it dawns on him. "Thank you for sharing that with me, Dani. I'll do my best to make you comfortable, okay?"

I shrug and finish my eggs. All of a sudden, I'm free of the burden of social niceties. I should have done this ages ago. "Did you catch anything?" I ask.

He lights up. "A snapper," he says. If only I could stomach making more fish-based conversations. Any remotely fish-related topic of conversation immediately lifts Jim's spirits.

I nod. "I'll make my Cajun cream sauce for it."

That's our deal: He catches, cleans, and grills the fish, and he makes the sides. I make the sauce. If you can make a good sauce, people think you can cook. I love every kind of sauce. I'd love to do a sauce book instead of a damn healthy vegan cookbook, but sauces don't feed the Fox image. Sauces imply oily, gassy, fat, foreign rather than clean, fit, healthy.

I can make all five of the French mother sauces, plus butter sauces and brown sauces. I'm not as big a fan of the tomato sauces, but I can do a few, and as far as I'm concerned, the sweet coulis are not sauces at all. A thought pops into my head of another idea for a YouTube channel—I could be the Saucy Saucier, where I wear lingerie and teach people how to make proper sauces while telling dirty jokes. Maybe I could do a tie-in with an OnlyFans account, where adoring fans could pay me to, I don't know, lick sauce off a whisk or something.

This is how I know that one day I will hit it big—the ideas never stop coming.

I wash and rinse my plate and take my ginger tea to my cabin. I'm never seasick, though I use it frequently as a gambit to escape work on *Serendipity* and *Aboat Time.*

Jim hasn't said anything, but I can tell the freshly ransacked appearance of my cabin is distressing to him. Maybe he can write it off to my manufactured spectrum disorder.

I am desperate for Wi-Fi. I spend hours—days, even—fantasizing about what is happening in the real world and how to best monetize this current plan. But Jim refuses to get Starlink, so in order to have Wi-Fi, we'll have to go to more populated areas. And even one cruiser spotting me, or us, will completely upend things.

I will wait the full twenty-one days—the longest I've ever gone without Wi-Fi—but not one day more.

CHAPTER

19

Royal Bahamas Police Headquarters

Inspector Knowles

Day 16

OFFICER WALTER KNOCKS on Knowles's open office door. "Inspector, a gentleman from San Diego, Anthony Diaz, is here and says he's a relative of Dani Fox."

Sawyer had mentioned an Uncle Tony on the missing persons form. He also said she was estranged from her family.

"Couldn't he have called?" she mutters. That's so American. Jump on a plane and go somewhere, uninvited and unnecessary, and spare no expense.

"Says he's been unable to get through."

"Damn it! Bring him in. And get some more people working on the tip line." An overly busy tip line is a failure of structure and process, the very sort of thing that gets under Inspector Knowles's skin.

"Boss, everyone is on it."

"Okay, okay." She'll have to call Nassau for more support. She's already made that call once. They offered to centralize calls and tips at the Nassau office, but she refused. This is *her* investigation, and Nassau cannot be trusted to give the same oversight that she would herself. As soon as you introduce another office, you introduce cracks for important witnesses to inadvertently slip into. But her small office can't keep up, and she knows she'll have to enlist their help soon.

A short, grim, jean-clad man in a Padres T-shirt enters her office carrying a backpack stuffed to the gills.

"Inspector Knowles," she says, coming around her desk and shaking his hand, taking in every detail of his appearance and alphabetizing his distinguishing features for cataloging in her mind.

"Anthony Diaz. Tony. I'm Dani's uncle—well, through marriage, but we helped raise her. She came to live with us when she was twelve."

"Please, sit. I'm so sorry you had to come all this way. We've been overwhelmed with calls. Can I get you to verify some information? And do you mind if I record this conversation? It's easier than taking notes."

"No, go ahead, unless—"

Knowles looks up. "Unless?"

His hands are fists. "If she does come back, will she hear this tape?"

"No, sir. I can't imagine a scenario where she would be allowed to, legally."

He seems relieved and gives permission.

Knowles verifies Dani's date of birth, and something that hasn't been posted everywhere online: her social security number. Maybe she'll finally get concrete information about who Dani is. She's heard the woman described as everything from petty thief to saint by the cruiser community and it's hard to separate fact from fiction.

"Sir, you said you raised Dani?"

"Daniella. That's what we called her. And we adopted her so she was Daniella Diaz, but I heard she's legally changed her last name to Fox."

Knowles nods. "I understand she's estranged from her family?"

"Her mother is dead. Daniella had no siblings. Her mother never identified the father. My wife died when Dani was fifteen."

"I'm so sorry."

"Thanks."

"Unfortunately, I've not yet been able to learn much about your adopted daughter. You've come a long way, and I can't tell you much more than you've probably read. She's missing. Last seen sometime late Saturday night or early Sunday morning two weeks ago."

He stands and paces the room. "I understand she may have been swimming in the ocean."

"It's possible, yes. That was her routine."

He stops and looks at Knowles. "Lotsa sharks here in the Bahamas?"

She nods. "Yes."

"Do you think that's what happened?"

"Shark attacks are incredibly rare but rest assured, we're exploring every lead."

"And the boyfriend?"

"Every lead."

"If a shark had got her, what would you expect to find? Body parts washing up?"

Knowles winces. People are always trying to entice her into baseless speculation, to lead her down the primrose path. She does not abide. "It is impossible to say, Mr. Diaz."

He blows out a sigh. "Daniella's mom was not a level-headed person. The social worker who came to talk to us said years of neglect and some abuse. My wife and I did all we could, but—we couldn't fix what was so badly broken."

Inspector Knowles sits up straighter in her chair. "What was broken?"

"We had her evaluated a few times after she came to stay with us. Initially they thought high functioning—Asperger's was the word then. Do you know what that is?" He's back to pacing.

"I am familiar."

"She didn't respond socially very well. Very reserved. Didn't seem to understand, fundamentally, how to act around people or how to identify, emotionally. She was highly intelligent and very focused. My wife worked hard to get her to understand social cues. We brought her to mass regularly and family gatherings—"

"No one we've spoken with has reported this." Knowles is perplexed. How could something so fundamental go unnoticed by all those cruiser types she interviewed, let alone her intimate partner? It doesn't compute.

"Well, it turns out it wasn't Asperger's." He looks away. "The work my wife did helped—outside the house. But with us she didn't see the need to act normal."

"What do you mean?

"She learned how to behave with other people. How to pretend. Does that make sense?"

Knowles's brow wrinkles. "If it wasn't a spectrum disorder, what was it?"

"Over the years we heard everything from bipolar disorder to oppositional defiant disorder and then, later, all the letters came in: BPD, NPD, ASPD. Bipolar, narcissistic, antisocial. We had new acronyms and words every six months. We felt bad for her, we really did, and we did our best. But by fifteen she refused to go to therapy and things got worse."

He drops onto the chair, seemingly exhausted.

"How?"

"As Daniella got older, she used what she had learned from my wife and others how to act, how to manipulate. She learned all the behaviors that go with relationships, but there was no feeling underneath. My wife used to say to her, fake it 'til you make it. And I think that's what Daniella does all the time. As she got older, her behavior became riskier. She'd meet up with men she searched out online. She's clever and she was good at not getting caught. But nothing we did or said had any effect. Nothing and no one could rein her in. Not fear of punishment, from me or God. Eventually her behavior caused rifts between us and relatives and friends and our church. Even with my employees."

"Can you elaborate on the kind of trouble? Trouble with the law? Did she have any arrests?" Knowles asks.

"No."

"Drugs?"

"No, no drugs. She stole things. Jewelry from a school friend, money from a relative. She uh, had a relationship with her teacher when she was fifteen."

"A sexual relationship?"

"Yes, with a woman."

"Dani is a lesbian?"

"Bisexual."

"Her boyfriend didn't mention it."

Diaz shrugs. "We didn't care about that so much. But the teacher attempted suicide. A few weeks later the woman's husband accessed her accounts and showed me what he'd found. Threatening emails from Daniella, screenshots of texts. We didn't press charges after what the husband showed us, and they left town. By the end of that year Daniella was causing these kinds of problems with the men in my shop. She was promiscuous, they were married, she got them to buy her things and give her money, there were jealousies and fights. It was a nightmare. We tried to be understanding, you know, because of her childhood. We took her to confession every week. My wife, Araceli, spent the rest of her life, on her knees, praying the rosary for Daniella. When my Araceli got sick, while she was dying and I wasn't paying attention, Daniella got into the motorcycles . . ."

"Racing?"

"Stealing them. Used my van to do it, little did I know. Sold them to chop shops."

"At what age?"

"Sixteen, seventeen. I was not myself for a long time after Araceli died. I woke up when some people came after her, to my garage. Some turf thing about parts. They threatened us with guns. I told her she couldn't stay if she wouldn't stop causing trouble. She agreed to leave if I did the paperwork for her emancipation. It was easy since she had her GED. She moved out and I haven't heard from her in eight years. Then I see her face all over the news."

"Was she ever caught stealing?"

"Not as far as I know. But I had a mess to clean up after she left. Someone torched my garage."

"Oh wow. I'm sorry."

"I'm not saying it was Daniella. I'm not saying it wasn't. I'd lapsed paying the policy when my wife was ill."

"You lost it all?"

"Burned to the foundation. I declared bankruptcy," he says. "I don't hold grudges, but I wouldn't be surprised if Daniella finally pissed off or stole from the wrong person. If she's still doing that kind of thing." He shakes his head.

"Did you come down here because you are worried about her?"

"Of course I'm worried about her. I want to know she's okay, but I don't want to reunite with her if . . . *when* she's found, you understand? So please, let me know when you know anything, and if she is alive."

Inspector Knowles nods.

Anthony Diaz stands and picks up his sack. He puts his hat back on his head. "Daniella may have changed a little over the years, her name or her nose or . . ." He gestures to his chest. "But if some guy was beating on her, he better sleep with one eye open. One of the guys in my shop grabbed her ass once. She broke his wrist with a wrench."

C H A P T E R

20

Platinum Star

Sawyer

Day 22

I COLLECT BRENDAN WEATHERBY at his boat, the well-maintained *Bacchus,* a Ganley 43 nearly a decade old. It's the Bentley of monohull yachts and I'd love to take it out with him for a sail but every time I've suggested it, he's demurred. For as long as we've been off Lee Stocking Island, I've never seen his boat leave the anchorage. Nor have I ever been invited aboard. You can tell a lot about a person by the boat they choose, though not so much in my case as I was hamstrung by limited funds. His boat suits him perfectly since he's such a traditionalist. Dani would say his boat is on brand.

It's early, around seven AM. Too early, apparently, for the handful of cruisers, kooks, and randos who come by in their dinghies, tenders, or power boats to stare or try to get a photo of me. We head to an anchorage off Castle Beach. Brendan, who has been out here for years and has partied with nearly everyone, has connected me with Jesse Jonas. Jesse and his husband have a YouTube channel, *Platinum Star*, named for their four cabin, four head Lagoon 450 catamaran. They bought the boat three years ago, outfitted her, and now take gay travelers sailing in the Bahamas for a week. Jesse is the captain, Donavan is chef and crew. What they charge is jaw dropping, but they seem to have no problem getting bookings.

Brendan thinks this is the perfect opportunity to tell my side of the story and he's vouched for me with his friends Jesse and Donovan. God knows I can't trust Brendan's judgment so I'll just have to evaluate their motivations myself. We arrive at the *Star*. She's a beauty and it's immediately obvious they have spared no expense with upgrading her.

Jesse and Donovan come out to the sugar scoop to greet us and help Brendan tie up. Jesse makes small talk while he gives me a quick tour of the *Platinum Star*. She has an open saloon and galley, a large dining table inside and out. The fly bridge has lounge seating as does the forward trampoline. She leaves me with terrible boat envy.

"I've laid out some breakfast, if I could interest you?" The question is asked to both of us but Donovan is focusing more on me.

"I'm starving," I say.

While Donovan pours us coffee and fresh juice, Jesse shares a typed sheet of paper with me. "These are the questions I'm going to ask."

I glance at the paper and my lip curls. "Courtney?"

Courtney was a useful idiot who is now becoming an embarrassment. Not that I feel shame about her, or our relationship.

"She's irrelevant."

"It's out there now," Jesse says with a shrug. "You need to address it."

I shake my head. I'm so sick of this shit. I'll decide what I need, not these two.

"You should listen to him," Donovan says, laying perfectly plated eggs Benedict with potatoes and hollandaise sauce in front of me. I wolf it down.

It's amazing. I haven't eaten anything this good in weeks.

Jesse frowns.

"Sorry, but this is so good," I tell them between bites. "I've been living off protein bars and fruit."

"That's sad," Donovan says. "Let me make you another."

I don't tell him no.

"Let's do a dry run," Jesse says. "Tell us about your relationship with Dani."

I shrug. "We were fine, in love, whatever."

"What do you think happened to Dani?" Jesse leans forward and meets my gaze directly.

"Not a clue." When it seems he's waiting for more, I add, "I sure would like her back."

"Okay, that's enough. Look, you have to put some heart into it," Jesse says.

"Some what?"

"Some *heart*, Tin Man. Are you sad she's gone?"

"Of course, but I'm angry that I'm accused—"

He holds up a hand. "No, Sawyer, you're not mad, you're sad, got me?"

I scowl. "Can't I be both?"

"You don't have that luxury when you're the prime suspect. No matter the provocation, you cannot come across as angry. When I ask you how you feel about your wife Emily's death, show the viewers your sadness."

"Okay," I say.

"I know you're a tough guy."

I raise my eyebrows.

"But this is a time for vulnerability. Genuine emotion. If you want to get the police looking in the right direction, it will help if you can convince some people that you didn't do it."

Donovan lays another plate with fruit and two eggs Benedict with a salmon base in front of me. I groan and begin eating. He sits across from me. "Listen to him. This boat? This is the boat that Jesse's PR and marketing skills bought. He fixed scandals in Silicon Valley for years. It's all about the apology tour."

"I'm not doing an apology tour. I've done nothing wrong."

"Dani seems to understand that appearances are everything, even if you don't. She's winning this game," Jesse says. "You have to respect the hustle."

I stop chewing. *What* did he say?

"You have to fight fire with fire. This doesn't have anything to do with truth or reality, Sawyer. Tell me you know that."

The food is forgotten as I stare at the man across from me.

My eyes narrow. "Have you met Dani?"

"No."

"Then how in the hell do you know—or think you know—what she's doing?"

He smiles a cold little smile and removes his sunglasses. I finally see him. Until this moment, he's camouflaged that inner frost well enough to fool me. This man is a master. All those loving touches and glances with his spouse. There are more people like him out here than I imagined. Maybe this is where they go when they leave that boardroom or the CEO position—cast out for ruthlessness with a golden parachute. Maybe he's here for the same reason most of us are: liberation from friends, family, and expectations of normalcy.

The mask is back on in a blink. "How do I know? Because it makes sense. At least, it makes sense to a creative." Jesse's expression changes again; he's all business. "You need to do your part to increase your likability in the long run, even if in the short run you're getting crushed in the public eye. You are a thoughtless or unkind boyfriend but never violent and never, ever, unfaithful. Dani has been careful with what she's put out in the first two videos. The last one was a little bit too much, if you ask me, the whole you-shaking-her incident, but I can't wait to see what mindfuckery she'll hit us with tomorrow."

It's hard to see the humor when it's your boat they're flying their drones over, throwing food at you and catcalling at all hours. I'm a sitting duck on *Serendipity*. "What she's doing to me—"

"Could make you rich. Have you seen the channel views? You can't buy this kind of exposure. Like it or not, you have Sonja to thank for that. I wonder if Dani had any idea how effective that woman would be at rallying the troops. Is it dumb luck, Sawyer, or is she a mastermind?"

He chuckles at my glare.

"There's nothing funny about this."

"For you? No. But you have to admit—Fox Finders? That was inspired," Jesse says. "And this all goes viral, playing to our biases. Men always kill the wife or girlfriend. White women are so valuable we'll do anything to find them. Laypeople can be helpful to the police and solve crime." He levels me with his stare. "Sawyer, if we thought you killed her, we wouldn't have you on. I'm betting this story has legs and we want to get in on it."

"I don't know what happened to her or where she is."

"I believe you. And, in the short run, it doesn't matter."

We run through the questions and answers three times before Jesse is satisfied.

We're ready to start and my stomach is finally full. The gear is already set up—headphones, camera, all of it.

Jesse stands up and starts some relaxation bullshit. I play along. "Tilt your head back—no, further, toward the sky—and close your eyes. Take three calming breaths. Now, without moving your head, open your eyes."

He's standing above me, two lemon wedges in his hands. Before I can blink he squirts them into my eyes.

My corneas are scalded.

"What the fuck?" I leap to my feet as he scurries out of the way.

Rubbing only makes it worse.

"I get the feeling you don't emote well, so we're cheating."

I'm holding my hands over my burning eyes and cursing, tears spilling down my cheeks.

"Now we're ready. Donovan?" he calls. "Be a love and bring up a tissue box."

I nod, still wiping at my watering eyes, as Jesse begins recording.

"Hi—I'm Jesse Jonas from the SV *Platinum Star* and I know you all are used to tuning into this channel to see us sailin', failin', cookin', and bein' naughty, but today I have a special guest. He's a fellow cruiser and he needs our help. His name is Sawyer Stone. I know you've all seen Sawyer on the news—and he's being courted for interviews by lots of media, but he's decided to come on our channel to share his story. Sawyer?"

I can't believe these guys are pimping my story for views to protect me from Dani who is doing the same damn thing. But my options are limited, so here we go. "Thanks, Jesse." I nod. "For those of you who don't know, my girlfriend, Dani Fox, is missing and I'll take all the help I can get to find her."

"Can you give us a bit of background on you, the boat, and Dani?"

"Sure. I'm Sawyer Stone, my grandfather started Stone Mustard, you may have heard of it or seen it on the shelves. I grew up sailing in Annapolis, Maryland. My wife, Emily Standish Stone, died in a tragic scuba accident when we were on vacation two years ago. After she died, I took to the sea to deal with the pain of that loss."

This "taking to the sea" thing is cheeseball stuff, but Jesse insisted.

"I'm so sorry. That must've been awful."

"It was." My eyes are still burning and leaking so I use my palms to clear my cheeks.

"Donovan and I are both PADI Divemasters. I'd like to know what went wrong, if you wouldn't mind sharing."

I hate talking about this. I try not to think about it. But now that Dani's missing, it's all anyone wants to know.

"I wish I knew. We shouldn't have been out at all, but we were too inexperienced to realize it. Conditions were bad. Maybe she panicked, or had an equipment failure? All I know is her diving buddy came up and said she had lost her in the murk. I went back down to look, and we found Emily unresponsive near the wreck we were diving." I pause here and tick off the seconds in my head as Jesse instructed. Long pauses are tough guy code for grief, so Jesse says.

"I'm so sorry."

I wipe my eyes and manage not to scowl. *Fucking lemon juice.* "We did everything—CPR, all of it—but she was gone. It was the worst day of my life." I clear my throat. A few times. Probably one time too many.

Jesse stares me down.

"How awful for you and her family. I can't imagine what that must have been like. Folks, the lesson here is that it pays to have experienced people taking you to the right spots and choosing the right weather window."

It's nearly a plug for his charter business, but not quite.

"We learned that the hardest way. We didn't know what we didn't know. Excuse me." I grab a tissue from the box. My eyes are still trying to flush the lemon juice out. "It never gets any easier to talk about."

"I'm sure it doesn't. After Emily died in that terrible accident, what happened?"

"Once the police completed the investigation, I flew her . . . back home . . ." I stutter here, because I want to say flew her *body* back home, but Jesse thinks that's too cold. ". . . with her parents and her sister to bury her in Connecticut. I stayed with the family for a little while. We were all lost."

This is such bullshit. I've never been lost. I'm not convinced Jesse knows what he's doing, but more than that, I want to beat her at this game.

"I'm sure you were." Jesse leans forward, his expression registering feigned empathy. This man is a master.

Jesse said showing my anger only solidifies people's ideas that I'm the villain, and Dani doesn't need any help from me in that department. Jesse had also said they wanted to keep me out of jail. I know that's a possibility and that's what made me put my back into it. I am *not* going to jail.

I take a deep breath. My eyes have finally stopped watering.

"I know there are some photos out there of me and Emily's sister, Courtney, online. She and I were able to love and support each other during the worst time in our lives. That's confusing to some people, and I get it. Our relationship grew out of the overwhelming grief we shared. When we were together grief turned into a hope for a love that maybe could replace what we lost. But it couldn't. People are making things awful for her and her family. I wish I could make it stop, for their sake."

"Grief makes you long for comfort from any quarter," Jesse says.

I nod. "Eventually I came to terms with the loss and took a look at my life and realized I wanted to go back to doing what I loved as a child. Sailing. Dani Fox and I met, and we clicked. We worked on the boat for a bit and have been sailing her for a year. We haven't gotten too far in our circumnavigation yet."

"It's so hard to leave this Bahamas paradise."

"I know, but we want to explore other parts of the world. To do that, I need my co-captain Dani. I want to make this appeal to anyone who may have seen her." Co-captain. That's rich, the notion that we are equal when she's barely competent crew, but Jesse insisted.

"We'll have a link in the comments to an app which allows you to make an anonymous tip if you've seen Dani or know where she might be," Jesses says. "When did you last see her, Sawyer?"

"Saturday night—at a party three weeks ago." I strive for sheepishness, but I don't know if it's working. "I was drunk. Really drunk. Falling down drunk. I don't normally drink to excess, and it hit me hard. And I'm so angry and upset with myself that I was incapacitated that night of all nights. The night she needed me. Someone has video, I think. I'll see if I can send it to you," I say.

Jesse's eyes widen, his lips twitching upward with glee for a millisecond before his features reshuffle themselves into furrowed brow concern. "Yeah, we'll post it."

"I didn't think to share it with the police, but I guess I should—it's the last time many of us saw her. I don't know if you've ever been falling down drunk," I say.

"A few times," Jesse says. Still no sign of Brendan below deck, exhibit A in the falling down drunk department. "On boats it's that much harder to be that drunk—on the best of days it can be hard to keep your footing out here if there's a swell. But when you're drunk, you're kinda dependent on people dragging you around, putting you to bed. I'm assuming that's what Dani did—though she likely had some help."

"I know, right? Getting someone who's absolutely wrecked on and off a dinghy, onto a rocking boat, down the companionway, and into bed, where I woke up the next day, is not a one-woman operation."

"Totally true. Unfortunately, we've had that experience on occasion here with guests. And Dani is tiny!"

"She would say, *No, I'm strong and tough.* But even the toughest, strongest hundred-five-pound woman would have trouble dragging my hundred-eighty-pound butt around."

"No doubt. She'd need help."

"Right. And we haven't found anyone who can tell us who helped her that night. Because whoever did may have been the last person to see her."

"There has been some speculation that a shark . . ."

"I refuse to believe that. I know people say that because she swam every day in the ocean and there are plenty of sharks here—dozens of species of sharks, we see them all the time—but only one person has been killed by a shark in the Bahamas in the last ten years. So no, I don't think she was killed by a shark."

"Okay, take it easy," Jesse says.

This is all scripted, but I marvel at how well this is going.

"I'm sorry, I . . . I just know she's still alive. I feel it. There's a link between us." I wonder if I'm laying it on too thick, but it's too late now. I'm going for it. "I know someone has her. And with all this focus on me and my past and people thinking I could ever hurt her . . ."

"Let's talk about that."

"Dani is an incredibly strong person—physically and emotionally. She's not my victim, she's not anyone's victim. She had a rough childhood and I mean terrible—and she would never put up with that as an adult. I know that for a fact."

"You have to understand, those videos—"

"I know. She was always comfortable sharing more about the good and bad in our lives than I was. I'm a private person. I don't love that she posted my temper tantrum—and that she didn't post the rest of the video. Sure, I grabbed her arms, but she shoved me, hard enough to unbalance me, and I landed on my ass."

Jesse smiles. "She may be small but she's fierce."

"Dani doesn't take crap from anyone, least of all me. I think if people understood that they'd stop this useless speculation and take a harder look at the boats that left the anchorage that night, or early the next morning. I wish the police would follow those leads."

"Sounds like you have a suspect."

"I don't want to say too much. I don't want to put her in jeopardy. But yeah, a few people sailed out that night or early the next day and the police should be using their resources to locate those individuals."

"Sawyer, you can see why this is so hard for folks to believe. Those videos reflect poorly on your relationship—and you."

I shake my head solemnly. "Dani and I are passionate people; sometimes our emotions get the best of us. She wants to show the realities of sailing, warts and all. You know what it's like, sharing a two hundred square foot interior space with someone for a year, and when things go wrong—"

"Do we ever. But it has to be said, I've never shaken my husband, Donovan."

I attempt an ashamed expression. I don't know if it's effective, but Jesse is nodding at me.

"I wish all of the videos were only her. I like watching her swim nearly naked with a speargun to catch our dinner as much as everyone else."

"I think you speak for most heterosexual males." He winks. "Tell me, are you a good partner?"

I sigh on cue. "Lately, not so much. So many things have been going wrong with the boat."

"Like?"

I groan. "Careful—you know how much cruisers enjoy complaining about boat repairs."

"God yes, we could talk about these damn boats and their problems for days on end."

"The water maker malfunctioned—that was an expensive fix—the dinghy disappeared, the engine needs to be overhauled, it's a lot."

"All in one year? That is some terrible luck."

I raise an eyebrow. "All in one *month*."

Jesse emits a low whistle.

"I was stressed, she was stressed. I think out here on the water all of us cruisers worry about the money drying up before the desire to stop sailing does. When things are going badly there's volatility—fights and arguments—but, and I want to be absolutely clear about this, we are not violent toward each other. I have never and would never hurt Dani. I love Dani and I'm desperately worried about her."

Jesse nods. "Anything else you want to say before we go?"

I take a deep breath. "I get why everyone is so focused on me. I know the statistics on domestic violence. But Dani and I are not statistics. We're real people who love each other. My soulmate is missing, and I want her back. Focusing on me isn't going to bring her back. Focusing on whoever took her is."

This has been a master class in Dani-style media manipulation.

I don't know why I'm surprised by how good I am at this.

CHAPTER

21

Serendipity

Sawyer

Day 23

I'M SITTING NEXT to Weatherby in a bean bag chair, sunning myself on *Serendipity*'s deck.

"It's Monday," Weatherby says.

"Is it?" I reply though I know full well what day of the week it is.

"Think another video's gone live?" he asks, putting down his beer and picking up his phone.

I sigh and pick up mine.

I'm not worried about whatever she's posted this week. The *Platinum Star* YouTube video I made with Jesse has nearly ten million views and climbing. There are plenty of haters in the comments but there are more who believe my side—maybe they can push the police investigation in a direction other than at me. Even cruisers are wading in, asking questions. I saw Zild mentioned by a few people. The tide is turning.

There the third video is, right on cue. It's another montage of sailing, snorkeling, and swimming with turtles.

There's a bonfire on the beach—before the fish poisoning incident. The camera zooms in on two figures on the beach who are having an intense, possibly drunken conversation with lots of aggressive hand movements. I vaguely recognize the woman in madras shorts as the wife of a Realtor who drones on endlessly about Florida real estate. The man with her I don't recognize; he looks to be a decade younger. He pulls madras-shorts wife back into the shadows and they start making out under a palm tree while the cuckhold Realtor stares gloomily into the fire twenty yards away. After a few minutes the woman stumbles away and rejoins her husband.

That's what happens out here. Hookups, drunken revelry, loud fights. All the stressors they thought they left in the suburban cul-de-sac or city apartment play out here, amplified by the weather, heat, alcohol, close quarters, and random failures of equipment on their boat home. Their fights echo through the bays where we anchor, or on the beaches where we party, unfolding in earshot or full view of us. Dani loves this stuff. The drama, the gossip, who's cheating on who, listening to their sad screaming fights. There are few secrets out here, no real closed doors, and Dani revels in it.

I couldn't care less.

She must be saving the poisoning part of the show for later because after ten minutes or so, the footage cuts back to the boat. Dani's sitting in the captain's chair in the cockpit, wearing a hat, and sunglasses.

I hold my breath.

"Sawyer went to help a friend with a fix on their boat." She removes her sunglasses to reveal a black eye.

My hands make themselves into fists.

It's very well done; she has always been good with makeup. There was a stretch where she was thinking about becoming an online makeup artist doing makeup lessons, apparently while reciting facts from random true crime cases, if you can believe it. Like so many of her cockamamie schemes, nothing ever came of it, but she did improve her already formidable makeup skills.

A single tear falls from the unblackened eye, and she wipes it away.

How many takes to get the tear to fall from the left eye so as not to smear the makeup on the right? Was a lemon involved?

"You're still *Sailing with the Foxes*, but you need to know the truth about our lives. It's very stressful right now. And . . . things happen."

It's all I can do not to laugh. She's that bad of an actress. Not that anyone will see past the tear.

I wish to God I knew where she was.

I fantasize about wrapping my hands around her smooth, thin, tan neck and squeezing, her body bucking under mine until the light goes out of her traitorous blue eyes. I've done it before. It's not difficult to choke someone into unconsciousness.

"That's the worst one yet," Brendan says unhelpfully, and stands. He's unstable on his feet going down the companionway and it has less to do with the swell and everything to do with the fact that he's been drinking all day. I check his cooler. Two beers and a hard seltzer. I grab the seltzer and open it, taking a few slugs. Then I take a beer and put it behind me, hiding it in the cushions. He won't stay once his stash is out.

When he returns, he looks into his cooler, frowns, and shrugs. He cracks open his last beer and suggests for the thousandth time that I get a lawyer. I suppress the instinct to choke *him* out while whispering "I don't have the money for that, imbecile" in his ear, but he's the last man standing, my only friend out here, so I refrain. My gut is telling me I need to leave now. But until I can put some money in the bank account, I'm on empty.

I stare moodily at the bar wall. Some genius has nailed up every random nautical thing that's washed up on the beach to the walls. There are parts of fishing nets, ancient buoys, and pieces of driftwood interspersed with photos of people holding fish, the pictures so old the color has washed completely out of them. To make matters worse there are fake fish, taxidermy fish, and even a few singing fish on a wooden board trapped in pieces of net. It's an interior design disaster.

Dani has been missing twenty-three days. My urge to flee ratchets up with every hour. If I had money to provision, I would be out of here.

"Incoming," Brendan says, looking over my shoulder.

It's three PM—the start of happy hour deals at the open-air Anchor Bar and Grill overlooking the beach. The scents of frying conch and shrimp waft around the place. The bottoms of my flip-flops stick to the rum punch and Mai Tai veneer atop the cement floor. I'm about to hit up Weatherby, the stingiest motherfucker on the planet, for money so I can get the hell out of this damn country.

I'm out of options.

I slouch a little in my chair.

I'm wearing sunglasses and a green John Deere cap pulled low, but I've been spotted.

"Hey—you that piece of shit Sawyer Stone?" drawls a beefy American in a white, sweat-stained golf shirt and ratty tan cargo shorts. "I hear you killed your girlfriend. It takes a real tough guy to kill a hundred-pound woman."

He's big—taller than me and close to 300 pounds, more fat than fit, but you never know how he'll do in a fight. You can't deny the role of mass in the calculation of force.

Brendan scoots his chair back about five feet and holds up his phone, filming.

"Bruh," I say to Brendan. "Chill."

"What'd you say to me?" the big man says, the slurring evident.

I catch the eye of the bartender who needs no signal, he's already on his cell phone, hopefully calling the police.

I stand smoothly, putting some more distance between us.

We're four feet apart when the guy lurches in and takes a swing.

He misses but regains his balance.

We dance around a bit. He's unsteady, his perspiring round face pinkened by some combination of sunburn, humidity, alcohol, and rage. One hit from that meaty first would lay me out. He has no fighting experience by the looks of him, and he's very drunk, but given our size difference, a worthy opponent. I let him take a few more swings, hoping for the arrival of the cavalry.

For God's sake, the police station is within walking distance.

He gets closer and almost gets a hold of my shirt.

On his next swing and miss, I spin around and take his back—he's got a hundred pounds on me but only three or so inches.

I get him in a standing rear naked choke. I cling on as he lurches about, crashing around into nearby tables. I wonder if I can stay astride this beast of a man for more than eight seconds.

Someone in the restaurant is screaming.

Weatherby is still filming, damn him.

I have little choice but to take the guy down—not difficult thanks to his inebriated state. I manage our trip to the floor gracelessly; he's on all fours and I'm still on his back. I've got my legs hooked over his hips now and lean my bodyweight to the side, toppling us. My forearm presses against the right side of his neck, but I don't have enough power with one arm to choke him to unconsciousness, so I leverage my other arm, pushing the blade of my forearm into his carotid. I could do more damage leveraging his windpipe, but the carotid is faster. He writhes madly.

Some part of me is aware choking this guy within an inch of his life in front of spectators is not a good look, but what choice do I have?

He's unconscious within twenty seconds.

I release him and stand.

Brendan stops filming long enough to toss a few bills onto the table.

We head out the front door, but the police are here.

"On your knees, hands behind your head!" an officer I don't recognize shouts.

I drop to my knees and lace my fingers behind my head. "Brendan," I hiss.

He looks at me.

"Get on your knees," I say.

His mouth opens and closes a few times before he does what I tell him.

Two officers handcuff me, then Brendan, while two other officers go into the bar.

"Didn't know you were going to go all Hulk Hogan on his ass, bruh," Brendan mutters. "I was waiting for you to bust out a tombstone piledriver or something. Kinda disappointed really."

I can't believe Brendan is shit-talking me under these circumstances, but I guess being in trouble with the police is not that disconcerting for the well-heeled set. What kind of world is it where a drunken lush like Brendan is better off than me in almost every respect? I don't know, but here I am living in it, on my knees, handcuffed, being watched by the two officers when I hear my name.

"Sawyer," a woman calls out again. She's coming down the sidewalk, pulling a Louis Vuitton suitcase, clad in a white, long-sleeve, button-down shirt, topped by a black leather harness with a jeweled neckline. A black leather accordion pleated skirt and cap-toe booties complete the outfit. All of it shrieks Manhattan, not the Bahamas. For a moment I think she's simply another tourist coming to troll me. But I know her.

Jesse's words echo in my head. *Low profile. No violence. No infidelity.* I've hit the trifecta of don'ts.

"Courtney, hey," I say, weakly. She hustles over but is shooed away by the officer guarding us. People are filming.

It is officially a clusterfuck.

When the other officers come out fifteen minutes later, the officer in charge tells the one guarding me to take me to the station and they call for an ambulance. He puts me in the back of the car and releases Brendan from the handcuffs.

The fight, such as it was, lasted less than a minute, but the fallout will exponentially exceed that. I hope this idiot hasn't had a heart attack or stroke; he should be conscious already after the choke.

"I'll meet you at the station. You were assaulted and defended yourself," Weatherby says this with all the privilege his status in the world has afforded him. "But until I can spring you from the lockup, remember, don't drop the soap." Didn't take long for that prep school privilege to reassert itself with a well-worn rape joke.

Courtney joins him on the curb. I watch them introduce themselves as I'm stuffed in the police car for the four-block drive to the station. I look out the back of the car to see Courtney shaking Weatherby's hand.

I arrive at the station minutes later. Inspector Knowles greets me, unsmiling. "Mr. Stone."

"Inspector."

"We'll process you here and walk you across to the jail."

"Fine."

And so there goes one of my life goals, avoiding a cell.

My adrenaline has died down and now I'm hungry and pissed. I didn't get my food before that sun-fried tourist trash assaulted me. They take my cell phone and boat keys and lead me down the hall back into the room where I was initially interviewed.

"Do you have any medication you will need for the next few hours?" Knowles asks, closing the door.

"No," I reply. "You need to see the video Weatherby made. The guy attacked me, totally unprovoked. I defended myself."

She raises an eyebrow. "Why did he attack you?"

"You know why. Those damn videos. People think I'm a killer and they're going vigilante on my ass." I owe Weatherby, big time. There can be no he said/he said here.

"We'll look at the tape."

Knowles leaves me in the room, but she's back within the hour.

"We're going to keep you a bit longer."

My spine stiffens. "On what charge?"

There's a pause. "You're simply being detained at present," Knowles says, evasive.

My eyes narrow. This is a stretch, and I had pegged Knowles as a by-the-book type. "It was very clearly self-defense."

"We'll get that all sorted out. We've notified the US Embassy's Consular Section."

Now they're throwing the damn bureaucracy at me. "Who?"

"When you are arrested in the Bahamas you have to be given the opportunity to speak with the embassy or consular officer."

"Thought you said I wasn't arrested?"

"We're still sorting it out. There is a process to be followed."

She is ice cold, this woman. Initially I liked my chances here. Lately, I'm not so sure. And I get how not good this is. But it's not my fault. "Can I have my cell phone? Don't I get a call?"

"No cell phones or other electronics are permitted in detention. Sit tight, Mr. Stone."

"Don't I get a lawyer or something?"

"You can discuss that with the US consular officer, if we get that far. We're still investigating."

"So I can't go back to the boat?"

"You may be with us overnight." Her expression doesn't change. I'm starting to sweat.

"Did you release Weatherby?"

"He was not detained. It's not only about who started it, Mr. Stone. It's whether the defensive or offensive response was excessive and injurious."

I don't like the sound of that. Who gets to decide what is excessive and injurious? The magistrate? Everything seems excessive unless it's your face the mountain of flesh is swinging for.

Detaining me is total bullshit. This backwater police department is going to be sorry they tried to do an end run around my rights. I'm an American, for fuck's sake.

"Get Weatherby's video—it shows I was attacked. You can see for yourself. And ask him to check on *Serendipity*."

"We're doing a complete investigation," is all she says.

I know, lady. I heard you the first time.

CHAPTER 22

Royal Bahamas Police Headquarters

Inspector Knowles

Day 23

INSPECTOR KNOWLES PUTS in a call to the deputy chief. Maybe this will be as good a reason as any to send Sawyer Stone back to the United States and let them deal with this mess. She fills the deputy in on the details and he tells her to ship out the instigator and keep an eye on Stone.

"Complete the investigation and update us. We're doing everything by the book," he says.

She's as by the book as it gets. But a viral suspect and a vigilante are now on her beat, apparently, and she doesn't have the resources for it—or the skill for handling the media. "No comment" and "We're still investigating" are the only two things she has approval to say to the public and she's been throwing them out with increasing regularity. The deputy chief told her to refer everyone to the public information officer, so that's exactly what she's been doing. Still, it's hard to feel in control of an investigation that has garnered so much public interest, and worse still, public involvement.

Knowles pushes down the thoughts about the unruly public intrusions on the margins of this investigation and focuses on the tasks she's prioritized for the day. God knows how long it will take to get DNA samples, including the one from the dress, back. Island time is the reality here. Stat, rush—you can check the boxes, but in practice they're largely meaningless.

Agent James walks in, grinning broadly. "An officer at the consulate reached out to me," she says. "Permission to ship this guy out? I could fashion a six-foot padded envelope and we could FedEx him to the United States, once and for all?"

"I would love nothing more," Knowles replies, "but I'm just off the phone with the deputy chief who told me to keep Stone and get the brawler off island." She stands and grabs her handbag.

"Where are we going?" James asks as Knowles closes her office door behind her.

"To the clinic to do as ordered."

"Have you seen the video Weatherby shot?" James asks.

"Yep."

"Pretty obvious Stone was attacked."

Knowles nods.

"But have you seen the clip posted on Fox Finders?" James asks.

Knowles stops in her tracks. "No," she says hollowly.

"It shows the choke at the end. None of the lead-up. And out of context it makes our guy look like a stone-cold killer. I've never been involved in an investigation that got this amount of public attention and interference. The villagers are sharpening their pitchforks and encircling the station house. Interference at every turn."

"Oh, it gets better," Knowles warns.

"How could it possibly?"

"The fella we're going to see, the American? Not only a tourist—he's a self-described cyber sleuth. He told Officer Moxley he was making a citizen's arrest."

James grabs Knowles's upper arm. "Hold up. Are you serious? A cyber sleuth? Investigating outside of a search engine dialogue box?" Her eyes glitter with suppressed humor.

"I am serious," Knowles says, rubbing her forehead. The cyber sleuth has induced an actual headache already. "I would like nothing better than to kick this whole ridiculous mess back to you all. You all should have to deal with your social media creations."

"We'd love to have him."

Knowles sighs and continues walking. "However, I still have a missing American woman, and we need to solve this case, which I had hypothesized as a likely drowning, until the dress was discovered. I am not beholden to Occam's razor. I am continually adapting my theories of a case to incorporate new information as it is uncovered. In this case, the dress changed everything."

"How?"

"Let's say he accidentally killed her. It happens—he's a cold son of a bitch and there's every indication violence was at least a small part of their relationship. She's shared that with people and the videos make it clear, maybe too clear. He's the most obvious suspect," Knowles says. "Anyone is capable of murder, given the right circumstance, and usually those circumstances involve drugs or alcohol intoxication. Stone checks all the boxes."

"And now we've seen what he can do in a minute to a three-hundred-pound man," Agent James replies, nodding at the white stucco building with a big blue George Town Clinic sign thirty feet away.

"But to get to him, you have to rule out accidental death," Knowles says. "Which I haven't. We know she swims straight out past the channel every morning—tempting fate. Early hour, overcast sky . . . those are certainly the right circumstances for a shark attack."

"Only no one saw her go out that morning," James says.

"Probably because they were all sleeping it off from the night before. *Serendipity* is anchored further out than most of the catamarans, because their monohull requires deeper water. Dani swims straight out to sea. It didn't even have to be a shark. Could be something as mundane as a leg cramp."

"And the dress?"

"That's what bothers me. We know she's a slob. Maybe she got a cut or used it to clean up fish guts or had the period from hell, but why stuff it in that drawer?"

"It's a Neiman Marcus dress. I seriously doubt she used it to clean up fish."

"You never saw the state of her cabin."

"I saw photos," James protests.

"Insufficient. For starters, photos do not convey smells. It took a full day to bag everything in there and that cabin is small. We bagged trash, dirty plates, soda cans from that room. There were bugs. And him being so orderly, that would be motive for murder in my household. She had lots of expensive clothes, kept in a terrible state in that cabin. It conjures a picture of mental unwellness. She must have been sleeping every night on a pile of dirty dishes. How does someone get to that state?"

Nothing gets under Inspector Knowles's skin faster than someone living unnecessarily in filth, and she feels her focus slipping. Knowles mentally squares up and turns back to the investigation at hand. "Why was the dress in the drawer—a drawer that was difficult to open, by the way—and not in her room? If Dani was the one who put it in the drawer, it would be the first thing she had put away. Perhaps ever. Our theory must fit the evidence, not the other way around. The dress is a problem. Also . . ."

"Also?"

"Everything only points one direction, to Sawyer. We all know why because it's been spoon fed to us. Sawyer Stone already has one dead intimate partner. There's another life insurance policy in play. He was blackout drunk the night of the disappearance. She confided in someone the night she disappeared about his abuse. It's those damn videos. A dozen of them are all sunshine, sand, and dolphins, then she disappears, and number fourteen drops and it's a doozy. I don't like it. Which is odd because there's nothing I like more than an orderly case with a clear-cut motive, but it *feels* all wrong. But I don't listen to gut feelings. Gut is bias."

"Gut isn't bias, it's intuition and it's invaluable," James puts in. "If he's killed another lover for the insurance money, he's an idiot. He doesn't strike me as an idiot. What odds do you give for him doing the first wife?"

"You know as much as I do. The whole world knows as much as we do. There's no point in wagering. We both know the Dominican Republic doesn't want to get dragged into this and if they're smart they won't let themselves. Their investigation was cursory, since there was no reason at the time to suspect foul play. They're under some public pressure to reopen the investigation, but without some impetus, like the parents winning a civil wrongful death suit or one of the witnesses coming forward, they won't."

"Right, and where's Dani's body? Without one, he could wait years for her to be declared dead. Which he seems to know. He would have thought this through."

"The truth will out, James." Knowles reaches for the clinic door handle. "You coming in?"

Agent James nods.

Knowles approaches the smiling woman at the reception desk. The colors are beachy and bright with shells and amateur photography of some of their least known attractions. *Doc should sell his work,* Knowles thinks. "Hello, Rhonda. Inspector Knowles and Agent James to see the patient, Chuck Spencer."

The woman's eyes get wide. "One moment," she says, picking up the phone. "Doc? The inspector is here to see the patient."

A tall, dark-skinned man comes from an adjacent hallway. "Hey, doc," Knowles says. "This is Agent James from the legal attaché's office of the FBI."

Dr. Fields smiles widely, showing an attractive gap between his front teeth, and introduces himself to Agent

James. They engage in a little flirtatious banter while Knowles makes small talk with Rhonda.

"We're ready to discharge him as soon as you give the okay," he says. "Come on back."

The patient is sitting at the edge of the hospital bed, putting on his flip flops. He looks even more pasty under the fluorescent lights of the hospital examination room. It's hard to imagine him fighting anything more formidable than acid reflux.

Dr. Fields makes the introductions. "Why don't you use my office? I have another patient coming in a few minutes," he says. He leads them down the hall. Knowles has been in this office a few times since taking this assignment for one case or another. The walls are a pale, soothing yellow.

Knowles takes Dr. Fields's chair and the other two settle in front of the desk.

"Mr. Spencer, we'd like to interview you about the events of this afternoon. Can you tell us what happened? And before you do, you should know we have viewed a video recording of the incident."

Spencer rubs his jawline. He's sunburned everywhere, including beneath the scruff on his face. "I flew in two days ago hoping to find that sumbitch Stone and get him to confess," he says.

"What is your interest in Mr. Stone?"

"He's a serial killer. I've been following the case. I'm a virtual detective."

"I am unfamiliar with this term," Knowles says, keeping her eyes fixed on the man in front of her, far too professional to let her feelings about the idea of "virtual" detectives show. "What does that entail?"

"I'm part of a group that connects and collaborates with other amateur sleuths around the world. We get online to discuss live cases, bounce around theories, and share information we've discovered about the crimes we're investigating. Most of us are people who have other jobs who are passionate about crime and finding criminals."

"Why did you assault Mr. Stone?" Knowles asks.

"It wasn't assault! The use of non-deadly force is permissible in the course of making an arrest," the man protests. "And I never laid a hand on him."

"You are not an officer. You have no standing to make an arrest."

"I was making a citizen's arrest! It is a right recognized in commonwealth countries, part of the Bahamian legal inheritance from its British colonizers."

"You are not a citizen." Knowles does not wish to confer an iota of authority to this would-be vigilante. He needs to get back to his place behind a keyboard and get the hell away from her investigation. "We've seen the video, and your actions were not justified under the circumstances. Actual law enforcement officials would classify your provocation of Mr. Stone and the actions you took against him as assault," Knowles says, her jaw set.

"Figures you're coming after me." Spencer is indignant. "If you did your job and arrested that wife killer I wouldn't need to be here. Do your fucking job. Serve and protect! You have everything you need to lock Stone up."

"We're in the middle of an investigation. We will follow our own protocols. What you do on the message boards does not constitute proper investigative technique. I understand that you are trying to be helpful, but you are *not* adding value here." She clears her throat. "Enthusiasm alone does not substitute for training and experience. There are procedures that must be followed. I certainly empathize with wanting to go around and punch everyone you suspect of wrongdoing. That is very tempting indeed. But you must understand, amateur investigators make my job more difficult. People with valuable information cannot get through to our tip line, because it is tied up with people who have read baseless theories on a message board and want to relay their insights on the case."

James steps in to bring the conversation to an end. "Sir, I am Agent James, I'm with the FBI—assigned as a legal attaché and working on the investigation with the Bahamian Police. I've spoken to our colleagues at the US Consulate in the Bahamas. You're going to be returned to the United States—"

"But my flight doesn't leave for two days," Spencer says.

"Rebook it. You can get a flight out today. Your work here is done," James says.

"And if I don't? I'm still recovering, and I haven't finished investigating," he says weakly.

"Dr. Fields has cleared you. If you don't leave here, you'll spend the remainder of your time in this country in jail, waiting for the magistrate, who will fine you and *then* put you on the next flight back to the States. Is that preferable?"

He scowls but acknowledges this with a brief nod. "I'll book it. I got enough information. Did you see him go after me? That's probably what he did to her—choke her and dump her overboard. It would take him ninety seconds. You all should have taken that professor up on his offer to track her body based on the currents. Can't see the forest for the trees, I swear."

Agent James steps forward. "I'll escort you to collect your belongings. There's a flight to Nassau in an hour. From there you can get back to the mainland." Agent James follows Spencer out the door and past Dr. Fields.

"You're sure he's fit to travel? We don't want him stroking out on the plane," Inspector Knowles says.

"He's in better physiological shape than his size would indicate," Dr. Fields says. "Had to give him fluids due to the dehydration and intoxication, but his blood pressure and heart rate are mostly within normal limits."

"How did Sawyer take him out so quickly?"

"My receptionist showed me the video. Lots of people in the comments called it a choke—and indeed, 'choke' is the term used in jiu-jitsu and law enforcement for what was done to Mr. Spencer. But technically choking is the act of airway blockage, for example, drowning in water or food obstructing the airway. These so-called 'chokes' are actually strangulations."

"That doesn't sound much better," Knowles says.

"It is though. Strangulation interferes with the normal flow of oxygen into the brain via compression of the carotid arteries or jugular veins, which in turn decreases oxygen intake and—voila!—unconsciousness. Once the pressure comes off the artery or vein, the oxygen supply is reestablished and all is well, the individual wakes up. A little groggy maybe," Doc says. "You probably trained on this."

"I did," Knowles says, thinking it through. "If you were to strangle someone with this method and throw them overboard, would that be effective?"

"You know I'm a family medicine physician—you're the one with the forensic team. But generally, no, because it's so transient. It only takes about ten seconds to 'choke' someone out, and they are only out for about another ten seconds. Which is probably as long or longer than it would take you to pitch them overboard. Then there's the mammalian diving reflex to consider, where the airway closes off to keep the water out. If you are trying to kill someone by strangling them, it takes a lot longer—four or five minutes and significantly more pressure, often involving the windpipe—all of which may be able to be determined, but not always, on autopsy."

"I see," Knowles says. And even with the prospect of having to strangle someone for minutes on end, Knowles could still see Stone doing it. Going well beyond the choke he executed on Spencer seemed well within the realm of possibility. Knowles wouldn't put it past Stone to be better briefed on the logistics of strangling someone than she is, despite her extensive law enforcement training.

Doc leans over her and clicks a bookmark on his desktop device, opening the Fox Finders group page. "Seems you have a number of laypeople avidly following this investigation," he says.

Knowles peers at the screen. "And there are thousands more each day."

"This Fox Finders group has four hundred thousand. Others have popped up." Doc puts Dani's name into the search bar, then looks at her over his glasses. "Sucks for you," he said softly. "But I can understand the interest."

"Can you? Because it mystifies me. All over a girl who, likely, got a cramp and drowned."

"Between the devil and the deep blue sea, the devil is a lot more interesting. And his dating history with one dead intimate partner and one gone missing is not going to get him far on Tinder. Bit of a red flag," Doc says.

Knowles sighs. "Not you too."

Doc raises his hands in submission. "Don't kill the messenger, but I can understand the viral aspects."

"How would you feel about dealing with half a million untrained people thinking they're doctors and doing their own research on your specialty?"

"I deal with that all the time—I don't have many patients who don't first consult Dr. Google before coming to see me. I am pretty much now always relegated to giving a second opinion. Always the bridesmaid, as they say," he says gently. "All I'm saying is that I would have second thoughts about being this fellow's lover number three."

"There are a few dozen scuba fatalities every year. Should we treat them all as homicides? They're nearly always the result of what befell Emily Standish Stone, according to the law enforcement investigation—panic, poor conditions, and inexperience," Knowles says. "Maybe he did it, maybe he didn't. I want to know what happened and use evidence to support it." She sighs. "A body would help."

Theoristical43 Least to most likely scenarios: abducted (aliens, human traffickers), shark attack, left his ass and ghosted him, overdosed and body dumped, had fight and BF murdered, went for a swim and drowned.

CHAPTER

23

George Town

Sawyer

Day 23

WEATHERBY AND I slide into the booth at the far back of the dark, quiet restaurant.

I was freed from detainment an hour ago. I was only kept in a room, not a cell, so I'm calling it a win and not an incarceration. I wouldn't have chosen to go to another eatery in this town, but I'm starving and need to deal with Courtney, so the Conch and Tonk it is. The patio outside is loud and teeming with tourists.

I can't help staring at her sitting across the table. She's so much like her sister. The nose and high cheekbones are the same; her eyes are brown where Emily's were blue, but they are similar in shape and filled with longing.

There is a reflexive stirring in my groin, but I tamp it down. Jesse's admonition is embedded in my psyche.

Courtney barely acknowledges Weatherby; her eyes have been locked on me since I came through the door. "My God, how are you? What can I do to help?"

"I may be beyond help. I'm being framed. This whole thing with Dani is complete bullshit," I tell her. "For all we know, she staged her disappearance. That's the only explanation I can think of for those videos."

Her mouth hangs open for five seconds until she snaps it closed. "That bitch," she says, softly. "Why . . . why would anyone do such a thing?"

I lean back in the booth, maintaining eye contact, and nod. "I'm not worried about her. It's what she's doing to me—and you."

"I know. It's so unfair. We've been through this. It's always the husband or boyfriend. Always. Terrible accident? Wife killer. Missing woman? Boyfriend did it. That's the only lens people filter information through. I'm so sorry, Sawyer. If it makes you feel any better, some of those keyboard warriors are even trying to pin Emily's death on me," she complains.

This does make me feel better, but I know better than to say so. Because anything that takes heat off me is a good thing. I wonder if there's anything I can do to deflect a bit more suspicion onto Courtney. If the internet groupthink had another explanation for Emily's murder, maybe Dani's disappearance wouldn't look so bad. But any theory of Emily's death at Courtney's hand is probably going to implicate me, so never mind.

"It's probably a splinter group no one pays attention to," I say. "There are always going to be alternate theory conspiracists. Whatever you do, don't speak to them—it only adds fuel to the fire."

She looks down, her cheeks flushed with shame.

"You've been talking to them," I say wearily.

Weatherby's eyes bug. "Girl, you need to stop," he says. "Those people are crazy. One of them attacked us this morning."

She looks up, nodding, fingers in motion atop the table as her self-soothing cuticle picking goes into overdrive. "I wanted to see if they had more information. And that boat . . . *Serendipity*, Trip? How could you name her that, as if you feel *lucky* things ended up this way? That's awful."

"That was already the name of the boat," I lie. "I haven't gotten around to changing it. It's a ton of paperwork." I avoid Brendan's eyes when he looks up from his drink.

"Speaking of names . . ." he says. "*Trip?* That's your nickname, Sawyer? You clumsy motherfucker."

"Yeah, that was Em's nickname for me—short for Triple, on account of being the third Sawyer Stone. I hated it then and I hate it now."

The color rises in Courtney's cheeks and she hangs her head like a scolded hound. She had languished in Emily's shadow, the not quite as smart, pretty, or successful sister, but she was no slouch in the obsessed with me department. Things were tight waiting for the life insurance after Emily died, and since Emily and I never had joint accounts, I squeezed Courtney for ten thousand. Her parents wouldn't have allowed it, but she paid my debts without a word. Though both women were in their twenties, their trustees still had complete control over them financially and wielded it in accordance with the parents' wishes. When I married Emily I underestimated her parents' influence over her.

We had an iron-clad prenup. It didn't take me long to realize I married the wrong sister. Courtney had a malleability Emily didn't. Emily both loved and feared her parents and despite her love for me would not go against their advice regarding our finances. Courtney, the less successful child, was largely ignored—until that dynamic was demolished by the death of Emily. I saw the parents reluctantly accept that the second-best child would have to be the recipient of their wisdom and control. Despite what people have written online, Courtney could never be tied to her sister's death—and still can't, despite the ridiculous cast of online characters lifting every rock and the stupid girl in front of me talking to these idiots.

Emily found her sister's interest in me hilarious. She might've found it less funny if she knew that I had fucked her sister dozens of times.

Courtney, now the sole heir to the Standish fortune, is sure to collapse under parental pressure, so what's the point. Besides, she's exhausting in her neediness. Emily's saving grace was being a workaholic. It's easy to get along with a wife you never see.

Courtney is not plan B.

"Emily's death was my fault," I say, hoping to hit the right note.

"You always say that," she says. "It was her own fault."

"I was stupid. We were stupid. Now that I'm an experienced diver, I know all the little things and all the big things we did wrong. A fly-by-night operator, bad conditions . . ."

Courtney leans forward, holding her hand up to stop my words. "I read that no one ever found the boat operator. That's suspicious, Sawyer. Maybe he was responsible, somehow."

She's gotten an earful from someone.

"Who can blame him?" I reply with a shrug.

"What?"

"Lawsuits. Wrongful death. Your parents wanted someone to blame, and the boat operator and I made good targets. So did her dive buddy, for that matter. No one wants to come forward and be sued."

She nods. Courtney's anxious nature makes it easy to convince her of dangers inherent in pretty much any scenario.

"I'll never understand why she agreed to go. She was always working," Courtney says, her voice barely above a whisper. She angles her body away from Weatherby and toward me. "You always thought good times with her were right around the corner. Well, they weren't. She was always that way. Neglecting you, putting work first." Each word comes out drenched in bitterness. "I don't know why you could never see her as she was. I loved you and I never would have taken you for granted like Emily did. I thought once she was gone we'd—"

"Your parents," I say.

"I know, but you could've stuck around."

"I couldn't, Courtney. You know why. We talked about it so many times. I only ever want the best for you, and I'm not that."

Could there be anything as boring as rehashing these exact same conversations over and over with Courtney?

"I wish all of this wasn't coming out. It's awful to be dragged into it," she said softly, twirling her hair.

It takes everything I have not roll my eyes. "Why did you come here, Courtney? Do you think I had something to do with Dani's disappearance?"

She looks up at that, brown eyes wide and drowning in unshed tears. "No! Never. I . . . I really wanted to see you. I thought you could use the support."

I need to tread carefully here. It's going to take some deft maneuvering to convince Courtney to bankroll me without ending up romantically beholden to her.

I take her hand. "When things between us couldn't happen, I was adrift. Then I met Dani. It was easy to be with her because it wasn't serious, you know? I knew she would never be my soulmate, not like we could've been, so there was no pressure." I wave a hand.

She nods and tears spill down her cheeks.

I pull my hand back with a glance around.

"I love you, Sawyer, I've always loved you. For me, it's always been you. But I know it was harder for you—it didn't look right to my parents, our friends. No one could have understood. I only wish you'd been willing to try. I don't care what anyone thinks."

Weatherby is more flushed than usual around the collar of his golf shirt and looking desperately for the waitress. Evidently, he's wildly uncomfortable with what's spilling out of

Courtney. It's going to take a stiff drink or six to override his flight instinct. Lucky for me it's not hard to get six drinks into him. I can't be seen alone with Courtney, not with the cyber sleuths and cruisers trailing me every time I venture out. I've no doubt they know exactly who she is—her picture is all over the Fox Finders page. Brendan is giving me cover here.

He flags the server down and she approaches us, hands full with water glasses. "What can I get you?" she asks, barely looking up from her pad.

Courtney and I order the fried conch and get the seafood platter to share. Brendan gets a hamburger and fries and a round of rum punches for the table. "Just in case you haven't endured enough punches this week," he says.

Courtney's lips compress and she shakes her head, but I laugh.

"I thought gin and tonic was your favorite," Courtney says.

"The rum punch is fantastic," I say. "If you don't want that, I'd do the Pirate ale."

"No, the rum punch is fine," she replies.

The waitress leaves.

"It's so unfair that she's the one with you, on the boat. She's not even that pretty—so trashy, Sawyer."

I will myself to relax. Courtney's petty jealousies haven't improved with time.

Weatherby is staring at me.

"I would trade everything—*everything*—to have Emily back," I say. "And I would trade all of that to give *us* a chance. But now is not the time."

"I'm sorry, Sawyer. I know." Courtney hangs her head, twisting her fingers together. "It is easier to try to find someone to blame. And I can't believe Dani's doing this to you."

I nod and my lips turn down. I learned a lot in my PR boot camp with Jesse. I'm a quick study.

"What do you need?" she asks.

I give Weatherby a meaningful look over Courtney's head.

"He needs money," Weatherby says, finally, wading into our silence. "He needs to resupply. He needs a lawyer. He may need to abscond to a country without an extradition policy with the US. Maybe Venezuela? You'd love the diving in Aruba, Sawyer. Or there's Bonaire, or Curacao. Maybe Cuba? Lots of people go there to get lost."

Courtney's expression is crestfallen at that bald declaration. She's imagined going on the lam with me. Some romantic daydream where she hoists sails and drinks gin and tonics in the sun with me at the helm on our way to the Seychelles.

The bartender brings over the drinks. Judging by his curled lip, he recognizes me. "We don't want trouble in here," he says. "Finish your drinks and food, then go and don't come back." The words are spoken softly and he leaves as soon as he says them, but it's another reminder that I need to get the fuck out of the Bahamas.

Courtney's mouth is open. She blinks at me a few times. "People are being so mean to you."

"Yeah, it sucks. I can't wait to leave this place," I whisper. "Please understand, you being here, as much as I love it, doesn't look good for me," I say. "I can't be seen as unfaithful to Dani. The police will use anything and everything to detain me again. And I'm getting killed in the press," I say. "Not that I care about what anyone thinks but as you can see, some of these people can make my life a living hell."

She nods, the corners of her lips turn down, and her eyes fill with tears again as I kill her dreams of us sailing away together. "How much do you need?" she finally asks.

I look at Weatherby, who is devouring his hamburger.

He swallows a mouthful and downs half his rum punch. "Twenty thousand," he says.

I act surprised by the sum. "So much?"

"You need a lawyer, and to get one they'll need a retainer. You need to fix your engine. And you need to restock your food stores. Thirty would be better."

Courtney pales; she's already shaking her head. She's only picking at the seafood platter, so I scoop most of it onto my plate.

"Whatever you can spare," I tell her, filling my mouth with shrimp, lobster, and conch. I slide across a card I've prepared with my account details. "No one else cares about me like you do, Court."

She looks from me to Weatherby. "Can I talk to you somewhere privately?" she asks me. "Can we meet up later or tomorrow?"

I nod.

I need the money.

I can't take the hit to my reputation.

But I need the money.

She fiddles with her phone for a few moments. "It's done."

I look up from my food. "What, already?"

"I'll give you anything you need, Sawyer, you know that."

"Let me resupply," I say. "Get fuel, do some engine maintenance, get lawyer names, then let's see if we can sneak you onto *Serendipity* tomorrow. I'll text you a plan."

She gives me a watery smile and I lean down to squeeze her hand. "Promise?"

"Promise."

I step outside into the Bahamas sunshine and smile for what might be the first time in weeks.

CHAPTER

24

Serendipity

Sawyer

Day 24

I COULD REACH UP and touch the ceiling in this cabin. Would prison be any more claustrophobic? When I first got *Serendipity*, she felt roomy. I enjoyed never having to bend down in the salon despite my height. My berth felt snug in a good way. Pretty much the whole cabin is taken up with the double bed, the corners of which are rounded to maximize the utility of the floor space. Shelves on the wall follow the curve of the keel and function as bedside tables. They are bare but for my water bottle and charging phone. A porthole on one side brings in some natural light above the waterline. Above the porthole, small cupboards offer a surprising amount of storage, more than enough for me to store my pared-down belongings. I used to love the jet-set feel of the rounded corners and leather furniture, like some sort of space-age bachelor pad. But the proverbial walls are closing in, and I am suffocating in here.

It occurs to me that I don't miss Dani as much as I would've thought. I am not lonely, but somehow, the way being aboard *Serendipity* used to feel like freedom has dissipated completely, leaving nothing in its wake.

My phone alerts me to receipt of a text: I'm being summoned to the *Platinum Star*. I would ignore it. I want to ignore it. But I can hear Jesse's voice in my head telling me Dani is winning. If I'm going to leave, I have to leave some cruisers with reasonable doubt.

I jump into the shower adjacent to my cabin and drain every last drop of hot water from *Serendipity*'s six-gallon tank. This is not as satisfying when there's no one there waiting to shower after you. I put on a Freeport Rugby FC T-shirt I earned by drinking six Kaliks in an hour at a local pub, together with some no-name khaki shorts and plastic flip flops.

Brendan, irritable and reeking, picks me up in his dinghy and we make the fifteen-minute ride in silence. There's some chop and his skin is a pasty gray yellow-green beneath his rosacea. I don't know how he gets up every day. I don't know how people let anything control them—drugs, alcohol, sex, food. Addiction is anathema to me.

Jesse's expression is flat when we clamber aboard. He's impeccably dressed, as usual, in a perfectly pressed white linen shirt and navy linen shorts. He looks cool, while I'm already sweating through my cotton shirt. I flash back to all those times being called down to the headmaster's office at prep school. I wasn't ever sure exactly what specific infraction among my catalog of recent misdeeds was bringing me behind the carpet this time, but it didn't much matter. It was a meeting to be endured, nothing more.

My opening gambit is a compliment, a solid strategy in almost all circumstances, and this time, was rooted in genuine curiosity. "How do you stay so cool out here in this heat?"

He stares at my sweat-ringed armpits. "Botox.

"In your armpits?"

He gives an impatient nod. "You might give it a try."

He must be Botoxed everywhere. The only hints of his displeasure come from his mouth. He's damned hard to read, and I'm not great at evaluating emotional cues. A failing Dani and I share that has gotten us into trouble a time or two.

"You couldn't simply lie low for a little while?" he says tightly. "Enjoy the positive reception our video was receiving? Let the narrative shift in your favor, that was too much for you?"

My lips flatten into a line.

"What's circulating looks bad for you, Sawyer. I warned you about the violence—"

"*He* came at *me*."

Jesse presses play on the laptop he has open. It's a CBS news clip on YouTube. I examine the footage of the bar fight. The guy doesn't try to defend his neck at all. Clearly, he's had no training for the ground game. It takes about five seconds from the time we hit the floor for me to get position on him for the rear naked choke and another twelve seconds before he's sprawled on the floor, unconscious. It's not easy from the vantage point of the phone to see exactly how I did it, but any jiu-jitsu practitioner would be impressed with the speed of the takedown and the choke.

"Stop smiling, damn it," Jesse says, scowling. "It looks like you broke his neck."

"Nah, it's just a good choke."

"This is damning stuff. Whoever might've been on the fence fell all the way onto guilty."

"First of all, none of this is my fault. What am I supposed to do? Let that flabby son of a bitch lay me out without defending myself? Him not being an athlete doesn't negate the fact that getting hit by three hundred pounds of flesh will do some damage, that's simply the law of physics."

Jesse's eyes narrow. "I'm not concerned about physics, Sawyer, I'm concerned about optics, the true fundamental force of the universe. Don't play the victim. We've discussed this. It's not a good look for you."

"I'm not playing anything. This is my fucking life, not some game."

"We need to fix this."

"Can we get our video, the one Brendan shot, out there?"

"How is that going to help?"

"It shows me being attacked. It's a better angle on all of this. Drum up some sympathy, give perspective."

Jesse lifts a brow and puts a hand out for my phone.

I point to Brendan.

Brendan pulls up the video and hands his phone to Jesse.

Jesse's mouth twists as he watches the interaction. He looks up at me and says, "You should have run away."

I cover my laugh with a cough.

Run away? Fuck no. I would rather die.

He watches the tape all the way through and closes his eyes. Finally, he sends the footage to himself and hands back the phone. "It would've been better if he'd landed at least one punch. You need to think about how every little move you make will be perceived. Let the danger manifest before you defend yourself from it. Then we have something to work with."

My eyes widen. "Bruh—Jesse—one punch would've laid me out. I'm starting to think you've never been in a bar fight."

Jesse arches an eyebrow at me. "It should be painfully obvious by now that I am a lover, not a fighter."

Despite the quips, I can see that Jesse is genuinely annoyed with me. I sit, deflated. "Where's Donovan?"

Jesse glares. "Not here. Why? You hungry? I've got some protein bars." His expression is snide. "Brendan tells me Courtney is here, but that cannot possibly be true, because that would be unbelievably imbecilic."

I acknowledge this with a slight nod. It is hard to dispute his contentions.

"I thought you were smarter than this. Get rid of her. Today."

"Not that easy," I mutter.

"You're being stupid. Let's review: Your girlfriend is missing, presumed dead, and instead of lamenting your loss and hunting high and low for any sign of her, you are busy getting into bar fights and plowing your dead wife's sister. Do you have any idea of how bad that makes you look? You are the villain of your own story, Sawyer, writ large. To put it in sailing terms, you are getting hoisted on your own petard."

"Tell me what to do and I'll do it." Jesse is a sucker for appeals to his authority, and trying to make him see my point of view is only going to protract this dressing down. Let's get on with it.

"Brendan, I have a job for you," Jesse calls. He unearths a bottle of Glenlivet twenty-five-year-old scotch from the storage under his seat. Brendan's eyes light up as if Jesse has produced gold doubloons.

Ten minutes later, Weatherby, scowling and clutching the scotch between his knees, motors us back to *Serendipity*, where Courtney is putting away supplies.

She comes out to greet us and her face falls at my expression. I don't have to look at the surrounding boats to assume there is at least one telephoto lens picking all of this up.

We climb aboard.

Her phone is ringing—it never stops ringing. "My parents," she says helplessly, turning off the ringer.

"You have to go," I say. "We're being watched and this—you here—is bad news for me."

Tears fill her eyes.

"Did you hear what I said? Don't give me that look, we're being filmed." I can hear the whine of a drone. "Smile, damn it." It's the wrong tone; her features collapse in grief. I exhale. "I just mean, if you want to help me—"

"You know I do," she says through tears.

I relay Jesse's instructions. Her eyes widen as Brendan comes up the companionway with her oversize purse that doubles as an overnight bag and drapes an arm around her, giving her a kiss on the cheek. "C'mon darlin'," he says.

"Please make it look good at the airport," I tell her.

She swallows hard and nods.

She and Brendan give me their brightest smiles as they push off, waving. I force a smile of my own and go down to hide in the galley.

Within hours the photos of her departure from *Serendipity* and her passionate embrace with Brendan Weatherby at the airport are posted in Fox Finders. I view their kiss on my computer screen dispassionately.

I hope the scotch was worth it.

CHAPTER 25

Somewhere in the Bahamas

Dani

Day 23

I'M TWO DAYS overdue for departure. We've been out in the open ocean in the middle of nowhere for the past three days. I've hinted, begged, and am getting ready to insist that we head closer to land when Jim decides to sail us near Rum Cay this afternoon. *Finally.*

Meanwhile, I've finished the edits on my rescue of the Bahamian boys and I'm sketching *Serendipity*'s logo in my notebook. I'll need merch when I return. Merch is an element that is underestimated by many business owners, but that is what separates the girls from the girl bosses. Merch takes hardly any time to set up, and then people are paying *you* to put your business name out there. Free advertising and an independent profit center? Yes please! Plus, get the right item positioned in the right TikTok video by the right influencer, and you will be buried in revenue. Absolutely buried. This is the destiny I manifest. No serendipity required.

"What's that?" Jim asks, peering over my shoulder at my sketchbook.

I jump a mile. This time when I growl, "Don't sneak up on me," my aggravation isn't feigned.

"What are you doing?" he says again.

It's obvious. I've got cost estimates for shirts, hats, bags, and sweaters in my notebook with *Serendipity*'s logo. Plus some logos for my boat name idea.

His expression changes from surprise to suspicion. He's starting to put things together. I must put my plan in motion. Meanwhile, I'm operating blind—I still have zero idea what's happening online. Maybe no one cares that I'm missing, or Sawyer wasn't as incapacitated as I hoped and left the anchorage early and all my breadcrumbs with Sonja were for naught. There were too many moving parts in my plan to be assured of success, but it all will come together with my trust in the universe.

"A while ago Sawyer asked me to do some sketches for the channel. I was revisiting them. It clears my mind to sketch. It's one of the self-soothing techniques I have developed over the years."

He doesn't believe me but he doesn't say anything more about it. All he says is, "I'm thinking we should head back."

"Absolutely." I nod earnestly. "Whatever you think."

"You should go to the authorities about the abuse."

My eyes go wide. "Are you sure? And you'll be with me?"

I'm not the best at reading people's expressions, but I think that was a sneer. He's clearly over the white knight role. It has taken a lot to get Jim from savior to this derisive place; I hadn't expected him to cotton on to my hustle so fast.

"Something tells me you won't need me," he mutters.

I didn't play my damsel role well enough after my supposed spectrum disorder was revealed. I've barely said two words to him in the past few days; I've been too intent on editing. Too focused. And now I will pay, as we are still not close enough to land for my taste.

Seduction to buy time is out of the question—that game requires a longer lead.

"Did you catch anything?" I ask.

"No, we'll have to eat frozen. Did you want to make a sauce?" I don't know the tone, but the sneering expression is back.

Damn.

I have lost my touch.

At least I have until morning.

I don't want to use the Rohypnol, and although the Benadryl won't work as well without alcohol, I'm going to try it in a smoothie. I'm tempted to add some rum, but I don't think there's any way to disguise the flavor. In the end I go with gobs of Benadryl. He downs it without a second thought.

After midnight, I knock on his door. He doesn't respond but it isn't locked. He's a very sound sleeper, I've learned, which is very helpful after the shenanigans I've been up to for the past few hours.

I shake him awake. "Wha . . . what? Dani?"

"I'm so sorry to wake you, I thought I heard dripping in my room."

"Is it raining?"

"No, can you please come see?"

He's a little unsteady as he follows me into the cabin. Must be all the Benadryl I dosed him with.

I put my ear against the wall. "Here. Listen."

He dutifully does.

I leave the room, telling him I have to pee. I close the door and, as quietly as I can, padlock the four industrial strength hasp locks I've installed on the outside of the door. I drilled the interior hinges yesterday when he took the dinghy out so he can't remove the pins from the inside. I caulk the door edges with a strong sealant, the way I did with the hatches for my cabin. It will take time to cure.

He's pounding on the door now and shouting my name.

"Enjoy the cocktails," I say and there's silence within.

He's found my special surprise. Five handles of Bahamian rum—nearly five gallons.

I considered bashing in his skull while he slept or overdosing him on insulin and weighing down his body and dumping it overboard—but then I thought about the shoe he caught with the foot still inside and how many tools there are to identify DNA and toxins. Accidental death is a whole lot less fun but much safer.

There's no water in the cabin, no tools to use to escape, no communication devices. I've left him a bucket.

He may claw his way out over time.

The sealant is probably a bit of overkill. But if it comes to it, I can hear myself explaining it to law enforcement: "I was afraid for my life. It was sitting out, and I thought I remembered how it worked." I don't know that it will hold him. Lucky for me, he upgraded the companionway door a year ago. It's not some flimsy wood, it's the latest in aluminum. Even if he gets out of the bedroom, he's not coming up through the companionway to the deck.

Heat, lack of water, rum.

It's the Bahamas that will kill him, not me.

I load up some garbage bags with things he'd need if he did get out. Food, water, insulin. I methodically go through the boat, loading the bag and dumping it out into the sea. I fill my gallon jug with water for my trip, then drain the rest of the water out. Search for and find the two emergency beacons and toss both the EPIRB and PLB overboard.

The fuel tanks are mostly full. It's tempting to set the boat on fire—I fantasize about watching it all burn as I ride away over the waves in the dinghy. There's nothing like a fully involved boat fire, and boats are insanely combustible. But they are conspicuous as hell and leaving Jim to the elements is the plan I'm sticking to, so I resist the temptation.

They won't be able to prove I sabotaged his boat, and by the time they find him, he'll be dead.

Jim helpfully showed me all the emergency equipment on the boat when I first moved aboard so I'm easily able to locate the lifeboat and his go bag. I toss the lifeboat overboard and dump our electronics too.

The go bag is coming with me; I'll need it if things get dire.

Saying goodbye to all that beautiful equipment is more painful than I expected but I've stored everything I need on a hard drive in a drybag. Once I'm back in civilization, I'll upload it to the cloud.

I short out the radio—I have to finesse this a little. I can't have this whole thing scream sabotage.

We're anchored pretty far off Rum Cay—a virtually deserted island heavily impacted by Hurricane Dorian—so I set the autopilot due east for Tenerife.

Of course, he won't get within three thousand miles of Spain with what's in the tanks, but it's enough to send him to sea and buy me some time. Maybe if I'm lucky he'll be mowed down in the shipping lanes.

He can't last longer than three or at the very most four days, even if he manages to get out of the cabin, now that I've stripped the boat.

As for me, I've fueled the dinghy. Now I need to head due west and get to the northern end of Long Island before daybreak. It's two AM and Jim told me the dinghy goes ten miles per hour.

Thunder rumbles in the distance.

I go through my mental checklist one last time. Even though I am fueled by adrenaline and moving as fast as I physically can, it still hits me how fantastic my plan is. It's innovative and accounts for every eventuality. It makes me sad that I will never get credit for it. I wonder if I will ever be able to share the details with Sawyer. He's the only one who I can imagine ever being able to tell, and the only one I've ever met who has it in him to truly appreciate the genius of what I've brought together. I don't know if he will ever be able to get past how I had to use him as a pawn in my plan, but if he can, he will surely be impressed.

Jim's still pounding on the door. One minute pleading, the next minute cursing.

I've been so absorbed I haven't heard him.

I drink as much water as I can hold and turn on the engine, starting the autopilot.

I put the go bag and the water in the dinghy. I'm wearing my full body UV protective unitard swimsuit, which is the least sexy thing I own, but I have put a lot of thought into my rescue outfit—it's in the dry bag with my bikini. I put on my lucky Dolphins baseball cap and shove my sunglasses into the backpack. I know there are things I'm forgetting but I have to go. Now.

I untie the dinghy as lightning fills the sky in the west.

The squall is headed this way.

CHAPTER

26

Somewhere in the Bahamas

Dani

Day 24

TWO HOURS LATER the dinghy is riding up waves as tall as me. I've strapped the go bag to myself because I'm afraid it will be pitched overboard at any moment. I'm also wearing a life vest—a first—because I have real concerns one of these waves will upend the boat.

I'm seasick and dehydrated from vomiting over the side.

I can barely see anything, let alone the compass.

It's no longer warm and humid.

Until today I've never been cold in the Bahamas.

But I know I will make it ashore.

Probably.

It's another two hours before I glimpse the lights of the cay. My every muscle is frozen or strained and uncooperative. I hope I'm in the right part of the island, but I can't even bring myself to care that much.

I somehow manage to get the dinghy to shore in the surf but my legs give out and I'm down, prone on the sand. My sluggish brain is telling me it's getting light. Get up. Camouflage the boat. I can't. I'm completely spent. The sky is gray, yellow by the time I force my frozen muscles to cooperate and lever myself into a sitting position. I groan and get to my feet.

There is a figure down the beach. Adrenaline gives me strength—between that and the hard-packed sand and boat wheels I'm able to drag the dinghy up to the scrub. Jim taught me how to pull it far up enough up the beach and out of the incoming tide. I cover her as well as I can. It takes me much longer than it should. Every muscle is screaming when I head back to the beach and head east. The person is heading toward me. I do my best to hustle but my legs are not cooperating. There's nowhere to go to avoid him, so I dig my sunglasses out of my bag and move higher up the beach where it's harder to walk. He's hugging the tide line. I keep my head down as we pass. He's elderly but going at a good clip. I'm practically limping.

He hails me with a wave, and I barely lift my hand in response, taking care not to look in his direction.

It's not high season and this isn't the most popular place on Long Island. It's pretty remote. I need a place to lie low for two days. Three would be better, but I've compromised.

I walk another five minutes and see a large white house with a smaller villa next to it.

Both appear deserted.

I check the beach in both directions. The man is far down the beach, almost out of sight.

I choose the villa. The doors are locked but the windows aren't so I climb in. It's clean but there's a sheen of dust on everything indicating it hasn't been rented in a while. Once I've scrambled through the window, I make my way to the front door to open it and grab my gear.

I take an ocean-facing room and drop my bag.

I check the fridge: empty. I still have two protein bars in the go bag and one packet of sports drink powder. I've emptied one water jug already.

My body shakes.

I'm nauseated.

I need a long hot shower.

I move the chest of drawers in front of the door.

If anyone comes to the house, theoretically I'll have time to go out the window.

I don't worry, I plan.

Encountering that man on the beach was not part of the plan.

CHAPTER

27

Long Beach Cay, Bahamas

Dani

Day 26

I'VE WIPED MY prints off everything in the house and left no trace of my occupancy. It's five AM in my little villa on the northeast side of Long Beach Cay. The tourist fishing boats may be leaving the marina soon and I need to be where they'll find me. I haven't eaten much these past few weeks and the last few days have taken a toll. I barely recognize myself in the mirror. The skin on my face is tightly stretched; there are half-moon bruises of exhaustion under each eye. I've picked up bruises and scratches all over my body from covering the dinghy. My stomach is still raw from all the vomiting. I revel in the fact that my physical state matches my tale.

I've chafed my wrists with sandpaper I found in the garage.

Rubbed a few inches of skin raw on my cheekbone.

I make a few fingerprint bruises on my forearm, then my neck.

I would kill for a cheeseburger and fries or fried conch and fritters but there will be plenty of time for that later. I move the dresser back into place, and cover my head with a scarf I found in a drawer. In the go bag that I plan on dumping, I've got the clothes for my rescue.

I opt for a blue cropped tank top and my shortest denim cutoffs. They are no longer snug, and no longer high waisted. They hang at the widest part of my hips, barely staying on my frame. The inseam is too long. I cut them off so they show off all of my tanned legs but barely any cheek. They're low-rise daisy dukes now, which is not the style, but I can bring it back with a million views of the rescue.

A rain poncho from the go bag covers the outfit. After dressing myself, I have to sit and rest. I'm so dizzy. They have water in the villa but I haven't hydrated well. I've tried to be very circumspect with my water intake. I need to be as dehydrated as possible. This part is hard—thirst is primordial. But I resist the urge.

I don't bother with my hair, because even beachy waves would look suspicious in a fleeing-for-your-life scenario, but I'm vain enough to put on a long-wearing matte lipstick the same color as my nipples, and a generous coating of waterproof mascara that's marketed as so long-lasting it's used on cadavers in open caskets. I should make a final pass through the house but I have to go. Getting rescue-ready has taken longer than expected.

I walk down the beach at the pace of an elderly woman. I remember reading once in a supermarket tabloid that your walking speed predicts how long you will live, and I try to calibrate my step to what I imagine a ninety-days-to-the-grave timeline would be. It's not hard. I feel bad enough for real to sell it.

The dinghy is right where I left it.

I pull it into the water, which takes longer than it should but is the fastest I can do it in my state, and pull the engine cord. It sputters and dies. I push the button to prime it and try again. It catches, but it doesn't sound too healthy. Motoring away from my temporary home, dumping the contents of the go bag as I head south, I have a fleeting thought that it may have been preferable to burn these items, but where could I have set a fire that wouldn't attract attention? That is the number one job of fire. I hope the ocean doesn't give me up. I imagine a fisherman reeling in the contents of my go bag, solving the mystery of my disappearance, and renaming his vessel *Aboat Crime.*

Jim was always so forthcoming with the information. He probably never realized how careful I was to absorb everything. How far from Rum Cay to Stella Maris on Long Island? Where do the tourists fish from the marinas there?

The boat's engine has quit on me twice in the last ten minutes and I'm starting to sweat when just after sunrise I spot it on the horizon. A small fishing charter.

I use my yellow rain poncho to flag them down.

They change direction to head toward me. I am ready for my closeup.

I sob as one of the crew helps me out of the dinghy and onto the boat. Four of the six people on board are filming.

"Dani Fox?"

"Oh my God, it's Dani Fox!"

White filters through the edges of my vision until it covers everything. I hope someone catches me, I'd hate to have survived all this and end up concussed. One last thought congeals before everything fades away: I sure did a fantastic job, pushing myself to the brink. Nailed it.

skipjackmancay87 she's been found. Dani Fox is alive!

PART III

CHAPTER

28

Serendipity

Sawyer

Day 26

THANKS TO COURTNEY'S thirty-thousand-dollar transfer, I've provisioned, dumped trash, and refueled. Everything is ready for my two hundred mile run to Cuba—a straight shot southwest. There are thousands of little islands where I can get lost and evade capture. I'll have to live on fish and the cans and dry goods I've stocked, but I can do the off-grid thing for a while—months even, before concerns about hurricane season and running low on supplies come into play. Cuba seems like the best bet for someone on the run from a global cruiser community hunting me with the intensity of Captain Ahab.

I'm not sure how I'll manage the sail by myself, but I can set proximity alerts for boats instead of taking watch. The prospect of being far the fuck away from absolutely every other person on the planet is incredibly appealing to me right now. Manning the sails on my own, not so much. It's stressful and frustrating trying to operate a system that, though it may be marketed as single-handed, is, in reality, premised on always having another set of hands available. I need to conserve fuel but I'm the one dealing with the sails even when Dani is on the boat. I entertain some idle thoughts about picking up some weathered, misanthropic first mate who doesn't speak English or want anything in the way of human companionship. Sailors and misanthropy go hand in hand, but even if a would-be first mate didn't speak English, that seems not to be a sufficient bar to awareness of the disappearance of Dani Fox.

I'm on the bow ready to pull anchor when the police power boat, lights flashing, comes into my line of sight, making a beeline for me. For a nanosecond I consider fleeing. I can almost imagine the slow speed chase that would ensue and how it would end, with *Serendipity* boarded and me in handcuffs for the second time this week and someone's drone footage of the whole thing shared on every forum and in every Fox Finders group. The drones currently swarming *Serendipity* have me longing for a shotgun. These fools have no idea how many skeet I blew out of the sky in my prep school days.

I will know no satisfaction today.

I never realized that one could run out of serendipity.

I make my way to the bow.

It's Inspector Knowles, Officer Walter, and a person I don't recognize steering the boat.

Knowles hails me.

I bring up a hand to shade my eyes.

"Sawyer Stone, permission to come aboard?'

I doubt she can read my facial expression from this distance, but my mind is racing trying to evaluate my options here. There's still a large part of me that wants to make a break for it. What will be inferred if I refuse to grant permission? Do they even *need* permission? I have yet to retain a lawyer with my windfall from Courtney. I had once planned on going to law school myself, but I wasn't cut out for the paper chase. Law school was too formulaic to capitalize on my intellect. It would've been three years learning how to think like everyone else, and for me, that would be a big step down. I'm regretting that decision right about now. Reasonable cause, search and seizure, constitutional protections. I know the buzzwords, but I don't know how they're actually applied. Especially when floating off the coast of a foreign country. All these thoughts flash through until I realize polite accommodation is my best move. Anything else connotes having something to hide. I'm not even sure if I have a right to an attorney, let alone the right to deny police access to my boat.

"Granted!" I shout. Have they gotten word through the island grapevine that I cleared out the marina bodegas of all their tinned goods, and Knowles deduced that I am about to go on the lam for real? Has another video dropped, giving her another line of questioning to pursue? Did Dani's body or parts thereof wash up somewhere? Worst case scenario, she's here to execute an arrest warrant. As Dani would say, if she were here: FML.

"We have news," Officer Walter says, raising his voice over the roar of their boat's powerful engine.

"Come aboard, of course." The officer I don't recognize deftly swings the stern of the aluminum police boat around to parallel *Serendipity* as I throw a couple of bumpers overboard to keep the boats apart. "Give me a second here," I say as I tie the rope to keep our boats together. Once secure, I motion for Knowles to board, and she confidently steps between the boats, and then turns back to offer a hand to Officer Walter, which he waves off with visible annoyance.

"Maintain three points of contact, Walter," Knowles instructs as he moves between the boats with more assurance than Knowles. The surf is a little choppy, and makes each boat move unpredictably and asynchronously. Still, Walter makes it across despite having reverted to only two points of contact as he jumps aboard the *Serendipity*. I hadn't noticed what a pedant Knowles is. God, it must be miserable working for her, with every task, no matter how menial, requiring a hospital corner.

"Dani Fox has been found," Knowles says without any preamble.

I notice how intently she scrutinizes my reaction. This is why they motored over so quickly—not to intercept my departure to Cuba, but to ensure that they could be first to break the news to gauge my response. Dumb luck for them that I have been too busy provisioning and preparing for my imminent departure to check the news.

I stare at them, wondering what notes to hit here. "Found? I . . . is she, I mean, found alive?" I strive for a hint of "Dare I hope?" in my voice. Any nuances of tone are lost, though, as I have to shout my reply over her engine noise. That police boat is so damn powerful. The thought of trying to outrun it is laughable. Given the size of those outboards they must use it to chase down drug traffickers at sea.

The truth is I would have been surprised if Dani was dead.

"Suffering from exposure and dehydration but doing well all things considered. She's at Doctors Hospital in Nassau," Inspector Knowles shouts back. She uses her hand to her throat to make the universal "cut" noise to the man driving the boat and he idles the engine.

"Is she hurt?" I ask. "Where has she been? What happened to her?" These seem to be the questions I should be asking, but what I need to know is, has she implicated me in any sort of felonious conduct in relation to her disappearance?

"She's being checked out," the inspector replies. "There will be plenty of time for questions later. She's asking for you, so pack a bag."

Good. Now I can find out what really happened and clear my name.

"I'll be right back," I reply.

I head down the gangway, through the narrow hallway, and into my cabin. I lean against the wall and take a few deep breaths. I wouldn't say I'm overwhelmed with joy, but there is relief and no little amount of curiosity. Maybe even a frisson of excitement. What kind of trouble has she gotten herself—and me—into? I consider my closet for a minute more than I normally would. I can almost hear Jesse's voice in my head telling me what to select to get camera ready.

There are four different shades of blue polos, slim fit khaki pants, and an obscene number of linen shorts, plus designer jeans with odd fading. I pull on a teal shirt, change into the linen shorts, and shove the rest in my duffel. Dani gifted me with this crap six months ago. I've never worn any of it but I have a feeling I'm going to need this wardrobe now.

Am I looking forward to seeing Dani? I can't put it in such simple terms.

She has my undivided attention.

I stuff underwear and toiletries into my duffel, grab my hat, keys, passport, money clip, and sunglasses, and lock the companionway door. "I need to contact someone to stay with the boat before I can leave."

The puzzlement is evident on Knowles's and Walter's faces.

"People have been coming by the boat, throwing things, pelting her with food and paint of some kind. I even had someone try to board her, but I ran them off. I worry about vandals and worse, what this could escalate into." Whatever else happens, however this meeting with Dani turns out, I need this boat.

Knowles's face is a mask of displeasure. I have negatively impacted the schedule she had formulated in her mind. That much is written on her face.

"How long will it take you to pull up anchor and follow us to the George Town Marina?"

"A half hour, give or take."

"Walter, give him a hand. We don't have all day."

Knowles motions to the police boat and boards moments later.

They head to shore.

With Walter's help, I ready the boat, pull the anchor in, turn on the engines, and follow them to George Town.

"You haven't said anything," Walter says as we get underway.

"I'm only thankful she's alive."

"From what I hear she's a little banged up; she needed to be rehydrated. She was found in a dinghy by a charter fishing boat at the crack of dawn."

"Adrift at sea?" My astonishment is not feigned. I don't know what I thought, but not that she'd had to escape whatever befell her by setting out in the open ocean in a dinghy.

Walter nods and bites his lip. "That's all I can tell you." Knowles has undoubtedly put him under strict instructions not to reveal details.

I make some sound that seems to satisfy him.

"I thought it was you," he says.

"You and the rest of the world. Fucking way off base, jumping to conclusions, total bullshit."

"You must understand, when this happens, from where we sit, it's nearly always the partner."

"I've been down this road before. Accused of having a hand in the death of someone I love. People I thought were friends turned on me once and now have turned on me again. Everything in my life, my past, scrutinized and cataloged. I wanted Dani found more than any of you. I told you to stop focusing on me and start looking at who might have her." I look over at him. "Who was it?"

"Inspector said not to say anything yet." It's a tell that Officer Walter is starting to feel more sympathetic toward me. He didn't only categorically deny my request for information, he pointed the finger at Knowles preventing him from giving me the information I want. It is a subtle shift, but it feels like a sea change to me. I can't believe I'm out of the woods on this thing.

"See? Still a suspect." I am making Walter feel guilty for sport. "Was she . . . hurt at all?"

"That I don't know, sir."

Now I'm sir.

I don't know who she was with, if she was forced, where she's been for over three weeks.

Now the police are looking at me with compassion. Acting as though they always knew it wasn't me.

I focus on getting *Serendipity* into the slip.

I'm pleasantly surprised when Officer Walter puts the bumpers out, takes the lines, and jumps off to tie them to the cleats. His effortless understanding of what needs to be done and when marks him as a fellow sailor. Drolly I wonder whether he is available to crew for me over to Cuba or the Canary Islands or fucking Point Nemo. I'm out of hot water, but that doesn't change my desire to get the hell out of the Bahamas. I don't know that I will ever be able to come back here. It reminds me of the time I got food poisoning from pork vindaloo from my favorite takeout spot. Five years later and the slightest waft of the smell of curry gives me the dry heaves. That's the Bahamas to me now. And I won't miss having it in my life as much as I miss Indian takeout.

There's another officer standing by the boat. Walter tells me he's to keep watch over her.

I grab my duffel bag and follow Officer Walter down the dock.

Several people film us with their phones. I ignore them.

"Why isn't he in handcuffs?" s woman three boats over swabbing the deck shouts at Officer Walter.

"Murderer!" her partner calls after us.

This draws the attention of several other tourists and locals, all who have their phones out to record us. I smile the smile of a man who knows how stupid those hecklers will look when word gets out. Smug satisfaction is powerful. I don't even feel angry toward Dani now, so potent is the thought of everybody in the entire world who was ready to pillory me for a crime I did not commit getting their well-deserved comeuppance. The police car is waiting, and we arrive at the small airport a few minutes later.

We hustle into a little prop jet already packed with half a dozen law enforcement officers—including Agent James. She's got her laptop out and is scanning whatever is on there. She looks up, unsmiling, when I board.

Walter and I sit and buckle into seats at the front of the plane.

This ought to be interesting.

I'm already dreaming up ideas about how our newfound fame can be best used for financial gain, other than Dani's YouTube revenues—which have exploded. We need to set up a Patreon account, stat. No one would've sponsored our page before out of fear I might use their funds to obtain legal representation or abscond, but now that people know I didn't murder Dani, we need to capitalize on our fame while we can. She's had a helluva lot more than her fifteen minutes.

CYBERSLEUTH ADMIN NOTE

James Marsh has been officially named by Bahamas LE a POI in this case. He may be sleuthed.

Speculation about the victim DF or her BF, SS will not be tolerated. Negative speculation of a victim is not allowed. Such posts will be removed.

Warnings, time-outs, or suspensions will be issued for those who violate our Victim Friendly rule.

CHAPTER

29

Doctors Hospital, Nassau, Bahamas

Dani

Day 26

I FLUFF MY HAIR and sit straighter in the hospital bed. I've done my makeup, though it wasn't easy. My hands shake as if I have delirium tremens. A nurse told me to expect it given everything I went through and the state of my electrolytes. Thanks to the IV hydration, I'm already feeling much better than I did when I arrived, but I could sleep for days.

"Are you ready to tell us what happened?" a woman police officer asks from where she stands next to the camera on a tripod to capture my story. She told me her name, but it slipped through and is now gone forever. She doesn't matter anyway. I smile and nod.

Her tone is gentle, and I'm being treated as the victim, but make no mistake, this is an interrogation. I need to bring my A game. If I can pull it off, this should be the second and final interview.

I don't tell her what I'm desperate to do, which is have a look at my numbers. How many YouTube views and subscribers have my videos generated? I'm desperate to read my own press. The universe better not have let me down after everything I went through. Abandoning my skin care regimen for three weeks has wreaked absolute havoc. *Havoc.* And you can't turn back the clock and undo that kind of damage.

How can I know if this will all be worth it without checking my numbers? Did my gambit work? Clearly it had some impact if a bunch of random tourists on a fishing boat knew my name. How well, though? Very well? *Spectacularly* well? But they were all olds, so for all I know they learned my name from some Bahamian milk carton or some other fuddy-duddy analog way. But if my channel *has* taken off, I can parlay that influence into infinite other directions—that's how you create a media empire. That's what normies like Jim don't get—you can't do one thing and stick with it and think that will always be there for you. You need fresh content. Reinvent. Reinvigorate. I wonder what my first offshoot from our cruising channel will be. I'm thinking of doing a tea channel, where I cover the gossip relating to other top-rated influencers. It's a natural fit, because I love gossip. It would be on brand. Easy to edit too. Got to think about the back end.

But first, interrogation. There are questions to answer, a boyfriend to acquit, and an innocent man to condemn. My baseline body language is being observed and recorded for later review. I am ready for this. These police investigators have no idea how much experience I have selling things on camera. And by things, I mean, myself. Countless hours prepared me for this moment.

Every aspect of my behavior has to convince the people in this room that I'm trustworthy and honest. Emotional pain isn't exactly in my wheelhouse but avoiding body language red flags will have to suffice. Good thing I went through that phase of watching all those body language analysis videos on YouTube where experts dissect the significance of the posture and demeanor of criminals. I've seen enough to know the video will be broken down and evaluated, movement by moment by someone, probably the FBI, for deception. I keep my lips soft. Compressing them can be a sign I am withholding information. Looking up can indicate I'm trying to remember something or be perceived as contempt or disdain. Lifting my chin, tucking my hair, using my hands, shoulders, if the so-called grief muscle shows in my forehead when I cry, all of it matters and it's a lot of cues to remember. I've been practicing in the mirror. Not much else to do on *Aboat Time*. But still there are a lot of moving parts here, and it's hard to keep them all front-of-mind.

My story can't seem too rehearsed, so minute details can be added but must be remembered to be repeated. None of this is evidence of guilt or innocence, of course, but if I can do this convincingly this should be the final retelling to law enforcement. Sharing my story of survival on television, on my channel, in interviews, may only be the beginning.

The videos released during my "captivity" sure did a great job implicating Sawyer. No doubt the internet, cruiser community, and Sawyer's unlikable demeanor has done the rest with a little help from Sonja. I feel like Dr. Frankenstein with my own monster creation in Sonja. I zapped some life into her with a few well-placed insinuations and unleashed her onto the world. A lot of people don't realize that Frankenstein is not, in fact, the monster, but rather the doctor who created the monster. I firmly believe in giving credit where it is due so I'm careful about that sort of thing.

But now, focus. Interrogation. Innocence. Why haven't I seen Sawyer yet? Perhaps Sawyer has been detained. Surely by now someone has realized that Sawyer's wife died under mysterious circumstances.

Maybe that's finally caught up to him.

Maybe he's tried to run.

That would be delicious. Even if it meant I never saw him again, it's a great arc.

My focus now is to convincingly rewrite my narrative with a new villain.

I sit up straighter in the hospital bed and clench the sheets between my hands.

I draw in breath and begin to tell my story.

"My name is Dani Fox. Three weeks ago I was abducted by a man named Jim Marsh and held captive aboard his sailing vessel, *Aboat Time.*"

I'm about to drop my first well-placed self-deprecating remark to make me seem more relatable to average people when the door to my room swings open and two more police officers enter.

Right on their heels is Sawyer Stone III.

I gasp.

I think that was the perfect dramatic reaction. Sawyer is at my bedside in an instant, his arm reaching over my body, and I have a brief flash of questioning whether he's about to rip the pillow from behind my shoulders and smother me with it. A glint I catch in Sawyer's eyes suggests a quick suffocating may not be out of the question. Instead, he goes for a wide armed embrace and buries his face in my hair. I feel a wave of relief wash over me, and I revel in the strength of his embrace for a long moment, before peeping through my eyelids to see how our reunion is being received by the assembled officers.

Inscrutable.

But now Sawyer's lips have found my ear, and he's whispering so low that only I can hear. "I have one question for you."

"Mhhmm," I reply with lips still pursed together.

"The fuck?" Sawyer's voice is tight with rage, and something else . . . incredulity, maybe? The reality of how much bad energy I'm going to have to dispel to get us through this phase hits me hard. I honestly don't have the strength for any of it. *Good vibes only*, I want to plead, but there's no way around the dark cloud of Sawyer's reaction that I now must reckon with. I must go through it.

Sawyer takes my hand in his and squeezes, painfully tight.

I inhale, my eyes fill, and the tears spill over. I hold up the hand not holding Sawyer's. "I'm sorry—" My voice breaks. I am still more exhausted than I've ever been in my life. It's easier to manufacture tears when you're this tired. Who knew?

"We're sorry to put you through this again, but we need to complete our interview," the Bahamian woman in the dark blue dress says. "Please walk us through your account of what happened."

I take another deep breath. "I talked to Jim at the party—"

"The party at *Xanadu* Saturday night?" she interrupts.

I nod. "We made plans to look at his TG-6," I say.

Sawyer notices the blank expressions in the room and comes to my rescue. "It's an underwater camera."

"Yes, sorry. It's an Olympus. He was excited about it—and I was in the market for one, so I wanted to check out all the features." This is true. Basing your lies on facts makes them both easier to remember and more authentic. I can hear the hesitation in my voice. "Sawyer . . ." I say, sneaking a glance at him, but he's stone-faced, not even blinking. "I think Sawyer got the wrong idea about me and Jim . . ."

I look down at my lap where his calloused, tan hand holds my smaller, fragile one. My manicure is in surprisingly good shape. I wonder if it's genetic.

I look up to see everyone's eyes on Sawyer, but he remains silent. He's not going to protest. He knows it's what I want. He knows I'm a liar and worse. Yet here he sits, playing the role of concerned lover so well. I didn't know he was capable of it.

Is it a relief that he won't be going to jail for murder? Has he seen my *Sailing with the Foxes* channel numbers? There's no Patreon account—not yet. But now that I've exculpated him, people will want to contribute to helping us get back on our feet and of course, getting the additional content. We are going to monetize our love.

If I can talk our way out of this investigation, that is.

"I am kinda . . . *was* kinda flirty. It doesn't mean anything, but sometimes it gives people, men, the wrong idea," I say, using my teeth to toy with my lower lip and casting my gaze down again.

The room is still silent. It's much harder to perform without any positive feedback. Sawyer remains stone-faced. As advertised, I suppose.

"Sawyer got pretty lit on *Xanadu*. He was way out of control."

There are nods around the room.

I sneak a glance at Sawyer. He looks almost sad. What's he going to say? He was drugged? If he were going to say that, he would've already. I shoot him a conspiratorial look, but his face remains implacable. It would have been nice to find out what he has been saying or what the internet has been saying before this interview, but I've seen enough police procedurals to know they kept us apart for my first brief initial video to see if we tell the same story. Even the victim is treated as a suspect.

"I think . . ." I turn to fully look at him. "I think it may be an issue, the drinking."

He seems to stop breathing but otherwise doesn't respond. That same almost sad expression is fixed, but his eyes meet mine and promise retribution.

We're in the public eye now. Every sip a slip. A single drink and he's "off the wagon." He knows he can't trust me to edit out his occasional beer or rum punch. Come to think of it, the alcoholic boyfriend trope could create endless drama. Something about how excited I am about this new idea must show in my face because Sawyer gives my hand an ungentle squeeze. I cast a helpless look Sawyer's way. "That night, at the party," he prompts.

"Oh, right. The Nilssons asked me to take him home. Sonja was worried but I told her I'd have Jim with me and we'd put him to bed. I knew he'd be okay when he woke up. We loaded him up in my dinghy—our dinghy—and brought him back to our boat. Jim tied up mine and his. After we put Sawyer in his—our room, Jim asked me to go back to his boat to see the camera."

My nose starts stinging and tears fill my eyes. I've never been so glad I learned to make myself cry on cue. "I said yes, even though it was late, because I was worried Sawyer might wake up and still be mad."

One of the police officers steps forward with a tissue. Sawyer takes it and hands it to me. I catch the raised eyebrows in the glances the two women exchange. I shrink a bit more to feed into the possibility that they see Sawyer as controlling. I'm hoping it's not that they think I'm feigning my tears. I try to flex my forehead grief muscles. I hope I'm communicating sadness and not confusion. I have deep regrets about the Botox I had done four months ago. There was a doctor on TikTok who said if you start doing Botox when you are in your early twenties, you will never need it later. That made so much sense to me. But now I need to call upon some wrinkles to convey my distress and I don't know if it's working.

"I didn't see the harm in it. We were friends." I have practiced this line over and over, on the *Aboat Time*, during the dinghy escape disaster, and in the mirror in the house I broke into on Long Island. It is hard to get the right amount of wistful regret in my tone or expression.

There are expressions of sympathy in the room, but no one says anything. The woman from the Royal Bahamas police is wearing the navy dress. I've forgotten who the one in the black pantsuit is. Unlike the others in the room, their expressions are guarded. Black Pantsuit's narrow-eyed gaze hasn't left me.

"He took me in to see the camera. Brought out his laptop. I was playing with the Olympus for a while. Then the engines came on. I remember thinking that was weird but figured maybe he needed to charge his generator or something. His boat is old. He hadn't come back in the room but I was getting tired, and as soon as I stood up to find him I realized we were underway!" This feels like the perfect amount of detail. "I went up the companionway and asked Jim what he thought he was doing and he laughed and said, 'Kidnapping you.' I swear I thought he was joking but he seemed off somehow."

"'Off' how?" This question comes from Black Pantsuit, but next to her, starched-up Navy Dress has raised her eyebrows.

"Maybe drunk or high," I reply. "I didn't think he did that anymore. I'd never seen him drink in public. He was always telling people he was sober but . . . he was on something that night."

The tears come in earnest now and my forehead is wrinkled for all it's worth.

"Can we give her a little break?" Sawyer asks.

"I'd love a ginger ale or Sprite," I whisper to him. "Or a sparkling water, any flavor. But not coconut or peach pear. So gross."

A can of Sprite is procured, and I am urged to continue by the tall Black woman in the pantsuit. Inspector something or maybe agent something. I didn't pay enough attention; it's unlikely the women are in charge.

I wonder if I'll be able to get this tape from them? It will probably be the most authentic telling of this tale that I'm sure I'll repeat dozens more times. That's the hope, anyway. If they won't release it to me, I can recreate it for my channel and maybe give our patrons special access. I try to telepathically communicate to Sawyer that he should record me on his phone. He is not empathic enough to receive my instructions.

Instead, Sawyer stands and stretches. I hand him my half-finished soda and he downs it in one swallow, then takes up his position on the bed.

"He kept me locked in my cabin at night," I say. "I don't know where we were most of the time. I think we were in the Bahamas but I'm not sure. He let me out to use the bathroom, sit on the deck a few times, but mostly he didn't trust me and kept me locked in the room. I begged and pleaded with him to take me back."

"Did he sexually assault you?"

"He tried—a bunch of times, a bunch of things." I shudder, and next to me, Sawyer's shoulders stiffen. "I don't want to talk about that. Please don't make me talk about that." I pause for five heartbeats. Somewhere around the third beat, the amusement bubbling up inside me makes the corner of my lip twitch. This is so much fun. I can make them believe anything. I catch Navy Dress staring at me. I tame that twitching lip corner and harden my features again. "He couldn't, you know, get hard, stay hard. Maybe because of all the drinking. Then he'd get mad and he'd slap me, never his fist, always a slap—backhand, forehand. He said he had diabetes and that's why his, it, you know, things didn't work."

There was a murmur from one of the officers in the back. I'm connecting with my audience, I can feel it. I'm trying to keep this rated PG. Maybe the backhand and forehand was a bit much. It smacks of tennis, not abuse.

"I kept thinking I'd make a break for it when we resupplied. Then he told me we had enough to stay out for weeks. I lost hope that anyone would find me." I pause here, close my eyes, and cover my mouth. "I tried the door every night. Sometimes I could see land. Most of the time I couldn't. Sometimes he'd leave in the dinghy with his gear; I could see through the hatches, but they were sealed shut.

"I couldn't even try to escape while we were out at sea. Sometimes in the morning he didn't let me out in time to use the bathroom and I had to go in a bucket." I don't know how shame looks or feels so I hang my head and drop my voice to a whisper. "I woke him up a few times, yelling to use the bathroom, and he didn't like that, so he left the bucket. I begged him to take me back to *Serendipity*." My speech is as halting as I can make it. Rushing everything out is an indicator that speech is rehearsed, and I don't want them to think that.

"Did anyone know where you were? Or where he was?"

"No one, as far as I know. I never heard or saw him communicate with anyone else. And I had no idea where we were. He talked about Mayaguana a few times. We mostly ate fish so I think wherever we were the fishing must've been good, but it's the Bahamas, right? So the fishing is good everywhere." I manage a watery smile and nearly all the men in the room are nodding. Empathy or agreement, either way it's good. They are with me. No matter the circumstances, it seems people enjoy fishing and national pride.

"How did you finally escape?" Navy Dress asks.

"I got him to come into my room in the middle of the night. I yelled for him. Told him something was leaking in my room. He was pretty out of it at night I think—probably all the drinking. I tripped him, shoved him down, and ran. I locked the door behind me, using what he had installed. I wasn't sure it would hold him and he'd left the caulk out that I guess he used on the hatches so I put it all around to seal the door. I used his navigation system to see where we were and try to get closer to land but I was terrified he would be able to break out of the room. As soon as I got the boat kinda near civilization—at least an island whose name I recognized—I lowered the dinghy and got out of there. The weather wasn't great and his dinghy wasn't the best. I don't know how much time it took to get near where I was rescued but it must've been hours. I didn't think to bring much water or gear. I was only thinking of getting away."

I've said too much. It sounds rehearsed. I need to slow down. I don't like the look on the police inspector's face.

"That was so brave," Sawyer murmurs. He holds me tight and looks down at me—his expression is admiring? Proud? What is going on with him? He's too good at this.

There are more nods around the room, with the notable exception of Navy Dress and Black Pantsuit. Now that I look at her closely, Navy Dress would do well to rethink her color choices. A bright hue would be so much more flattering to her complexion. I make a mental note to create an opportunity to advise her later. If I facilitate a little glow-up for her, maybe she won't be so hostile to my energy.

But now, Navy Dress and Black Pantsuit wear nearly identical expressions of skepticism, while everyone else's face has sympathy etched in it. I have to carefully navigate the sentiment around them if they are going to go after me, the victim, still suffering the effects of exposure.

I put my head in my hands. "I'm sorry," I mumble. "I'm so goddamn tired."

It is the second true thing I've said today.

Sawyer puts his arms around me.

"Can we give her a break now, please? And for the love of God, can you please go find that monster, Jim Marsh?" Sawyer says.

Is he baiting me?

"Of course," the American woman says. "May I ask a follow-up question or two?"

The Bahamian woman nods.

Maybe she *is* in charge.

"Can you explain how you got the black eye we saw in the video?"

"I got hit with the boom," I say softly. "Sawyer warned me about it a million times, but the wind shifted so we were tacking and—blam! I was lucky I didn't get a concussion, right, Sawyer?"

I can feel him nod, his chin moving my hair as he holds me to him.

"It wasn't recent?"

"Oh no, it was months ago, on our passage here from Florida."

"What about the dress?" someone calls out from the back of the room. This isn't a very well-organized interrogation.

I blink.

Blink blink blink. My eyes are darting all over the place.

I drop my head to cover my distress. I'm sure my entire body language is screaming, "Liar, liar, liar."

I forgot about the damn dress.

Crap.

"When we were moving Sawyer into his cabin, I cut myself," I say. "It wasn't bad."

"Then what did you do?"

"The dress had blood all over it before I even realized. So I changed real quick before I went with Jim to see the camera."

"You put the dress in a drawer?" The Bahamian woman is asking this; her tone is kind but her expression is steely.

My head tilts.

"I thought I left it on the floor of my bedroom," I say.

Every pair of eyes in the room are on Sawyer.

Every single pair.

Shit, shit, shit.

His arm around me tightens.

"Maybe I did stuff it in a drawer?" I say haltingly. "I was rushing out of there."

"But why would you stuff a bloody dress in a drawer?" Navy Dress asks.

"It was in the kitchen, right? I think I was going to try to get the stain out with cold water when I came back," I reply.

The woman's eyebrows nearly reach her hairline. "Cold water on an expensive silk and spandex dress?"

"Is that not right Ms., er?" I ask. When in doubt, bimbo it. I look around the room wide eyed, lips slightly parted.

"Inspector Knowles of the Royal Bahamas Police Force."

"Hydrogen peroxide," an officer pipes up from the back of the room. "That's what you need to get bloodstains out." I catch the narrow-eyed glare Knowles shoots at him, so I jump in.

"When I am wanting to get a stain out, I search on cleaning TikTok for tips, and after a few videos, the algorithm is always successful in distracting me so much that I forget I was doing laundry in the first place. Shove the dirty clothes in a drawer and get on with life. Then a week later, when you're wanting to wear that same dress again, you have to go back and search for the same stain removal all over again but now add "old" as a search term. It's totally different now. Like old grass, old chocolate, old blood. Time is so fleeting. So, do you think that hydrogen peroxide would work on my dress? Is it too late to try that?" I finish babbling and crane my neck to see the man at the back of the room who offered up the suggestion, giving him a grateful smile.

"It's in evidence," Inspector Knowles says, punctuating every word, as you do when speaking to an imbecile.

I am duly chastened and slump in the bed.

"I think we're done here. Whatever else you have to ask her can wait. She's exhausted," Sawyer says, coming to my rescue.

He is looking so hot to me right now.

"When can I come back home to *Serendipity*?" I ask him. "I'm kinda ready to leave here, no offense."

There are murmurs of reassurance from everyone in the room save Navy Dress and Black Pantsuit.

Sawyer helps me lie back down and follows the people filing out of the room. I snagged his phone during our embrace—I'm not much of a pickpocket, so he probably knows, and as the door closes, I key in his passcode, open the browser, and search my name. I can't believe my eyes.

Holy *wow.*

CHAPTER

30

Royal Bahamas Police Headquarters

Inspector Knowles

Day 27

Inspector Knowles balances the white paper clamshell takeout container crammed full of sausage, eggs, and toast in one hand and closes her office door after Agent James. James takes her seat on the sofa in the corner and sets down her Diet Coke and pastry.

Knowles shovels in a few forkfuls of the eggs before laying down the utensil. "What are your thoughts?"

"I am trying to apply Occam's razor, but I am not sure which explanation is the simplest. I keep waffling as to whether I believe the Fantastic Ms. Fox or not."

"Have a look at this and see if this helps make up your mind." Knowles turns her computer monitor around to show Agent James a clip from Dani's interview that she had already queued up. Video Dani is explaining how Jim Marsh tried to rape her. Knowles presses pause after a minute or so. "It's the most harrowing part of her story and you see right there, she is suppressing a smile. That is duping delight, I'm sure of it."

James studies the freeze frame. "I see the mouth twitch, barely. It's incredibly subtle, but I saw it. Play it again for me."

"It is fleeting, I grant you, but it's there." Knowles resets the video to the tag, and plays the clip again, this time with the sound off. "Even with everything at stake, Dani is enjoying the hell out of telling this story. She is taking great delight in duping us—and that is a strong indicator of psychopathy. Of course, a microexpression like this does not substantiate charges, but it sure can give us a direction for our investigation." She closes the video window and refocuses her attention on Michelle. "So what's our next move, Agent James?"

"We need to find Jim Marsh. If there are holes to be poked in Dani's story, poke them we must."

"Jim Marsh is probably dead," Knowles says.

"No doubt. But if he is, there might be evidence she killed him . . ."

"And if he's still alive?"

"If he's found alive—and that's a big if—it's going to be he said, she said," James says. "And I wouldn't want to be him. She's a pretty little liar and people don't seem to need much convincing—present company excepted." She sips her Diet Coke.

Knowles rubs her forehead. "People believe her. Even my own staff—the commissioner, the deputy commissioner . . . are we the crazy ones?"

James shakes her head and takes a big bite of her sugar cinnamon donut twist. "She picked a guy with a record. No one wants to dig too deep. The public, the media, our bosses—they have their victim, their wrongly accused, and their villain. End of story."

"Did you see her start to cry about how we misconstrued her videos and investigated poor Sawyer Stone? Meryl Streep she ain't," Knowles says. "Every time I survey her reaction to some external stimulus, there is at first a pause, a blankness about her. Like software is compiling inputs."

"I heard they're flying out to New York to sign a book contract and be interviewed on a few morning shows. I haven't been in this line of work as long as you, but already I have learned the fundamental truth: crime pays."

Inspector Knowles groans and leans back in her chair. "Maybe we're being too cynical, James. Most criminals are caught. Most will pay for their crimes in some way."

James snorts. "Most criminals are stupid."

She has a point here. Knowles has a lot of faith in adhering to tried and true investigative procedures, but usually the quarry is not quite as intelligent as both Sawyer and Dani seem to be. Will it take some creative, maverick technique to bring them down? Knowles is more comfortable by-the-book than out-of-the-box. "We know this whole thing stinks like a week-old fish, but we've got nothing on her. How do we crack this one?"

James shrugs. "I think the key will lie with Jim Marsh."

"By all accounts Marsh is a model citizen. No one in the cruiser community ever said he set a foot wrong," Knowles says, setting her jaw.

"Maybe lately, but Marsh has a sheet for assault, disturbing the peace, public intoxication—"

"All offenses a dozen years old!"

"Alcoholics relapse," Agent James says gently. She finishes her donut, wipes her hands with the napkin, and shrugs. "Don't kill the messenger. This thing is only going one way in the court of public opinion. Hers. If we're going to charge her with anything, we need evidence and a considerable amount of it. So far, we have bupkis. No footage that contradicts her story. No witnesses who saw them, wherever they've been in the past few weeks." She leans out and tosses her can in the recycling bin.

"She cannot get away with this," Knowles replies.

James sighs. "Maybe we've got this all wrong. Maybe the scuba thing was an accident. Maybe Jim Marsh is a batshit-crazy stalker."

"Maybe this down-on-their-luck, broke-ass couple lucked into making millions with their YouTube channel."

James frowns. "Wait—when did she get monetized?"

"I'm sorry?"

"When did her channel start making money?

"I have no idea."

James opens her laptop. "Okay, I'm in the *Sailing with the Foxes* channel." She skims through and is silent for a few minutes. "Hoo boy, Vero, the subscribers and views on this thing are insane. Tens of millions of people have watched each of those seventeen videos. They must be absolutely raking it in. I think it may be worth contacting YouTube to see when they monetized. Look, they already have a Patreon account. That's new."

"A *what* account?" Knowles asks.

"Patreon. It's a subscription payment model for fans and a way for creative types to generate money without algorithms and the lot. Fans pay a monthly amount for exclusive access to extra content from their favorite vloggers, musicians, whoever." James turns her screen to face Knowles.

Knowles looks over her reading glasses. "How much money are we talking?"

"Well, it's based on views for YouTube, but the exclusive content patron bit is tiered, usually. They are asking twenty-five dollars per video for basic and it goes all the way up to two thousand dollars for exclusive one-on-one chats. We may need to subscribe to the basic—they promise GPS access to wherever they are in the world."

Knowles feels her mouth drop open. "They are essentially wearing a tracking device for law enforcement! Who does that?"

"Most of these sailing channels, it seems. They're doing a special meet and greet for the VIP patrons tomorrow."

"So, basically they've made a killing," Knowles says, summing it up.

James snorts. "Literally, figuratively, or both?"

Knowles shakes her head. "What a world."

"If she monetized days before the kidnapping we might be able to show . . ." Agent James begins.

"I barely know what you're talking about," Knowles says, "but it sounds pretty damn thin."

James closes her laptop. "I know."

"Who does this kinda thing?"

James shrugs. "I think you're asking rhetorically, but the answer is psychopaths. The garden-variety criminals you've encountered in your career probably don't have enough impulse control to pull off the long cons. It's the clever ones who get away with it—financial scams and the like, skating just this side of the law. We get a lot of those in the FBI. Her, I'm not so sure, but it's possible. Women are harder to figure, there's still so little literature on them. But with the women there are certain behaviors and schemes like blackmail, playing the victim, preying on family members and friends."

"She checks all those boxes."

"I'd love to know what she was doing before she met up with Sawyer."

"You think they're what, some kind of social media–style Bonnie and Clyde?"

"It's possible, birds of a feather and all that," James says.

Knowles frowns. "You'd think psychopaths would avoid one another."

James nods. "They can't trust each other. But there are some studies that indicate a propensity for young female psychopaths to hook up with older male psychopaths. Have you checked out that CyberSleuth group lately?"

Knowles groans. "God no. Don't tell me."

"They're doing some deep dives on Jim Marsh. Attempting to link him to some unsolved cases in areas where he's lived. Unfortunately, he's lived all over."

Knowles leans back in her chair and covers her face with her hands.

"Anyway," James says, standing. "I'm going to appropriate Walter's office for a bit. I've got some paperwork to submit."

Knowles resettles herself in her chair as the door closes behind Agent James. She pulls up the CyberSleuth site and searches through the latest posts. Interest in Dani and Sawyer has waned; their thread is near the bottom of the page. At the top of the page, the thread with the most activity is called "Find Jim Marsh."

Knowles clicks on the link and reads the first comment from crimegroupie12356.

Folks, Marsh had a white truck from 2013–2017 and lived within 40 miles of the last place she was seen!

Background on Hazel Whitmore Disappearance in Kansas City, Missouri

On the morning of October 13, 2016, blonde, fit, young 25-year-old (see the pattern!) Hazel told her husband, Banner, she was planning on running several errands in town after teaching a yoga class at the Everly Fitness Center. She stopped at Clothing Connection, a store near her home in Parkview around 3:00pm after teaching her yoga class. The clothing store was the last confirmed sighting of Hazel. It is believed by authorities that after leaving the store she drove to the Weston Bend State Park to go for a run. According to an eyewitness driving on Timber Road through the forest that afternoon, a woman resembling Hazel was seen running along the road wearing red shorts similar to those she had worn earlier that day. Investigators initially believed Hazel to have fallen victim to the elements or potentially been attacked by a mountain lion; however, they later suspected her husband Banner after uncovering evidence of an affair. Banner had an alibi: his lover. Additionally, a woman driving through the area from where Hazel disappeared claimed to have seen a white truck in the area around the time of Hazel's disappearance.

Sailing with the Foxes Channel
YouTube

Hi friends! It's me, Dani. Thank you for all the likes and subscribes and supportive comments. As you know, I had scheduled most of my previous videos to run in advance, from footage from our travels this past year, but our goal now is to give you brand new updates on our journey every Tuesday.

I posted my first video today—it's me and Sawyer rescuing two Bahamian boys from a pretty terrifying rip. I had no idea that less than twenty-four hours later I'd be the one who needed to be rescued! Check it out! And as always, like and subscribe.

We have a new Patreon account and it would slay if you could become a member. Our patrons are such an important part of our Foxes community—or the Fox Hounds, as we affectionately call them. They are the dream manifesters, and I've got so many dreams I want to manifest.

I've missed *Serendipity* and all of you so much. I've been to hell but now I'm back and I plan to tell you what happened in next week's video, with exclusive extended footage of my rescue for our patrons and extra exclusive content, including the AMA you've all been asking for—for our VIP-status patrons only! I promise the VIP material hits different.

I have some healing to do but there is no better place to do it than out here on the water with my love, Sawyer. I can't wait for you all to feel his true vibes! So click like and subscribe, sponsor us if you can. We hope to see you soon! Wishing all you Fox Hounds fair winds and following seas.

12 million subscribers
50 million views
76,000 supporters on Patreon

CHAPTER

31

Royal Bahamas Police Headquarters

Inspector Knowles

Day 27

THE GEORGE TOWN Police Force building happily reflects the noon sunrays with its fresh coat of pink paint. The pastel exterior is in keeping with island vibes but isn't what you'd expect for a building whose purpose is to investigate and document the very worst of human behavior. Down a dark hallway, tucked away in a back corner the way she likes it, Inspector Knowles squints at some blurry scanned documents on her computer monitor. The office is drab, with mismatched office chairs and inadequate lighting. A few months ago, her boss tried to force a new office furniture suite to "keep up appearances," but Knowles turned him down. "Have you never heard of shabby chic? It is all the rage this year."

Knowles stretches and glances at her cell phone. She really should check in with James about lunch. Surely she's finished her paperwork by now. She's seen Walter strolling the halls, chatting as if the investigation is over.

Knowles tries to ignore her ringing phone as she attempts to decipher the Dominican police reports that she had called up from archives, but eventually she gives up and answers.

"Knowles? I have good news and bad news," Campbell says.

She closes her eyes for a brief second, hoping against hope for a tidy resolution to this case. "Tell me the good, Chief Inspector."

"We found a boat this morning," he says.

She inhales sharply. "*Aboat Time*?" She texts Agent James and gets out her notepad and pen.

"Right."

"And Marsh?"

"Comatose. Airlifted to Doctors Hospital."

"Can you bring *Aboat Time* here?"

"That's the bad news—and why I'm calling. We weren't the first on scene. Or the second or the third. The whole damn thing is contaminated by cruisers and cyber sleuths or whatever they call themselves. Someone posted her location when the AIS was switched on—which we assume Marsh did. There were so many cruisers surrounding the *Aboat Time* when we got there, it looked like a damned regatta. Do you know what the people who boarded told my officers? That they were there conducting an investigation."

Knowles groans so loudly Officer Walter comes to her door.

"Some idiot started CPR without checking for a pulse. Broke a few ribs on the guy. They filmed themselves, went through the place. It's beyond bad and already all over the internet."

"Any chance you can bring the idiots who boarded the boat in? Print them, do eliminations, get statements?"

"We got there hours after they did, Inspector. The evidence chain isn't just broken, it's obliterated. To make matters worse, turns out some responsible adult reported the AIS signal to us *yesterday*. But it didn't get through since our channels have been overwhelmed by conspiracy theories and supposed sightings of this individual, Jim Marsh, and his boat. Meanwhile, others who found the signal posted it online and launched the citizen corps, as it were."

The acid comes up Knowles's stomach and explodes in her esophagus. She swallows, searching her desk drawer frantically for her antacid. She pops two in and chews the citrusy-flavored chalk.

"I'll call the ACP to see if they want to send another forensic team here."

"Did what you find fit? With her being held captive and all?"

"Looks like Marsh made it out of the cabin and into the galley. There were hasp locks all over the door, sealant around the edges. Just like she said. Must've taken him a long time to bust through. He's all beat up. We'll run it for prints and DNA but given the scene . . ."

Knowles sighs.

"Here's the interesting part. There were no cameras, computer equipment, diabetes medicine or medicine of any kind, and we had confirmed he was an insulin dependent diabetic."

"There should've at least been a camera, a T-6 Nikon something or other," Knowles says.

"No cameras. Boat wouldn't start. Autopilot was sending the boat due west, to Morocco or somewhere. Fuel tank is dry. No reserves."

"Sabotage?" Knowles muses.

"There's more. The watermaker was busted. There was no water in the storage tank. Radio not functional. No lifeboat or beacon. No WIRB or IRB. Some empty rum handles."

"His friends said he'd been sober for a dozen years. Never allowed alcohol on the boat," Knowles says. "Do we think he had some?"

"Could've been the cruisers partying in the crime scene."

"Are you . . . please tell me you're joking."

"Nope. Quite a few people on the boat were intoxicated. There's some video footage online of them hoisting the rum handles. When we got there they were all empty. Emptied by Marsh or the boat brigade, we'll never know."

"Damn it."

"Judging by the maintenance, tools, clothes—this was a very organized individual and a very experienced sailor," Campbell says.

"That's certainly what others who knew him said. Thanks for the call," Knowles says. "I'll make my way to Nassau."

"No rush. He's isolated in the ICU and not conscious," Campbell replies.

Agent James walks through the door as Knowles hangs up the phone. "What's going on?"

"It's her. The *Aboat Time.* We were last on the scene."

"What do you mean?" James asks.

"I mean the damn cruisers got there first!" Her hands make themselves into fists as she paces the room.

James's mouth drops open. "Holy hell. And Marsh?"

"Critical condition, comatose." Knowles rubs her face with her hands.

James checks the social media apps on her phone. "It's leading the news. 'Boat girl kidnapper found.' There's a ton of footage here with people on the boat," she says, scrolling. "Good God. There's video of people propping him up and carrying him around like it's *Weekend at Bernie's*, the monsters. Complete contamination."

"What I would like to know is, was it intentional to weaponize the web sleuths and lookie-loos? To corrupt evidence, and introduce so much noise into the system we cannot even conduct a normal investigation? Could that vapid girl be capable of orchestrating this?"

"Would she have to?" Agent James asks. "When terrorists targeted the World Trade Center in New York, they didn't know that flying a plane into the tower would ignite the jet fuel, which would overcome the building's fireproofing, which in turn would superheat the steel support beams on the floors hit by the airplane and cause the entire building to collapse. Maybe Dani's plan never even considered the actions of the keyboard warriors and web sleuths. Maybe her plan was nothing more sophisticated than leveraging the outsized impact of being a missing white woman. When your plan is to sow chaos and destruction, you are going to get some unexpected outcomes."

"You may be right. In one of her videos Dani herself said we should be careful in life not to make things more complicated than they need be. Of course, in that case she was demonstrating how to apply liquid eyeliner, not how to foil a murder investigation. Regardless, what should have been a *20/20* episode is now a multimillion-dollar empire with podcasts, a YouTube channel, sponsorships, and patrons. My team tells me they're shopping for a new catamaran," Knowles says tonelessly.

"Living the dream. Still, if I were Sawyer, I'd watch my back."

Knowles shakes her head. "She needs him."

"Does she?" James asks.

"Those boats don't sail themselves."

"People are expendable. And my guess is she's as good at sailing as she is at housekeeping."

"Maybe, but I think it would be hard to find another fox willing to live in her disgusting den."

James laughs. "Touché."

"We do have one thing, but I'm not sure how it will pan out," Knowles says.

"Anything. Please."

"I just received a report from an officer on Long Island." Knowles picks up a sheet of paper from her desk and hands it to James. "Here, I printed it off for you."

James scans it. "This looks promising. This old man says he saw Dani Fox on a beach two days before she was found by the fishing boat. 'The individual was wearing a unitard of some sort—wetsuit, UV clothing.' She had a backpack and was headed west down the beach near Stella Maris." James looks up.

"Is he reliable?" Walter asks.

"He's eighty-eight, has bad vision and worse hearing, but look farther down. His son says his dad's quite the ladies' man and he's sure. Recognized her from the news."

"I don't know why she'd be on that beach two days before she was found at sea."

"I'm going to take my team to search. We might need to access some of the properties near where he saw her."

CHAPTER

32

Royal Bahamas Police Headquarters

Inspector Knowles

Day 30

KNOWLES RUBS HER blurry eyes, takes a sip of coffee long gone cold, and shudders. She blinks at the clock on the right-hand side of her monitor. How many hours has it been since she took any time away, even for a moment? She's been chasing evidence from tip reports to message boards to interview transcriptions. Around and around it goes. The lack of a window in this space makes it hard to judge the passage of time and she has nowhere else to be. Not until this damn thing is unraveled.

An unexpected knock on the door isn't enough to tear her gaze away from the greenish glow of her screen. "Come in," Knowles says absently, finally looking up to see Sonja Nilsson framed in the doorway.

How did Sonja find her way to Knowles's lair without being stopped? Where on earth is Officer Walter? Raw emotion oozes from the woman, and Knowles doesn't have the patience to engage. "May I help you, Sonja?" she asks.

May I help you find your way back to your boat and out of my country? Haven't you done enough?

"You found *Aboat Time*," she says.

"We did."

"And Jim," Sonja says, her voice breaking on his name. Her eyes are bloodshot, red rimmed, and swollen. "They said it doesn't look good for him."

"Can I get you a cup of coffee?" Knowles asks, tapping into a reserve of patience she didn't know she had.

Sonja shakes her head and dabs at her nose. "This is a farce. Jim didn't kidnap Dani."

"I understand he was—is—a friend of yours," Knowles says.

"Yes. For years, we've been meeting up here or in Florida. He and Anders fish together. Jim's a good man. He did not kidnap Dani Fox. He has grown kids that have to listen to this bullshit on television. None of it is true."

"We're investigating," Knowles says. "I understand your concerns. Has your husband not come with you today?" Her spouse had been a moderating influence in her first interview with the woman, and she could really use some of that moderation right now.

Sonja weeps. Collapsing into the metal chair next to the door, she digs through her woven bag and produces more tissues. It's several moments before she can speak. "Anders said I shouldn't bother coming, that I had contributed to all this, created this internet monster that came to destroy us, Jim, our community, everything. I post and post about how good a man he is but no one will listen. They say terrible things about me, and they look for things to hurt Jim. Even our cruiser friends are divided over this. I took down all the Fox Finders sites but people have replaced them with Marsh Finders sites."

Inspector Knowles comes around her desk and puts a hand on Sonja's shoulder. "I'm glad you came and spoke for him. I've had many people tell me that Jim Marsh would never kidnap a young woman, never do any of these things."

"Never, ever," Sonja says simply.

"People have told us he'd been sober for a decade or more."

Sonja nods and blows her nose into the tissue. "I wish they had never come here," Sonja whispers. "They're inhuman."

"I know people who would agree with you there," Knowles says. All the things she loves about the law—the rationality, motive, enforcement, justice, rules—are being upended here. And she's powerless to stop it.

Tears run down Sonja's weathered cheeks. "There will be no justice for Jim, will there?"

"We're still investigating. It may take time but I have to believe the truth—whatever it is—will come out."

Sonja gives a humorless laugh. "They're too smart to leave evidence."

Knowles sits back in her chair. "You think Dani and Sawyer cooked this up together?"

She gives the detective a sardonic look. "Sawyer knows Jim. Jim was the kind of guy who helped all of us. When stuff broke, Jim knew how to fix it. He was helping Dani with her video editing. If Sawyer doesn't dispute Dani's story, he's in on it."

"We've looked into Jim Marsh's past. There are some red flags," Knowles says, as gently as she can.

Sonja stiffens.

"I'm not accusing him of anything, mind—I'm saying he wasn't a saint."

"He's an alcoholic—he had a drug problem," Sonja says. "He was in jail for a time, but he did rehab. He was open about all of that. And yes, he had a fascination with Dani Fox—that was obvious to all of us. But he wasn't a stalker and he would never kidnap anyone. His boat and his channel, his cruiser friends were everything to him. She left him for dead and if he survives . . ." She wipes her face with a tissue.

"He'll wake up to being investigated," Knowles finishes for her.

Sonja nods. "Anders and I are going to stay. We're going to start a cruiser fund for his legal defense. There are plenty of us out here who know what the Foxes are."

"You told me not too long ago that you believed Dani Fox to be the victim here."

Sonja sits up straighter in her chair. Her tone is defensive. "I am a trusting person. I believed what she told me. 'Trust women,' right? Well, Dani Fox is not a woman; she's a monster! She looked me dead in the eye and told me she was a battered woman. She had bruises on her throat, her arm. What choice did I have but to believe her? And the whole time she was plotting against my friend. She made a fool of us all."

CHAPTER

33

Royal Bahamas Police Headquarters

Inspector Knowles

Day 31

Agent James arrives at the station wheeling her bag, Diet Coke in her left hand.

"This really is it then," Knowles says, shutting the door and taking a seat on the far end of the couch. James sinks into the other end.

"That's it for now."

"Thanks for all your help."

James nods and takes a sip from the can.

We conducted a thorough investigation into facts and evidence, we can't get too caught up in the outcome. That part is always out of our control," Agent James says. "There's not enough either way. So far."

"It doesn't bother you at all that Marsh might be convicted? Already has been in the court of public opinion?"

"Marsh, for whatever reason, got conned and absconded with the wrong blonde. That's on him. Hopefully, he'll only pay with his reputation and not his life," James says.

"The world is literally paying her to tell her bullshit tale. Don't we have an obligation to dispute it with the facts?"

"What facts? What evidence? Tell me and I'll stay and help you make the case against her, against them." James tips the remaining soda into her mouth, then pitches the can into the recycle bin.

Knowles is silent.

Knowles leans forward, her chair creaking. "Do you remember back when we agreed on reality? Before the social media stampede, before cyber sleuths and Facebook and everything viral?"

"We never agreed on reality. Before social media it was newspapers, magazines, tabloids, broadcast news, gossip, and the pulpit. Social media doesn't always make our jobs harder. I've lost count of the number of criminals I've found through their social media accounts. Some of them have literally provided evidence against themselves with their narcissism and posts and failure to turn off their geotags. Technology helps as much as it hurts us in law enforcement. With these two though, controversy will only serve to keep them in the public eye and ignite their popularity and reach."

"Truth and reality don't matter because the prevailing public perception is that Marsh did it?"

"You of all people know detective work still matters." Agent James stands and grabs the handle of her carry-on suitcase. "Keep at it. There may be evidence out there. Enough to create doubt if not to convict. And Knowles, even if there's never enough evidence, at least you know they have each other."

"Each other?" Knowles echoes blankly.

"If Sawyer killed his wife, won't it give Dani, at a minimum, a few sleepless nights to know he's capable of that? Meanwhile he's hooked up with someone who threw him under the bus and backed over him for fame and money. Now these two are tied to each other, on camera, and under a watchful public eye in the cruiser community and online. Maybe that's its own kind of justice."

CHAPTER

34

New York, NY

Sawyer

Day 31

THE LIGHTS IN the studio are bright. I'm wearing makeup for the first time in my life. "Thank you both so much for coming on the show today," Jenny Kirkpatrick, the bright, bubbly young host of *Morning in America*, says.

"Happy to be here," I reply.

"Thanks for having us on to share our story," Dani says. Have I ever heard her so subdued? Is the national audience freaking her out? I reach across to put my hand over hers.

She smiles at me, mechanically.

"There have been so many things said, Dani, about your ordeal. There's been an outpouring of sympathy from the global community—but there have also been skeptics, some of them within your own cruiser community," she says.

Dani gives her a sad smile. "Yes, I try not to read the comments," she says.

A few in the audience laugh.

"Can you tell us a bit about what you experienced?"

Dani gives her halting, tremulous, eight-sentence account. She does it reasonably well. I know it's rehearsed ad nauseum—Jesse has been coaching us since it all dropped—but it mostly works. If she's more subdued than usual, people will chalk it up to recovering from trauma, not irritation at being scripted by Jesse Jonas.

"I wouldn't say I'm used to it—does anyone ever get used to being treated cruelly? I grew up in very difficult circumstances. When those people come at me in the comments I say 'bring it' and double down on my commitment to my mental health."

She looks at me and then the interviewer who is nodding along.

"When I was in that cabin—terrified and lonely, locked in that hot, airless space—I knew, somehow I *knew* I'd find my way back to Sawyer."

"I'm so sorry," Jenny says, dabbing the corner of her eye with a tissue. "What happened to you is every woman's worst nightmare. That you survived—"

"I'm not a survivor, I'm a thriver," Dani interjects.

I don't have to look at Jesse to know he's rolling his eyes.

"You are indeed a thriver, Dani Fox," the host says.

First one or two, then *dozens* in the audience stand, applauding. Moments later the entire audience is on their feet.

"I had to do something to stay sane," Dani says, softly, ducking her head and twisting her fingers, hiding her Cheshire grin.

I attempt a spontaneous, awkward, one-armed hug on the couch we share and she leans in.

She gazes up at me adoringly, another Jesse-ism. Then she visibly perks up, straightening and pulling away. "But the key, for me, is physical fitness and eating well. I have a new workout channel: *Get Fit in the Water with Dani.* It's all things you can do in the ocean, lake, or pool, with only a noodle, a kickboard, and some resistance bands. You can find the link on *Sailing with the Foxes*. We have to get our mental, spiritual, physical, and emotional health together any way we can, especially after enduring trauma. There will always be cruel and abusive people. But you can overcome anything by keeping spiritually centered, healthy, and fit. Find a new vibe."

It's a bit of an awkward segue. But the audience is nodding along with her.

Jesse's handiwork is all over this interview and it is as effective with Dani as it had been with me. His fee is astronomical, and Dani fought it, but I lobbied hard. He is our agent, our coach, and our manager now. His own channel is booming too, and we've planned a crossover video before we leave for Panama. Our rising tide is lifting his boat, and I trust his judgment in all things media. Which is to say, in all things. You can probably imagine how Dani feels about that.

"It's so true, isn't it? There have been so many studies showing the link between regular fitness and improved mental health—endorphins and whatnot," she says, turning to me. "What about you, Sawyer?"

I take a breath. "Being accused of hurting the two women I loved most in the world didn't come anywhere close to the pain and abuse Dani suffered. I'm here to love and support my girlfriend after the trauma she's endured at the hands of a madman. Dani and I are committed to living our best lives. I know Emily wanted that for me, as I know Dani's mother wanted that for her."

"Can you tell us more about the accident with your wife?" the interviewer asks, leaning forward.

Jesse and I have been over this so many times, complete with facial expression cues, that it's rote. "I want to take this opportunity to say to anyone out there who wants to scuba. Get certified. Go with an experienced dive buddy. Go with a reputable organization. Last but not least, make sure conditions are going to be good. Diving can be dangerous, but the risk can be mitigated by following the rules. Emily and I didn't follow the rules and I lost her. Dani and I scuba and snorkel and free dive all the time now on *Serendipity* but only with a buddy, with excellent equipment, and when the conditions are near perfect. Be smart and safe."

The interviewer doesn't take the bait. "There have been some rumors online about you and your dead wife's sister—"

I grimace. "Nothing is sacred. I was very close to my sister-in-law, both before and after my wife's death. Losing a young, beautiful, brilliant person is devastating for parents, siblings, and spouses. Our collective grief has been crushing."

I search the audience for skepticism and see none. The breath freezes in my lungs as I spot Courtney Standish in the middle of the second row. I can only hope no one else recognizes her. Her face is drawn and pale and she's locked in on me. Even from this platform I can see the bags under her eyes. She swipes at her blotchy face as she weeps into a tissue. As soon as we finish I will text Jesse to run interference. I glance over to see him nodding, smiling, and giving us the thumbs up.

I smile back and reach for Dani's hand.

CHAPTER

35

Long Island, Bahamas

Inspector Knowles

Day 33

Officer Walter is like a schoolboy with his nose pressed up against the oval window of the puddle jumper that is bringing him and Knowles into Stella Maris Airport. He completely blocks her view.

"One would think you had never seen Long Island from the air, Officer Walter."

"I'm keeping an eye out for the wild goose you're after, boss."

His ribbing is good-natured, and she lets it slide, confident that her suspicions about Dani's tale of survival are enough to keep pushing the investigation forward. She doesn't need moral support from a soul. Less than an hour since wheels up in George Town, they're back on the ground.

The superintendent of the Long Island division has taken it upon himself to meet them at the airport, in full uniform, standing stiffly in the area where the shuttle bus drivers pick up tourists for a stay at the luxury resort nearby.

"Inspector Knowles," he calls out as she and Walter make their way down the jetway.

She gives Whitfield a nod. It's been five years since she'd met him at a training seminar on domestic violence interventions.

"Superintendent Whitfield. Thank you for meeting us. This is Officer Walter, assisting with this investigation." Whitfield's serious expression remains in place as he nods in Walter's direction and sweeps his arm toward the parking lot, where a white Jeep emblazoned with the RBPF seal and the slogan "Working Together for a Safer Bahamas" awaits. In the more populated precincts, you would expect the superintendent to be driving an unmarked sedan, but out here in the hinterlands, there's not as much emphasis on hierarchy. The Jeep is practical for the uneven roads in these rural areas.

"I've arranged to meet the witness at his home. He wasn't very enthusiastic about coming to the precinct," Whitfield said. "You should conduct the interview, Knowles, since apparently we didn't do a thorough enough job on the first go-round."

His petulance is surprising, although a typical manifestation of police territoriality. She smiles and nods and puts on her most congenial face. It's best not to respond to those kinds of comments, even with banal reassurances. They drive the rest of the way in silence. Even Walter has the good sense to abstain from wisecracking.

The Jeep pulls up to a modest turquoise-blue house with freshly painted white shutters at the side of a quiet, dusty road. On the porch is the would-be witness, awaiting their arrival on a white molded plastic chair. He springs up out of his seat as they approach, more nimbly than expected by the look of him, with his lined and leathery face and white, grizzled beard.

"Inspector Knowles, this is Shorty Lockhart. Shorty, Inspector Knowles would like to ask you about what you saw on the beach the other day." Shorty flashes a grin at the group, looking not the least put out.

"Now tell me, Mr. Lockhart . . ." Knowles begins.

"Shorty, please. We're very informal here."

The nickname bothers Knowles more than it should, for the man is of average height at least, and by no reasonable metric would qualify as short. Knowles refrains from asking about it, sensing it will result in a long-winded tale, immaterial to the objective of this interview.

"Shorty. Tell me what you saw that day on the beach at Stella Maris."

"The American. I saw the American girl. A small blonde lady, wearing something that covered her like a wetsuit, but thinner. Like the bodysuits those Kardashian gals wear, only it was swirled with blue and white. She had a hat on—maybe from one of those American sports teams."

Knowles makes a note. A bodysuit is not one of the clothing items found with Dani when she was rescued by the fishing charter, but she had heard she occasionally wore UV-protectant clothing. There had been some bagged from her cabin.

"What kind of sports team?" Walter asks.

Shorty squints. "Orange and blue, maybe? If I saw the logo . . ."

Walter pulls out his phone. He and Shorty and he put their heads together over the device, presumably looking at American sports logos.

Please don't let the Dolphins cap be the only cap Walter shows him. "A variety, eh, Walter?" she says.

"Got it, boss."

As Walter scrolls, Shorty says, "No, nope, no. Kinda like that but no. Hold up, go back." He peers at the screen. Walter pinches out the screen with his thumb and index finger to blow up the image. Knowles notes there's a touch of cloudiness in Shorty's brown eyes that are framed by a web of smile lines. The beginning of cataracts? Not too surprising given his eighty-eight years. Something sure to come up if it ever went to trial. She should be so lucky.

"That looks like it! Yep, that's it. I'm sure of it. A dolphin. With those orange-and-blue markings."

Knowles nods and makes a note in her book.

Walter's triumph is plastered across his face and she frowns at him. Dani was rescued in that hat, it's been all over the news. It's helpful, but marginally so. Knowles turns toward Whitfield and shows him a photo of Dani's rescue. She's in cutoff denim booty shorts with the white bottoms of the front pockets exposed and a light blue midriff-baring tank top, with a Miami Dolphins blue-and-orange ball cap completing the outfit. She's clenching a backpack in one hand and a yellow rain slicker in the other.

Whitfield raises a brow, nodding.

"Sir, please continue," Knowles says.

"Shorty."

"Shorty, please continue."

"Her hair was wet, she had just come in from swimming in the ocean, and she was walking up the beach real slow like you would if you'd just been swimming at the break of dawn. But she had a sneakiness about her."

"Sneakiness? How so?"

"When she saw me coming, she moved farther up the beach, away from the ocean, where I was walking along the tide line. She raised a hand. I watched her. I saw her head up to the houses, the ones the tourists rent, the Airbnbs. Then a couple days later, I see this same lady on the news."

"Why do you think the woman you saw on the beach was the American you saw on the news?"

"She jiggled just the same, in all the same places." Shorty smirks. "She had a booty on her."

Knowles sighs. Not an ideal witness. Still, she couldn't discount his story.

"Can we go for a walk to where you saw her? Or should we take the Jeep?"

After some discussion, they all pile into the Jeep and drive for about ten minutes. The group clambers out and heads down to the shore.

"Show me where you were standing when you saw her."

He points. "North of here, just a little ways down. She was walking toward where we are now." He turns around and they all turn with him. He points at a group of houses further up the beach. "She turned up in there."

Shorty points to the modest but picturesque beach houses that are perched up overlooking the beach, set slightly back so they aren't actually on the sand. "I really enjoyed watching her leave." He winks at Walter.

Whitfield's lips are turned all the way down at the corners. "These are seasonal rentals, mostly vacant this time of year. It's a quiet cove, feasible to come ashore here unseen." Despite his earlier recalcitrance, it appears Whitfield is coming around to the idea that there's something worthy of investigation here. There is a possibility coalescing. "I'll summon a few officers to conduct a thorough search of these houses and look for signs of entry."

"Thank you, superintendent." Knowles has to suppress her smile. It's been a push to get authorization from her own boss to travel here. Everyone has moved on. Everyone but Knowles, Sonja, and Jim Marsh, that is. The chief inspector only acquiesced to this additional interview because he's as much of a stickler as Knowles. Dot the i's, cross the t's, finish the investigation, file the paperwork.

"Why would you search all those houses then? Why not just the one she broke into?" Shorty asks.

Knowles spins around on her heel to face Shorty again. "Mr. Lockhart. Where exactly did you see this woman go?"

"Through the window! I watched her climb right up and through the shutters with my binoculars—I watch the birds. Both kinds. I watched the American go." He laughs gleefully.

The mottled color making its way from Whitfield's collar indicates his displeasure. His team failed to elicit this particular salient detail in his interview with the witness. "Why didn't you report this break-in? You see a crime committed right in front of your nose and you don't phone the police to help your neighbors?" Whitfield says, scowling.

Shorty's nostrils flare. "They're not my neighbors; they're not even Bahamians. Tourists, part-timers, renting to other tourists and part-timers. I figured the girl forgot her key or lost it on her swim. She was a pretty girl. What harm could a pretty girl do? Crawl through a window, no harm." He's near shouting now.

Walter jumps in to calm Mr. Lockhart down. "No worries, man. Of course not. You're fine."

Knowles gives Walter an approving nod. They need to keep this witness compliant, cataracts and all.

"Let us switch gears here," Knowles says. "Superintendent, I feel that we should move from search to evidence collection. Let's seal off that cottage and process it as a crime scene. Sooner rather than later." This could be the only opportunity to gather untainted evidence. The cyber sleuths have not managed to insert themselves into this aspect of the investigation—yet. Some leads cannot be chased down from behind a computer screen.

Whitfield pulls out his phone. "Once I get the address, I'll attempt to get permission from the homeowner," he says.

It's a few hours before sunset when the Canadian property owner can be tracked down and a bit longer as faxes giving consent go back and forth between Long Island and Vancouver.

The crime scene technicians are onsite, protecting the scene, waiting for the go-ahead. Walter has busied himself with cultivating a collegial relationship with the star witness. Whitfield, back at the station, dealing remotely with the owner, finally calls Knowles with permission to enter and gives her the authority to oversee the scene.

Knowles smiles. There isn't any way Dani Fox, as messy as she is, has stayed somewhere without leaving fingerprints, trash, and hairs behind. There will be plenty of evidence in this cottage—if, in fact, the witness is right and she was here. Knowles puts on gloves and shoe covers and enters through the front door, following the two evidence techs in their blinding white suits.

"Ma'am," one of the white Tyvek suits says in a leading tone once they're inside.

"Find something?" Knowles's tone is sharper than she intends. Her hands tremble.

She follows the tech down the hallway, careful not to contaminate any surface, straight to the back bedroom. The tech gestures to something small on the wooden floor, near the edge of the single bed. Knowles drops down, ungainly on all fours, face level with the floor, holding her breath.

A cluster of blue and white threads. Denim.

They're aligned with an even straight edge; the threads have been trimmed from the edge of frayed fabric. She takes in the room again. There's a full-length mirror directly in front of this spot at the edge of the bed.

"Mudda sick." The Bahamian patois of Knowles's childhood bubbles out with the shock of this realization, at the vision crystallizing: an image of Dani, sitting on the edge of this bed, looking at herself in the mirror, trimming her denim shorts.

Knowles sits back on her heels, staring at the pile of fabric.

"Bag it."

She pulls out her mobile phone, scanning the images online of Dani on the charter boat shortly after her rescue. Pictures she posted on Instagram, posing with rescuers.

Simultaneously worn out yet alluring, blond highlights glinting in the sun.

She's wearing denim shorts.

Denim shorts with a frayed hem.

Denim shorts that are stowed away in a Royal Bahamas Police Force storage locker, to preserve evidence of the crimes Dani alleges were committed against her.

"Fingerprint every surface. Inside and out. Pull everything from the drains."

Knowles smiles at Walter, who's standing in the doorway, fist pumping the air.

"Gotcha," she whispers to herself.

CHAPTER

36

Punta Cana, Dominican Republic

Ella

Two years ago

SOMEONE TAKES THE stool next to me.

Hello, handsome.

He doesn't even glance over; he sits there, in all his shirtless glory, staring at his phone.

I automatically uncross my legs and run a hand through my hair. I reach for my soda water, bumping his elbow in the process and spilling some on the bar.

He turns to face me, and, right then, I know.

He steals my breath.

Kindred spirits, soulmates, love at first sight—whatever you want to call it.

I like to think he knows right away too.

My smile vanishes, and as we stare at each other, unblinking, his smile gels.

He is impossibly handsome and perfectly fit.

His name is Sawyer, and he isn't some midlife, middle management, middling golfer.

He doesn't bother trying to charm me, nor I him.

His wife is working in their hotel room, so he invites me on the sailing excursion he's booked.

Sawyer grew up sailing an old luxury yacht, the *Colonel Mustard* on the Chesapeake Bay. He spends most of the trip talking to the captain about the need to replace the rigging, the condition of the sails, weather conditions, the reef, and on and on.

I watch dolphins frolic off the bow, enthralled by their speed, their agility. The wind is calming. It is the perfect Punta Cana day.

I have an inkling of what it might be like, living on the water, being nomadic, sailing from one paradise to another. I'm not naïve—I know it takes money, and much more than I have.

After snorkeling, lunch, and a rum punch, Sawyer is more animated, talking about his dream of buying a boat and sailing it around the world. He knows what to buy, he could do at least some of the maintenance.

"So do it," I say, stretching out my legs over the edge.

"Buy a boat?" He laughs. "With what money?'

"You said your wife is rich."

"Ironclad prenup," he says, flatly.

"How much do you need?"

"Seventy to a hundred thousand to buy an outfitted blue water boat, then to live aboard and travel you have to plan to spend two or three thousand a month."

"That's a lot."

"Food, gas, slip fees or mooring fees, repairs, insurance are expensive."

"No joint savings?"

"We have some savings and I'm the beneficiary of her life insurance policy. That's about it. Days like this I can't remember why I married a girl who wants a house in Connecticut and two kids. I thought that might be enough. But it's a gilded fucking cage and the only saving grace is that she works sixty-hour weeks." He laughs but it is mirthless.

"Once you figure out what you want and how to get it, you do it," I say. "Be true to yourself."

"Sage advice from a twenty-one-year-old. Give up everything and buy a sailboat?" He shakes his head. "They only make it *look* easy on YouTube."

"Who makes it look easy?"

"Cruisers. People who sell it all, buy a boat, and go sail."

Now he has my full attention. "Do you know any?"

He laughs. "Not personally, but YouTube is full of them."

"There are YouTube cruiser channels?" I ask.

"Dozens of 'em."

"So they sail around, record themselves, and make enough money to keep sailing?"

Sawyer shrugs. "Yeah, I guess. Some of them pitch products, some sell mugs or shirts with their boat name, some have patrons who sponsor them."

"And they make money at this. Like influencers?"

"Yup. Most of the successful channels post videos every week."

He tells me the names of some of the channels and I look them up on my phone.

"Want another?" he asks, springing to his feet and shaking his empty red cup at me.

"Sure," I mumble. I barely hear him. I am all in on this sailing thing. We only need a plan to make it happen.

I find Sawyer the next day at the swim up bar, half drunk at noon. "She's screwing around on me," he tells me, before I can even ask what's wrong. "She works constantly but still finds time to fuck one of the partners. She wants a divorce."

He is some combination of livid and incredulous and can barely sit still.

The bartender is giving us the side-eye.

"Calm down," I say, my expression revealing none of my excitement.

He could've been a tough sell on my plan, so this turn of events is serendipitous indeed.

"And she was able to *hide* this from me. Me."

I put on my hat and take out my phone. "Sawyer, let me call a guy, then we'll go for a walk on the beach and figure something out, okay?"

I take his hand as we walk down the path from the hotel to the beach.

"Marcos? It's Ella. I want to book a dive for tomorrow, for three people. We need gear. What? Who cares? It's weather and could always change. I'll bring cash."

CHAPTER

37

Atlantic Ocean

Sawyer

Day 35

"DANI, CLEAN UP your fucking mess."

I catch her smile before she turns away.

"I'm dead serious. The sink is so full, I can't clean my own shit. Enough already."

"Maybe it's payback."

"Payback for what? I'm the one you set up. I'm the one who almost ended up in jail because of your scheming."

"You want to talk scheming, Sawyer? You have a million-dollar life insurance policy on me." Dani's tone is dangerously cold. "You really are a one-trick pony. You'd never have been able to collect. Where's the insurable interest? We're not married or business partners."

She still doesn't get it—sure, I got the policy, but I made it look like it was *her* doing. On paper, I was merely the beneficiary should her life meet a tragic, untimely end. And you can't get much cheaper than a term life policy on a twenty-three-year-old female non-smoker. I'd go hungry before I stop that annual $547 auto payment charge on my card. "So, we're doing this now? Fine. I got the policy because you thought we needed it after your miscarriage—"

"My *what*?" She laughs. "I miscarried? What about your vasectomy?"

Now it's my turn to be smug. "You talk about having a baby—who's to say we haven't tried and failed? Vasectomies are reversible."

"Still, it looks pretty shady, Sawyer, collecting on a wife *and* a girlfriend."

"If I'd known about your plan, I wouldn't have needed mine."

"It was better that you didn't know. More authentic." She says this very quietly with her back to me. I know why. She's got a camera with a voice recording device stashed in the bookshelf behind me. She needn't bother—I've turned off her gear for this conversation. I'm not going to be blackmailed. And thanks to Rod Zild's gear—including a camera finder that I keep in a safe in my cabin—she won't get as much on me.

"What did you use? Rohypnol? GHB?" I wolf down half of my sandwich and lean back in the banquette. It's a rhetorical question; she never reveals her methods.

She shrugs and smiles her most self-satisfied smile.

I switch tactics. "Do you still want a baby?" I ask, putting the second half of my sandwich down.

She stares, trying to read me, but she can't.

Her eyes are slits.

I lie to her, she lies to me. Such is the nature of our relationship. I have no illusions about what I am or what she is—our relationship, such as it is, works because we are so alike. We're not continually running scams on each other—what would be the point? Not having to pretend around each other the way we've had to pretend around others our entire lives had been liberating.

But now I'm seeing more of the risks that come with her impulsive schemes. Stealing a valuable ring from a boat with only four other guests aboard was stupid and careless. If I hadn't been able to slip it into Linda Fenwick's pocket we could've gone down for that. If Dani had drowned during her attempt to get from Marsh's boat to Long Island, I'd probably be wearing an orange jumpsuit about now. Just as I'm realizing the downsides of keeping her around she's got me locked in a fucking gilded cage, with thousands of people now tracking our every move via GPS thanks to their VIP Patreon access.

All that income goes straight to Dani. She's shut me out of the YouTube revenue, the Patreon account, and the book deal. She needs me right now for the channel, and I need her to get a new and better boat in Panama, but my eyes are wide open.

Everyone is expendable.

I can sell *Serendipity* but it's not exactly a liquid asset, not like the tens of thousands pouring into her accounts these days. That's why I need access to her fan base. I didn't study finance in college for kicks. I've got several ways to leverage her huge platform that don't involve makeup tutorials or swim lessons.

"*You* don't want a baby," she says finally.

"Neither one of us wants a kid. You think it's a way to generate more revenue and views. Maybe it will, but you're messing with our brand. There's plenty of money to be made with an exercise channel, sponsorships, and all the other things you've gotten us into."

She opens her mouth.

I hold up a hand. "That's not a criticism. We're rolling in money—well, you're rolling in money and we're on our way to trade this in for a catamaran—so, once again, you've fulfilled every fantasy."

She preens and, finally, sits across from me. "But we have to offer more and better content."

I groan. This thing she's done has shifted our dynamic. I don't know what I can say no to anymore.

"We need to have episode previews before they are released to the public, access to a monthly live chat, exclusive updates, ad free video, and opportunities for meetups." She uses her hands to tick off items. She loves this as much as I hate it and, although I hate to admit it, she was born for this.

"And access to investment opportunities," I say and stuff the rest of my sandwich in my mouth.

Her eyes narrow.

Maybe closing the door on Courtney was a mistake.

Courtney could be manipulated easily.

But Emily and Courtney's father called during our media tour. He told me he still controls Courtney's trust for two more years and will cut her off completely if she makes the same mistake as Emily, then he'll tie me up in court in a wrongful death suit. Given his rage and his money, he could easily put a hit out on me.

I don't need the headache.

When crypto tanked, I knew Dani would come up with something, same as she knew I'd never go along with what she dreamed up.

"The idea of making more money with a baby on board doesn't sell you on it? We can get a nanny," she says. "A hot nanny who helps edit the channel would be amazing. Give off some real *Tiger King* vibes." Her tone is cajoling.

"Crew doesn't stay with us."

She shrugs. "A whole lotta nannies then."

I put down the sandwich. "If we have a child and film our family life, we run the risk of exposing ourselves. Having 'nannies' that we fuck, or fuck with, is not a good idea. Didn't you learn from Marsh that it's hard to keep the masks in place twenty-four seven on a boat?"

"Have you no faith in my editing?"

"We'd be under a more powerful microscope. We're hedonists, Dani. Sex in paradise, naked sailing, drunk fests, cruiser drama—we're expected to be narcissistic. Family values is not in our repertoire; at least it's not in mine."

"What if I've already put a plan in motion?"

I toss up my hands. "You don't need my consent to get an embryo, donor sperm, a surrogate, whatever. It isn't worth going to war over. Let's see what happens from here."

She studies me. "What's that mean?"

"Your planning, your execution, it's well done. But you haven't learned to follow the thing all the way through. Tie up the loose ends. Not because you're squeamish, because you're arrogant. Haven't you ever wondered why Captain Marcos Reyes never showed up to identify you, even after all this, *Ella*?" I ask.

I've only managed to manipulate Dani a handful of times, but when I have, it's been to excellent effect.

I sold her on my wife's infidelity, and she came up with the scuba accident.

Dani was the one to turn off Emily's air.

It was Dani who wrestled my wife in the depths that day.

Her mouth drops open. "You—"

"Me."

I did not relish the experience; it was a rushed job. I lured Marcos Reyes away from the island with a cash offer and the threat of an impending lawsuit from my father-in-law against us both. Reyes picked me up in his skiff and we went out to sea—far enough to avoid having our cell phones tracked, I told him. What an idiot. I threw him overboard, incurring a broken finger for my troubles. It would've been better for him if he hadn't known how to swim. I wonder how long he lasted.

Daniella Diaz, Ella, Dani Fox. Whatever name she uses, she will always need me to clean up her messes.

CHAPTER

38

Doctors Hospital, Nassau, Bahamas

Jim Marsh

Day 35

THE CLOUDS DRIFT outside my window—shades of coconut, raspberry, and orange, all the sherbet flavors from my favorite frozen treat in childhood. I don't know that I've ever seen such a beautiful sunset. I stare, drowsy, drugged, and happy, until the clouds turn blue and purple, until the stars come out.

I glance around the dark room.

I'm in a hospital gown, attached to monitors, hooked up to an IV.

God.

I must've been very drunk.

Was I driving?

Did I kill someone this time?

Pain filters through my medicated state. Each inhalation brings a sharp, stabbing pain.

Wait.

I don't drink.

Not anymore.

Not for twelve years, ten months, and . . .

What day is it?

I move my arm to shield my eyes as the throbbing in my temples escalates, but I can only move it a few inches.

I try again and there's a clank.

I'm handcuffed to the bed rail.

It all comes back to me.

Dani Fox.

The second time I wake, there's a woman in my room sitting next to the hospital bed, drinking from the largest travel mug I've ever seen.

"Gotta get me one of those," I mumble, my voice scratchy from disuse.

She looks up from the folder in her lap, eyeing me over her reading glasses. "Jim Marsh, I'm Veronique Knowles, inspector for the Royal Bahamas Police Force." She flips out a leather wallet with a badge attached. "If you're feeling up to it, I'd like to ask you a few questions. May I record our conversation?"

I nod, grunt, and try to sit up in the bed, belatedly realizing the handcuffs have been removed. I fumble for the bed control and elevate the head of it as much as I can tolerate, holding a hand to my torso to alleviate the immediate pulsing pain left of my sternum. Broken ribs. I look longingly at the pain medication pump button lying on the sheet, then push it just out of reach.

Not going there.

The inspector puts her badge away and takes out a black electronic device, lays it on the hospital tray between us, and touches the screen. "I need verbal consent, please."

"Yeah, sure, record it. What can I tell you?"

"I'd like you to give me your account, to the best of your knowledge, of how you ended up in this hospital."

"Dani Fox," I mutter. But Knowles waits for me to elaborate. "She trapped me on board. It took me the better part of two days to break out of the cabin, but she'd padlocked my new companionway doors. I'd just upgraded to aluminum, 'cause that's what you want to have in a following sea—it adds strength. Keeps thieves out too. I knew there was no way I could break out of there. But I managed to turn on the beacon..." I pause, thinking. "That's all I remember. She'd dumped my water, food, medication. She left me nothing to drink but a few handles of rum. That's downright evil."

"Mr. Marsh, did you kidnap Daniella Diaz Fox?"

A laugh sputters out of me, and I gasp, pressing a hand to my chest. "Is that ... is that what she told you?"

Knowles doesn't respond; her pen remains poised over her legal pad, her gaze on mine.

"No, I didn't kidnap her." I almost want to roll my eyes at how ludicrous the thought is, but really, nothing about this is funny. "I thought I was *saving* her. She told me Sawyer was abusive and she needed a safe place. But the way she acted on board didn't line up, and after a while I started to question everything she'd told me. I'm a hard man to con. But let me tell you, she's a nightmare to have aboard. I told her I was taking her back to George Town. That's when she locked me up. I'm not sure how this"—I gesture to my broken body—"happened. She didn't break my ribs."

Knowles's expression is impassive. "No, that was the ... the people who discovered you. Some of your cruisers."

I scowl at her. "Cruisers wouldn't do this to me."

"It was, uh, unintentional. A misguided attempt at CPR."

I shake my head. "I must've been in a pretty bad way if that was needed."

Her lip curls in a wry smile. "It wasn't. You were in a diabetic coma."

I nod. "I feel like I've been hit by a truck."

"Mr. Marsh, was Ms. Fox held captive on your boat against her will?"

Another laugh escapes me but brings a wave of pain that takes my breath away. "Captive? *Kidnapped*? That's nuts."

She nods impassively, but I can tell she believes me. "Dani has been telling law enforcement, the media, and anyone who will listen that you held her against her will for weeks aboard *Aboat Time*."

The relief I'd initially felt at being released from the cuffs is replaced by something a lot closer to rage. I try to keep my voice level. "Well, let's put her under oath. I'd like to press charges for what she did to me—and my boat!"

Knowles sighs. "Unfortunately, it's not that simple. For one thing, Dani and Sawyer are together again—on *Serendipity*—and, according to their social media, on their way to Panama."

"Then get those assholes back here. She locked me up! She must've drugged me—"

"Your toxicology screen was negative for drugs and alcohol," Knowles says.

I stare at her.

"You're serious. You really think I *kidnapped* Dani *and* held her hostage for, what, three weeks? On *Aboat Time*? That's the craziest thing I ever heard."

Knowles looks away.

"You *can't* believe that," I say, starting to panic a little.

She stops writing on her pad and looks at me, unsmiling. "What I believe doesn't matter. What I can prove or disprove is what matters."

I sit up straighter in the hospital bed, ignoring the pain. "I'll tell you the whole story—under oath. I'll tell the whole world. I tried to *help* her and this is how she pays me back? Leaving me for dead, locked up on my boat with no means of survival!"

Knowles nods but offers no advice.

"Look. I've been sailing out here for years. I'm part of the cruiser community. I've got friends who can vouch for me."

Knowles sighs again. "Yes, we've heard from many cruisers. They've started a legal defense fund for you."

"I don't need that—I didn't do anything wrong! It's Dani Fox who needs that!"

"My supervisors see no reason to doubt her story—not yet—but I'm here to document your account and see what can be discovered before charges are filed—"

"File the damn charges!" I yell.

"—against you."

"This is insane."

"Perhaps. But Daniella Diaz Fox has been giving her account of events for a while now. She's got a lot of people out there who see her as the victim. You were accused, tried, and found guilty in the court of public opinion before you even regained consciousness."

The way she says it, so matter-of-factly, makes my blood boil. "I—"

Knowles holds up a hand. "But here in the Bahamas we don't accept the findings of the court of public opinion. We're still investigating and following active leads." She sighs and puts down her pen. "I'll level with you. We don't have clear corroborative evidence yet for *either* of your stories. Is there anyone you saw or spoke to during your time away? Anyone who may have seen you both?"

I stare at her; the breath leaves my body in a long, flat sigh. "No. No one."

Knowles looks at my monitor, I follow her gaze. My vital signs are flashing red.

"You need rest. I'll come back in the morning." She stands to gather her things. "Focus on your recovery, Mr. Marsh. What you assert, what she alleges—none of it may be enough to warrant charges or extradition. There's no loss of life or property. We *are* still investigating," she says, but her shoulders slump and I wonder who she's trying to convince—me or herself. "But my supervisors may not be interested in pursuing *either* allegation with zeal."

Which explains the lack of handcuffs. Sounds like they may not be pressing charges against me. But I have something else to say. "The thing I don't understand is why." I fist the bedsheet with my hand.

Knowles looks up. "Pardon?"

"Why would she say that? Why would she *do* any of this?"

Knowles folds up her reading glasses and puts them into a black briefcase with her papers. "We don't know for sure. But her disappearance sparked millions of likes and views on her YouTube channel …"

My heart rate ratchets up; the machine bleats a warning.

"*Millions* of likes and views?" I echo.

"Millions," she confirms.

The driver of engagement.

I'm her fucking foot.

CHAPTER 39

Atlantic Ocean

Sawyer

Day 36

DANI FOLLOWS ME up the companionway steps. The reflection of the sun off the Atlantic is dazzling. There's only a slight breeze so we're motoring for the second day. I check the weather app on my phone.

"You are either on my side or in my fucking way, Sawyer. Choose wisely."

I hit record on another app before I shove it back in my shirt pocket. "I'm here, aren't I?"

"I'm the victim, Sawyer—nothing and no one will change that."

"Marsh came out of the coma," I say.

She waves a hand dismissively. "Who cares about Jim Marsh? The internet sleuths are busy fitting him up for other crimes. They've gone after him way worse than they ever went after you."

"I'm not talking about the public. I'm talking about the investigation."

She laughs. "What investigation? They have their man. Who's the public going to believe? What evidence do they have? Don't you get it yet, Sawyer?"

"Police say there's a witness, from a beach near Stella Maris on Long Island Cay. I'm sure they're scouring the place as we speak. What are they going to find, Dani? Did you, for once in your life, manage to clean up after yourself? How confident are you that you didn't leave DNA or fingerprints or even trash behind while you bided your time there, waiting for Marsh to die?"

She pales.

"Supremely confident," she says, over the sound of the motor.

It's an admission of sorts and the app recording in my pocket may have picked it up.

"I get it, Dani. I lived through it. Perception matters, not reality. Unless, of course, there's evidence. A witness and a few fingerprints aren't likely to make a case. Or are they?"

I pause, watching her face. She's terrified, maybe for the first time in her life.

"I'm just glad we've sold them on our perfect relationship, and I'm happy to do my part in service to your version of events. I won't turn on you. But I *will* need access to the accounts and subscribers."

Her eyes narrow, her upper lip curls. "No fucking way. You'll blow it all on crypto again."

"Crypto will make us rich."

"*I* made us rich," she says, her face flushed with rage. "*Twice.*"

I take the helm.

The wind is picking up.

I may get the sails up yet.

She spins and goes back down the steps.

Something smashes in the galley.

I take out my phone and save the file, taking the time to password protect it.

I smile.

It's a perfect day for a sail.

Three hundred miles to Panama.

ACKNOWLEDGMENTS

WE WOULD LIKE to express our heartfelt thanks to our extraordinary editor, Jess Verdi of Crooked Lane Books. Working with you has been an absolute joy, and your professionalism and encouragement have made this journey exciting and fun. Thank you to publisher Matt Martz for believing in and supporting our project. A special shout-out to Heather VenHuizen, whose incredible design has brought our book cover to life—we absolutely adore it.

We extend our gratitude to the entire Crooked Lane team, whose dedication and support have been invaluable. Thank you to Thai Fantauzzi-Pérez, Rebecca Nelson, Melissa Rechter, Dulce Botello, Mikaela Bender, Madeline Rathle, Stephanie Manova, Megan Matti, and Doug White. We are overjoyed to have found such a wonderful home for *On the Surface*. Your collective efforts have made this dream a reality, and we are appreciative of the opportunity to share our work with the world. Thank you all for your passion and expertise.

We would also like to thank our early readers, critiquers, and enthusiasts—Anne Berube, Kim Bidermann, Nancy Ciepley, Tracey Crawford, Annalise D'Andrade, Kara Danner, Caryn Graham, Jessica Graham, Kristen Jones, Stephanie Oppenheimer, and Kelly Wraight. Your insightful feedback fueled our passion for this project, and we are truly grateful for your invaluable contributions.

We are so grateful for the love and support of our respective families: Chris, Aspen, and Ryker, and Shane, Hazel, and Wren, throughout the writing of our debut thriller. Your encouragement and understanding made this journey possible.

To everyone who played a part in bringing this book to life, thank you for being a part of this adventure.

—RG + LMW